MISSION COMPLETE

-A Fiction Novel that Could Be a True Story-

10/22/09

Capt. Lawrence S. Wigley, USN (RET)

*To Lily W. Gordon —
With best wishes for fair winds
and following seas.*

PublishAmerica
Baltimore

© 2005 by Capt. Lawrence S. Wigley, USN (RET).

All rights reserved. No part of this book may be reproduced, stored in a retrieval system or transmitted in any form or by any means without the prior written permission of the publishers, except by a reviewer who may quote brief passages in a review to be printed in a newspaper, magazine or journal.

First printing

ISBN: 1-4137-4913-5
PUBLISHED BY PUBLISHAMERICA, LLLP
www.publishamerica.com
Baltimore

Printed in the United States of America

This novel is dedicated to my wife Shirley, and my children, and to the other wives and families who support their husbands and loved ones while they are underwater protecting the security of the United States.

/1/ MISSION ASSIGNED

The weather in late December was typical of that to be expected in Groton, Connecticut, the "Submarine Capital of the World." The recently fallen snow and twenty-knot northeast winds, compounded by the freezing temperature, made driving treacherous.

Commander Bruce Stewart carefully maneuvered his decade-old automobile through the naval submarine base down to Pier Six on the Thames River. Not much traffic to contend with at this time in the holiday season.

It was now seven-thirty in the morning on the twenty-first of December. He remembered that last year had set all records for cold weather and snow. Bruce was confident that this year, 1989, would top all previous records.

Bruce, as commanding officer, had the ultimate responsibility for one of the United States Navy's most modern, fastest, and deadliest nuclear attack submarine, the *USS Jackfish* (SSN 945).

As his automobile stopped in the parking space at the head of the pier designated C.O. 945, he could see his charge safely moored against the submarine base pier in the Thames River.

Much activity on his ship and the adjacent pier was in progress.

The high tempo of activity on the pier was not normal for this time of the year, particularly during the Christmas stand-down period. During this holiday period, operations normally were relaxed somewhat. This permitted the crews of the submarines in port and the ashore support personnel to take some well-deserved time away from the pressures of their profession to enjoy their families and loved ones.

Seeing the current activity on the pier, it was obvious to the most casual observer that the *Jackfish* would be underway soon on a very important mission. The actual underway time was to be before noon today.

Bruce, a 1971 graduate of the United States Naval Academy, had been in command of this sleek black sinister-looking vehicle of destruction for forty months.

Prior to graduation, there was not a doubt from any who knew him that Bruce was destined to be one of the leaders of the Navy. His leadership had been well demonstrated during his assignment as brigade commander, the highest position of responsibility for a midshipman at the Academy.

On the football field, he expertly directed the Middies as their All-American quarterback to the best Navy season in over a decade, beating Army soundly and performing as the upset victors in the Cotton Bowl.

He was promoted to commander two years ahead of his classmates, was the first of his group to be assigned to command at sea, and should be promoted ahead of schedule to captain early the next year.

Bruce also had been valedictorian in his Naval War College class and concurrently earned master's degrees in systems management and computer science.

This Christmas was to be the first one during his four years in command of *Jackfish* that he would spend with his wife and children.

Bruce had been "at sea submerged on special operations to support the defense of the United States" the past three Decembers.

These words—"to support the defense of the United States"—appeared on the three Navy unit citations awarded to *Jackfish* and the Navy cross and three legion-of-merit medals personally presented to Bruce for his role as the captain of the ship.

No other details were provided on the citations germane to these highly classified and dangerous missions except the inclusive dates. This type of citation was normal for awards presented to attack nuclear submarines performing special highly classified operations in close proximity to Soviet combatants.

Jackfish had arrived in its homeport of Groton, Connecticut, on the fifteenth of December after a long and arduous eight months at sea.

Most of the period had been spent submerged, conducting hazardous and daring independent missions in close proximity to Soviet submarines and surface combatants.

The submarine performed superbly throughout operations under the pack ice of the Arctic, in the north Atlantic Ocean, and the Mediterranean Sea.

Each mission was followed rapidly with messages and letters of the highest praise for Bruce as the commanding officer and for the crew of this premier ship.

The submarine received the battle efficiency "E" for being the best ship in the squadron of twelve nuclear attack submarines for the last three years Stewart was in command. In addition, *Jackfish* was acclaimed on numerous occasions by the chief of naval operations, the fleet commander, and the submarine force commander as the top ship in the Atlantic fleet.

Since returning from the deployment, Bruce and Ann laid plans to be able to fully nurture the wonderful time together. An eight-month separation left much to make up.

However, these plans changed rapidly after a single telephone call from Bruce's boss.

The evening before, the captain of *Jackfish* received an urgent call from Captain Bill Walter, his squadron commander. Bill informed Bruce that a meeting of the utmost importance was to take place at his headquarters in thirty minutes. Bruce was required to be present.

As Bruce approached the entrance to the conference room five minutes before the scheduled meeting time, he was amazed to see an armed Marine on duty. He had never seen this type of security at the headquarters before this.

After presenting proper identification, he was admitted.

Bill was already present and nervously handed his premier commanding officer a cup of coffee. Not many words were exchanged between the two. Walter's nervousness was out of character, revealing that the matter to be discussed was of the greatest importance.

At exactly nineteen hundred hours (7:00 p.m.), four people entered the room preceded by the noise generated by the Marine sentry as he snapped to attention.

This was another clue that something big, with big people, was happening or was about to happen.

The four people entering the room included the submarine force commander, Vice Admiral James Dale; his operations officer, Captain Bob Beck, carrying a packed briefcase; and two men in civilian clothes.

The latter two in civilian clothes were introduced as Warren Andrews of the State Department and Vice Admiral Donald Hasting, the top intelligence specialist assigned to the president's national security council. Andrews was an assistant secretary of state.

After the normal salutations and introductions, the meeting commenced.

Vice Admiral Dale made the opening remarks by stating, "The mission to be discussed here is of grave importance to the survival of the United States and world peace." He emphasized, "The information received during the briefing will not," he repeated, "not, be discussed with anyone, including any crew members of *Jackfish*." The admiral continued, "In addition, the sensitivity of the mission is such that there will be no operations order written for the conduct of the operation."

This lack of an operational directive from higher authority was most peculiar. Even on missions of the highest classification in the past, Bruce had always received operational directives.

Admiral Hasting conducted the briefing with Warren Andrews, adding germane information as the discussions progressed. The meeting lasted forty minutes. It seemed to be an eternity to the young commanding officer.

Bruce at first was intrigued. As more information was provided, he became sullen and internally distressed. The briefing was incredible and beyond anyone's furthest imagination—unbelievable!

Admiral Dale's closing orders were for *Jackfish* to be made ready to get underway no later than noon tomorrow, proceed to the area of operational interest, and accomplish the assigned mission prior to midnight on the twenty-fourth of December.

The successful completion of the mission was to be reported to the chief of naval operations by an unclassified FLASH message in the clear, reading, "MISSION COMPLETE."

The admiral stated, "All United States and Allied communications receivers throughout the globe will be listening to copy this transmission. It is that important."

In closing, the force commander directed Bruce's squadron commander to provide the maximum assistance to ensure *Jackfish* was underway on schedule.

All the participants except Bill and Bruce departed.

Each reaffirmed to the commanding officer of *Jackfish* the urgency and national interest of this mission.

As he departed, Warren Andrews told Bruce that the president sent his best regards and that he had personally selected him for this operation.

Bruce could appreciate the sincerity of the advisors and could also sense that each one left the impression that they were glad he was assigned the mission rather than they.

Stewart and Walter, the remaining two participants of the briefing, sat dumbfounded, looking at each other for a few minutes. It seemed like an eternity full of bad dreams. What they had heard discussed and directed didn't and really couldn't have happened.

Mission Complete

Captain Bill Walter, being a top-notch squadron commander, had anticipated support action would be required. He had his complete staff assembled awaiting directions.

The captain of *Jackfish* immediately knew what his top priorities were.

He first called his executive officer, Lieutenant Commander Dave Brown.

Dave was a recently selected commander with a superior professional reputation in the submarine force.

"Dave, this is the captain. *Jackfish* will have to deploy no later than noon tomorrow." After a slight pause he continued, "I want an immediate recall of the crew. It is now eighteen thirty and I want a meeting with the crew in two hours in the commodore's conference room at his headquarters."

It was emphasized to Brown that this was a matter of grave importance and that no excuses would be accepted for all hands not sailing with the ship.

"All personnel on leave within twelve hour's traveling distance from the submarine base will be recalled."

Dave delayed his response anticipating some additional information, and then gave the captain a less than cheery, "Aye, aye, sir."

Bruce knew his exec would get the recall accomplished expertly.

Some of the crew would be beyond the range of returning within the underway time. They would be replaced with submarine-qualified men from either the squadron staff or from other submarines attached to the squadron. Those assignments would have to be determined tonight.

The next order of business was to telephone the ship's duty officer to direct that immediate steps be taken to get *Jackfish* ready for underway operations.

This process of getting the ship ready for underway operations normally started at least forty-eight hours before a normal scheduled underway of a fast attack nuclear submarine. However, this was not to be a normal scheduled underway.

The duty officer, Lieutenant Ray Jones, was directed by the captain to call in the standby duty section to assist in making the detailed prerequisite checks, valve lineups, and electrical and electronic checks necessary for starting up the nuclear reactors and propulsion plant and the associated engineering plant in preparation for at-sea operations.

Bruce then telephoned the engineer officer, Lieutenant Commander Tom Scott at home. He wanted to be assured that Tom was aware of the situation so that he would be prepared to support the readiness of the ship.

The complement of *Jackfish* was one hundred and thirty men, well

9

qualified and dedicated. Fourteen were officers. Most of the crew had served with Bruce in his previous ship and volunteered for assignment to *Jackfish* to serve him again.

Tom, the chief engineer, was responsible for five officers and forty enlisted men in the engineering department.

In addition, he was directly responsible for all propulsion equipment, electrical power, water supply, life-support equipment, the reactor and its ancillary equipment, plus the auxiliary components and systems that support the ship.

Tom had been the engineer of *Jackfish* for fourteen months and was a superb performer.

The engineer responded to the captain's call just as Bruce knew he would.

"Captain, I'm packing my traveling clothes and will report onboard within the hour. I have already talked to the engineering duty officer and have given him his directives."

"Thank you, Tom. Will see you soon."

Bruce hung up the telephone, confident his chief engineer would take charge and that his end of the ship would be ready to support the mission as he had done so many times in the past.

The ship had been in port only five days. Since this was a stand-down period, a time for rest and recreation for the crew after their extensive at-sea deployment, no major derangement of machinery or other equipment had taken place.

The squadron commander and Bruce then laid out plans to accomplish what remained to be done for the ship to get underway as scheduled.

These items included getting the Submarine Base Repair Department, on a high-priority basis, to reinstall the type twenty-four periscope.

This periscope was damaged during the last operation under the pack ice of the Arctic.

Although the backup periscope had been used successfully for the remainder of the deployment, the capability of the primary scope, both optically and for electronics intercept, far exceeded that of the secondary periscope.

In addition, sufficient consumables and spare parts were needed to replace those expended on the lengthy voyage, plus, of course, topping off the food supplies.

After a slight pause, Bruce put forth a request to his boss. "I need to load into *Jackfish* three Mark 56X torpedoes."

His request somewhat surprised the squadron commander, but after what was discussed earlier, the term surprise was only relative.

The Mark 56X torpedo was the most revolutionary submarine attack weapon ever developed by any country.

The torpedo completed its initial test phase without any problems. The rigid at-sea operational test was scheduled for early next year.

The torpedo was dual-explosive capable containing six hundred pounds of equivalent TNT conventional charge with an optional five-kiloton nuclear charge. The weapon had multiple sensing devices and detonating modes for use against any type submarine or surface target.

The torpedo was powered at speeds up to eighty knots, to distances of thirty thousand yards, by a compact highly enriched uranium 235 nuclear reactor. This power plant was similar to that used by the Soviets for some of their long-lived satellites in the late 1970s and 1980s.

"Although the nuclear option has never been tested, I will need the top-secret combination to set this mode of detonation should I get into an extremis situation," Bruce continued his discussion. "With the near-impossible demands placed on my ship and me, I will need anything and everything that could possibly provide me the slightest edge."

As usual, he was absolutely correct in his appraisal of the situation.

Without hesitation, Bill gave approval for the torpedo request. He would provide Bruce with the combinations to the weapons in the morning.

"Of course," continued Bill, "this authorization for use of nuclear capable weapons will have to be cleared up the line to the president."

Bill knew that under these circumstances the president would give him the go ahead.

Bruce felt relieved by Bill's agreement. Now he did not have to go over the head of his friend and boss to get permission to load these valuable assets.

There was no doubt in his mind that *Jackfish* would sail tomorrow with the nuclear capable torpedoes onboard.

The available food and supplies in *Jackfish* were routinely topped off and ready for emergency underway operations. However, the supply had gotten down somewhat during the recent underway period, but not below the level authorized by directives of the force commander.

Prior to underway operations, Bruce always ensured onboard supplies and food sufficient to last at least one hundred and thirty days submerged without any outside assistance.

With fifty minutes remaining until the "all hands" briefing with his crew,

Bruce hurried down to *Jackfish* at Pier Six, a two-hundred-yard walk from the commodore's headquarters.

As he boarded his ship, he was met with a snappy salute and "Good evening, Captain" from the topside security watch.

In the background, he could hear the ship's 1MC general announcing system echo "*Jackfish* arriving," the customary notification that the commanding officer was boarding the ship.

Bruce stopped momentarily to admire his charge. It was hard to envision that when you look at a nuclear attack submarine from on deck, only one fifth of the ship is visible above water.

Also, the uninitiated did not realize the complexity of the piping, equipment, wires, electronics, and electrical gear compressed within its steel shell.

Jackfish, four hundred and sixty feet long, displaced nine thousand tons submerged, operated at flank speed of forty knots submerged, and was fully maneuverable to a depth of two thousand feet.

The deadly arsenal of weapons in the ship included the nuclear tipped long-range Axehandle tactical cruise missiles and both conventional and nuclear long-range torpedoes of sophisticated design.

The BQQ-22 series sonar suite installed in *Jackfish* was the "eyes and ears" of this stealth underwater vehicle.

This system was the culmination of the efforts of a team consisting of the most renowned acoustic geniuses and acoustical engineers, coupled with the best computer processor personnel and design engineers this country could assemble.

The results were beyond all expectations, allowing the good guys to keep the acoustical edge over the ever-pressing Soviets.

The sonar system in *Jackfish* recently had the Mod Six installed, thus putting its system a margin ahead of any other BQQ-22 system.

Jackfish was the lead ship in the class of the most sophisticated and most deadly submarines ever put to sea by any nation. The ship used well the highest technology and most advanced engineering principles known to man.

The Soviets had attempted on the highest priority to emulate this warfighting platform at any cost.

The top Soviet experts in submarine design, construction processes, computer experts, submarine weapons analyses, and the Kremlin test and evaluation teams were assembled in a matrix team organization.

They used project-management principles and had a blank check authorized. Getting information germane to *Jackfish* was the number-one priority of the vast Soviet international spy network.

To date, however, they had been unable to get any useful data to successfully integrate the weapons system, sensors, communications, engineering quality, quieting main propulsion drive assembly, electronics, and habitability into their own *Jackfish*.

The United States Central Intelligence Agency and Naval Intelligence personnel had kept good tabs on the Soviet progress in this area.

Not to be surprised sleeping by some successful breakthrough in their technology, our establishment continually worked to upgrade all the systems in our ships, striving always to maintain that small edge of superiority that meant survival in a shooting confrontation.

At the present time, *Jackfish* was the only operational submarine in the class. This ship was delivered to active duty in 1985.

Then our government went into a pacifistic and anti-defense-spending mode. All defense spending was drastically reduced and our country's defenses weakened.

The next in the *Jackfish* class of submarines, *Tigerfish* was delivered two years later. Unfortunately, this magnificent submarine had been lost at sea with the complete crew this fall while operating in the Mediterranean Sea. A recorded underwater explosion and debris documented its fate, but the cause was yet to be determined.

The third ship of the *Jackfish* class had just successfully completed sea trials.

With a more aggressive administration now making the decisions in Washington, D.C., the construction rate of these underwater warriors should accelerate significantly.

The captain passed through a twenty-five-inch diameter personnel-access hatch, climbed down a twelve-foot vertical ladder, and landed on the first-level platform inside the submarine.

This access hatch formed the boundary between the inside of the submarine and the ocean.

The day's duty officer, Lieutenant Ray Jones, greeted his captain.

Ray's primary billet in *Jackfish* was the weapon's officer, a full-time job that he had performed superbly during the last eleven months.

"Good evening, Captain."

"Everything is proceeding on schedule with no major problems encountered."

The initial report from the officer responsible for ensuring that all prerequisites got done for the ship to make the underway on schedule was encouraging.

"Very well, Ray."

As the captain proceeded past Ray into the bowels of the ship, he looked the young officer in the eyes and stated for effect, "This is an important mission and more eyes will be observing us than I would like to acknowledge."

It was obvious by the querying look on Ray's face that he didn't fully understand what was happening and was hoping for follow-up information.

Bruce was hurt at not being able to provide any amplifying details to the men who had followed his orders religiously in the past without question and without complaining.

He also understood the many personal sacrifices his men and their families had made for him.

The two proceeded from the bow compartment into the operations compartment and thence into the wardroom. This was the living space or the "home away from home" for the ship's officers.

After he poured a cup of freshly brewed coffee, Bruce explained to the young lieutenant the directives he had been given, that there would be an all-hands meeting at twenty hundred tonight, and that the ship must be underway no later than noon tomorrow.

He stared at Ray and said in the most serious voice Ray had ever recalled hearing, "Ray, trust in me. This is a national emergency of the highest magnitude."

Immediately this officer knew nothing more was going to be said about the details of the operation and more importantly, this was indeed a serious and possibly dangerous mission.

He reconciled himself to the fact that this was the end of the conversation and resolved that he would perform to his maximum to support his leader.

Bruce reviewed the detailed check-off sheets used by the duty officer to prepare the ship for underway. He also took this opportunity to obtain status on the items out of commission and being repaired.

"Ray," the captain continued, "the engineer officer will arrive shortly and the squadron duty officer and repair officer will be onboard within the hour. This should take up some of the workload you currently are burdened with."

The leader of *Jackfish* then proceeded into the attack center to talk to his duty section by means of the ship's 1MC general announcing system. He picked up the hand microphone, delayed momentarily while mentally organizing his thoughts, then pushed the actuator button on top of the microphone.

"Let me have your attention please, this is the captain speaking."

All work ceased throughout the ship as men listened intently to the words of their captain. Hopefully they would get some details of the forthcoming operation.

"I realize we have been home for only five days after a long deployment and are looking forward to Christmas and the holidays with our wives, families, and loved ones.

"Regrettably, a crisis of the most important and urgent nature—one that imperils the United States, our loved ones, and the peace of the world—is in the making."

After a slight pause, Bruce continued. "The force commander evaluated all the submarine units to see which one is best prepared and most capable to carry out this mission. We are directed to get underway no later than noon tomorrow and will be out to sea for an extended period."

Bruce stopped talking momentarily to let the impact of the disappointment recede and to regain his crew's attention.

"I will meet with your shipmates within the hour to give them the same information, and also to inform them that all hands will report onboard by zero eight hundred tomorrow morning ready for underway operations.

"By department head approval, tonight's duty section will be permitted to depart the ship from zero eight hundred until no later than eleven thirty tomorrow morning. Although not much time, this period will allow you to get together your things necessary for going to sea and to spend a short time with your loved ones."

There was no doubt in the minds of any *Jackfish* sailor the sincerity of their captain and of the importance of this mission.

He continued his transmission. "I regret this inconvenience to you, a crew that has performed superbly in the past. I assure you this mission cannot be avoided. Our successful accomplishment will provide the opportunity to enjoy Christmas and the holidays next year.

"Thank you for your support in the past. I ask for the same unwavering support in the days to come. God bless each of you and your families and loved ones. Thank you."

The click of the microphone indicated the captain was finished his transmission.

Speculations abounded as crew members attempted to read between the lines of the captain's words and digest what had been said.

One thing was clear and was agreed upon by all hands. This mission was important and *Jackfish*, the best ship and crew in the submarine force, had been selected to do the job to ensure it got done correctly.

Although each person in the ship scoured some, and some outwardly bitched and complained about their personal hardships and plans they had made, each was proud to be serving under the command of Captain Stewart and as a member of *Jackfish*.

As Bruce started to depart the attack center, he saw Petty Officer McGann starting to energize the ship's inertial navigational system (SINS) equipment. McGann was an electronics technician first class with nine years in the Navy.

Although the ship had two other compasses, the SINS was the backbone of the navigation system. This elaborate electronics equipment consisted of gyroscopes and accelerometers that related the movement of the ship in all directions. Coupled with true speed through the water and over the ocean floor as well as true north, the SINS gave a continuous report of the submarine's position.

This information allowed *Jackfish* to remain submerged and travel long distances at high speeds, and still have good assurance of the location of the ship.

In addition to providing the much-needed navigational data, SINS provided accurate inputs for launching the deadly Axehandle missiles and torpedoes carried by *Jackfish*.

McGann was an expert electronics technician who had continually maintained his SINS in peak operational performance.

Bruce was very impressed with this young sailor—so much so that he had recommended him for selection into the limited duty officer program. This program allowed the best of the top enlisted personnel in the United States Navy to move into the officer community after four years of Navy-paid college education.

Bruce had no doubts, especially with his two-page endorsement of praise and platitudes, that McGann would be selected.

"Good evening, Petty Officer McGann. How's your pride and joy?" Bruce asked as he approached the technician. There was no doubt that he was referring to SINS.

McGann glanced up in respect but didn't want to take his eyes off the oscilloscope that was providing him valuable calibration information.

Mission Complete

"Captain. It will take eighteen hours for the SINS to be in top-notch operation."

"With ten hours of work and then going into fast align, I will have the unit operational to support the underway. Once at sea, I will fine align the system to peak performance."

A smile appeared on Bruce's face coupled with a nod of acknowledgment of the report.

As he turned to make his exit from the ship, he put his hand on McGann's shoulder. As from a father to a special son, he stated, "Thanks for your continued outstanding support. Keep up the good work."

"*Jackfish* departing" heard throughout the ship on the ship's 1MC general announcing system indicated to those onboard that their leader was departing the ship. They knew he was en route to the commodore's headquarters to brief the remainder of the *Jackfish* crew.

As he walked up the pier, Bruce was oblivious that the temperature had fallen to freezing, of a cold wind blowing across the Thames River, and of the falling snow adding to the already compressed snow underfoot.

It had been just over two hours since his initial meeting directing the mission. It didn't take too much time for the increased strenuous pressure, a result of that meeting, to start to weigh heavily on Bruce.

As he sloshed through the elements, he started to question his ability to carry out this assignment.

What if I fail? he thought. *What if I have a medical problem and my executive officer doesn't know the mission objective? Have we had time to ensure the reliability of all important equipment and sensors? Did I wear the crew out during the previous deployment? What if there has not been enough time for the men to "recharge" the batteries necessary for them to operate at peak performance?*

These thoughts continually raced through his mind. *If the answer to any of these questions is in the affirmative, the future of the United States and the consequences of this unthinkable future would be my fault as the captain.*

The words of Joseph Conrad's *Command at Sea* raced through his thought process. "In each ship there is one man who, in the hour of emergency or peril at sea, can turn to no other man. There is one who alone is ultimately responsible for the safe navigation, engineering performance, accurate gun firing, and morale of his ship. He is the commanding officer. He is the ship. There is not an instant during his tour as commanding officer that he can escape the grasp of command responsibility."

"Good evening, Captain." Dave's words broke Bruce's trance as he found himself at the steps leading to the commodore's headquarters.

Dave Brown was standing on the steps. The collar of his heavy bridge coat was up around his ears, and a light coating of snow covered the beak of his cap and shoulders.

"A nice evening for duck hunting," uttered by the captain didn't pack the gear to relieve the tension that had generated within Bruce nor the anxiety of his executive officer.

As the two professionals approached the conference room, Dave reported, "All but twenty of the enlisted men and two officers are present. Of this number, twelve of the troops and one officer are in the area but could not be located. Messages have been left for them to report to the ship. The remaining absentees are on authorized leave out of the area and will not be able to make it back on time."

"Dave, give the required replacement rates to the squadron staff after our meeting. Ensure their personnel people understand my preference is for bachelors and volunteers, if at all possible."

Dave provided these requirements to the squadron chief of staff as he entered the room. Bill Walter also was present and concurred to the request.

The executive officer was assured that qualified replacement personnel would report prior to noon tomorrow ready for extended at-sea operations.

It was now twenty hundred on the twentieth of December. Slightly over four days remained for the completion of the mission.

Bruce started to perspire and it was reinforced that time was indeed at a premium.

As he entered the briefing room, the chief of the boat, Master Chief Petty Officer Andy Tiernan ordered, "Attention on deck."

Tiernan, known as the COB, was the direct liaison between the enlisted crew members and the commanding officer and the executive officer of *Jackfish*. He had proven himself completely capable of carrying out this responsibility over his last fifteen months in the billet.

The captain walked upright and with authority as he took his place at the podium.

He then ordered the crew, "At ease."

Bruce, a strong advocate and practitioner of the chain of command, realized he first should meet with the officers. Then he would give them the information and an opportunity to discuss the issues and make recommendations and comments.

The department heads then would scope out the tasks with their division officers and leading petty officers.

This was the normal modus operandi of management practiced in *Jackfish*.

To fulfill the task ahead, Commander Stewart knew this was to be one of the many exceptions of good management practices he had prided himself on over the years.

His crew seated before him anxiously awaited the information that necessitated their being assembled under crisis conditions just five days before Christmas, after being home less than one week.

Bruce repeated the briefing that he just provided to the duty section aboard *Jackfish*.

Disappointment was obvious. However, these men had learned from experience and under extreme pressure that their captain would not ask this of them had it not been a national emergency.

In closing, he emphasized, "It will be up to each department head to ensure his commitments are met. The ship must get underway at noon tomorrow." He added, "I desire each man to have as much time home as possible within the limited time remaining. Liberty is to expire at zero eight hundred in the morning."

A work plan to allow the duty section some time home was directed to each officer in charge of a department.

"Attention on deck" was sounded as he commenced his exit.

As he passed Dave, he told him he wanted to meet with him and the navigator, Nat Olsen, in the ship's wardroom after the department heads' meetings.

Prior to returning to his ship, Bruce took this short break in his time-sensitive schedule to make an important telephone call.

"Hello, Ann. Sorry I did not have the opportunity to call sooner."

The call was short and after the telephone was cradled, Ann knew four things. She was reassured her sailor husband loved her. Although not directly told to her by Bruce, she knew there was a sensitive submarine operation brewing. Also, she would have to pack his at-sea clothes, and finally, this was to be the fourth Christmas in a row they would not be together.

Although underway operations without much notice had occurred many times in the past, Ann suddenly got a cold chill over her body. For the first time in a very long time, she was frightened.

/2/ MISSION PREPARATIONS

As the captain returned to *Jackfish* that evening after his crew briefing in the commodore's headquarters, it was obvious that his able crew was accomplishing much to ensure the ship made the underway on schedule.

During a normal evening, those men not on watch in the engineering spaces or carrying out assigned duties in the forward part of the ship or topside of the submarine would be watching movies in the crew's dinette. This was the eating and galley area that was transformed into a theater at night.

This area also provided the crew the space to relax, eat popcorn, munch on goodies, build giant "Dagwood" sandwiches, play acey-ducey, and write letters to their loved ones.

One of the incentives to being stationed on a submarine was that the food freezer and chill-box doors were never locked, and the contents were ever so inviting and always available.

On Sunday mornings when *Jackfish* was operating at sea, the crew's dinette area was used as a place for worship. A member of the crew from each religion was the lay leader to lead the services.

The Submarine Base chaplains provided prepackaged service material prior to the ship getting underway. This material was used as the foundation for the services.

This evening no movie was being shown.

Bruce proceeded to the wardroom, removed his winter clothing now wet and damp from the inclement weather, and drew a large mug of black steaming coffee.

While he sipped his refreshing and warming beverage, he dialed the Quartermaster's Station on the ship's internal telephone.

Mission Complete

"This is the captain. Please bring the catalog of navigation charts to me in the wardroom."

With professional haste, quartermaster first class Bierman presented the captain a large catalog showing all the ocean areas of the world divided into squares. A number was assigned to each area.

It didn't take Bruce long to locate the navigation chart he needed. This chart was numbered 145. It covered the East Coast of the United States down to Cuba and extended greater than fourteen hundred nautical miles to seaward from the cities of New York, Groton, Connecticut, Washington, D.C., and Norfolk, Virginia.

Bierman departed, catalog in hand, with directions to return with chart number 145, navigational plotting equipment, and some sharp pencils.

This had been a long day already and there still remained much to accomplish.

The tension was starting to show in Stewart's face. He untied his shoes, a mechanism that he realized long ago started the "relax circuit" in his strong computerized body. This body was exceptionally cared for, and in reciprocal action, it returnd to him the stamina and long hours when called upon to do so.

Reflecting upon his study at the Naval War College in Newport, Rhode Island five years ago, Bruce rememberd the key theme of the Soviet threat seminars and lectures. This major theme was that you must thoroughly understand the Soviet thought process and weaknesses and then exploit these weaknesses to defeat him.

This intelligence would be applied during the preparations for and of course during the execution of the mission.

With his sleeves partially rolled up, elbows on the table, and his head rested in his hands, the captain attempted to develop the mindset of a Soviet submarine skipper.

He had much experience at close observation of the Soviet adversary during his many lengthy submarine operations against the Russians during the past decade.

Most of the operations were associated with the cold war environment or "touch and feel operations"; however, one operation was a short torpedo shooting crisis with Soviet submarines three years ago. This operation was precipitated because the political decision-makers in Washington, D.C. erred in evaluating diplomatic signals from the Soviet Union.

As a result of this crisis action, Bruce was credited with sinking one of the top Soviet nuclear attack submarines in a classic Hollywood underwater dual. Unfortunately, our side lost two attack submarines in the engagement.

Bruce personally briefed this mission to the newly elected president of the United States. After the briefing, the president awarded the young commanding officer the first Navy Cross Medal that had been awarded to a submarine officer since World War II.

Bruce and the president had been personal friends ever since.

This briefing was the first of many special and dangerous operations by *Jackfish* that had come to the president's attention over the ensuing years.

A knock on the door broke the captain's concentration.

Petty officer Bierman returned with the requested chart and navigation equipment. These tools included a set of dividers, parallel rule, pencils and a circular slide rule.

This latter navigational aid was a simplistic device with two rotatable wheels. One wheel was for setting speed in knots and the other for distance in nautical miles. Both wheels indicated against a fixed index of time in hours. By selecting two of the three variables—speed, distance, and time—the operator was able to solve for the third variable.

In his short meditation role as a Soviet submariner, Stewart calculated that his adversary would not push his weapons or systems to the maximum range, as was the norm for American military tacticians and operators.

Thus, with a fifteen hundred nautical mile missile range, Bruce applied a safety factor of twenty percent with the expected launch point now twelve hundred nautical miles from the target.

The Soviet decision making process would elect to station the launching submarine outside the normally traveled merchant lanes of the Atlantic Ocean and be outside or on the outer edge of the range of United States Maritime Patrol airplanes.

The submarine would be in deep water, arrive at the launch point early to allow a sufficient amount of safety time, and remain submerged until after sunset.

The sun would set in four days at seventeen fifty two hours (5:52 p.m.).

His assumptions and planning had to be correct. There would be no retake of the examination. No second chance would be available to save the future of the United States and the free world.

Soon the executive officer and Lieutenant Commander Nat Olsen, *Jackfish*'s navigation officer, entered the wardroom.

Nat was the first to speak. "Good evening, Captain. Another cup of coffee?"

Mission Complete

After pouring a cup of coffee and topping off the captain's half empty mug, they both sat down, ready for the next piece of the puzzle to be put in place. Both Nat and Dave reported that they would be ready to support the scheduled underway at noon tomorrow.

They then sat quietly and sulked somewhat.

Both waited for their captain to provide them some details of the forthcoming mission. This routine of thoroughly discussing all aspects of the mission had always been carried out in the past when preparing for high priority operations.

The astute captain sensed their uneasiness and cursed to himself at the Washington hierarchy that prohibited him from taking his two trusted shipmates, warriors, and friends into his confidence.

After he slowly sipped his coffee, he withdrew his green pocket notebook, thumbed through it rapidly, then told Nat, "Plot this position—latitude twenty three point seven degrees north, longitude seven two point one degrees west. Label this location as Point Alfa."

Only the captain knew the significance of this information. As reported by Admiral Hasting during the initial mission brief, torpedoes at this location had sunk the United States frigate *USS Forbes*.

This datum was to be the starting point for developing the search and attack plan to be used by *Jackfish* to carry out the assigned mission.

He took a set of dividers from the navigational plotting set and spread the dividers to measure twenty degrees of latitude on the chart. This measure was equal to twelve hundred nautical miles. The point of the dividers was placed at Washington, D.C. With the outstretched leg of the dividers holding the pencil lead, an arc was drawn on the chart.

This procedure was repeated with the point placed on New York City. The arcs crossed at a location with latitude twenty-five degrees north and longitude fifty-eight point nine degrees west.

Bruce then repeated the procedure for Norfolk, Virginia, and Groton, Connecticut.

These last two arcs were drawn just to assure the plotter that the arcs would pass to the east of the described position greater than twelve hundred nautical miles.

His seamanship knowledge and nautical expertise were correctly confirmed. Now he knew he had reasonable assurance that he had bracketed the location of the launch submarine.

As he slowly returned the dividers to their proper stowage location, he told Nat, "Label this location where the arcs cross as Point Bravo."

The depth of water at Point Bravo was over thirty-two hundred fathoms, or over nineteen thousand feet. It was at the outer edge of Maritime Patrol Air range, outside of the normally traveled shipping lanes and approximately five hundred and forty nautical miles southeast of Bermuda.

This location met all the prerequisites the captain had developed in his strategy meditation session as to the launch point for the Soviet-Cuban attack.

Nat measured the distance between Point Alfa and Point Bravo and reported to the captain and executive officer that the distance was six hundred and twenty nautical miles.

Bruce was the only one who knew the significance of these two points as he recorded the accumulated data into his green pocket notebook.

Mentally he calculated that it would take a vessel at an average speed of five knots to travel this distance to arrive at Point Bravo about nineteen hundred hours, or seven o'clock the evening of December twenty-fourth—Christmas Eve.

Nat, now more excited about the mission since he was taking an active part in the preparations, continued to follow Bruce's directions in applying lines and arcs to the chart.

A sixty nautical mile circle was ascribed around both Point Bravo and Bermuda. A one-hundred-and-twenty- and a three-hundred-nautical-mile semicircle were drawn around the mystic Point Bravo with the diameter line on an axis of zero-four-five and two-two-five degrees true.

Dave continued to observe the planning and mentally attempted to piece together the objective of the mission.

He remained reserved and quiet, not at all his normal character. He was still sulking somewhat about not being briefed by his boss on the details of this obviously significant mission. Naturally he would be provided the details of this highly sensitive operation shortly—or would he?

Normal modus operandi in *Jackfish* was for the captain, Dave, and Nat to discuss the details of an operation, establish the objectives, and then develop a primary plan of action. Then alternatives or contingency plans to take care of the "what ifs" would be developed.

This allowed three astute minds to integrate their thoughts, usually with one playing the devil's advocate, to ensure that all details of the mission were covered.

In addition, should something happen to the captain, the executive officer, as prescribed in the U.S. Navy Regulations, would ascend to the position of the commanding officer of *Jackfish*.

Mission Complete

This was not to be the case for this operation, the most sensitive, most dangerous, most time restrictive, and most vital to the survival of the United States that Commander Stewart and *Jackfish* had ever been called upon to execute. He would have to complete the mission as a one-man show.

Bruce directed his navigator, "Mark a position at latitude forty-point-two degrees north and longitude seventy one degrees west. Label this position Point Charlie."

Point Charlie had a depth of water of one hundred fathoms.

Nat stated for concurrence, "To get to Point Charlie, we will travel eighty nautical miles on course one-six-five degrees true from a position between Block Island and Montauk Point located on the most easterly tip of Long Island."

Both Bruce and Dave nodded in agreement.

"Point Charlie is the location we will submerge the ship assuming we have no interference from the Soviet AGI."

The Soviets routinely had an AGI, or spy ship, stationed in this area. The ship was heavily loaded with electronic gear to monitor submarine operations.

The thought entered Bruce's mind that *Jackfish* might not make the return trip and the crew might instead remain buried at sea in their iron coffin, as many of Bruce's dolphin-wearing friends had done in the past.

He recalled a statement made by Winston Churchill in his book *The World Crises:* "But at the outset of the conflict we had more captains of ships than captains of war."

Stewart quickly dismissed these doubts. After all, he had seen the best of his enemy in mortal battle and had returned victorious. He was without a doubt the best of the best.

To regain some of the waning camaraderie of his exec, Bruce looked across the table and stated, "Dave, we need to evaluate the area within the sixty, one hundred and twenty and three hundred nautical mile circles generated around Point Bravo. Specifically, we should be looking at just the northwestern semicircles with the diameter of the circle on a line of zero-four-five and two hundred twenty-five degrees true.

"Using the Sonar Prediction and Analytical Data System (SPADS), get the time to search out each area with our newly upgraded MOD Six sophisticated sonar suite, the best speed and depth for searching with the underwater search gear, and the environmental conditions that would be present."

With firmness in his voice, but at a lower voice level, the captain continued. "And also, the target we will be searching for is a U.S. submarine of the *Jackfish* class with the same sonar system installed as us, but without MOD Six installed."

This last statement caused immediate silence.

Eyes staring at the captain from the two officers in attendance and a slight opening of their mouths left little doubt at the shock factor that had been delivered by Stewart.

Bruce knew that both men were deciding whether to question the speaker as to the classification of the target or just hope more information would be forthcoming.

The SPADS was the most modern piece of ancillary sonar equipment using the latest development of sophisticated high technology known in the United States. The system had been installed in the *Jackfish* just two weeks prior to the submarine's last deployment.

The company that developed the SPADS completed a very successful accelerated test and evaluation program to meet this schedule.

This magnificent computer system, a lightweight minimum volume microprocessor network, had almost an unlimited memory.

Environmental data for all oceans of the world covering all seasons of the year was one of the parameters in the SPADS that was used for solving the risk assessment equation.

The weapons performance effectiveness of every weapons system known in the civilized world, and the characteristics of every ship, surface, and submarine in active service by any country, friend and foe alike, were available in the memory disc of this system.

By inserting into SPADS the search area of interest; attack weapon; expected target speed; the specific target by name preferred, or second option by class; and the type class of the searching ship, the SPADS then would output the desired tactical data.

This data would include the best speed to use in sonar search, time to complete the search of the area, and the number of torpedo weapons to be launched at the target for an eighty percent kill probability.

In addition, the SPADS provided the maximum detection range for the attacker and the most important information to the hunter—the maximum range the enemy or huntee could counter-detect you by his sonar system.

The latest addition to the SPADS contained the name of the commanding officer of every war fighting ship known. The system had a rating profile that rated each captain based on a scale of one to ten.

This score was based on such factors as overall professional expertise, tenacity, time in the job, war fighting ability, physical condition, faithfulness to his spouse, leadership, engineering and training ability, and expected reaction time to emergencies.

This commanding officer's evaluation module had just been added to the SPADS program for solving the risk assessment equation to refine the solution even finer.

Many times this factor would be the deciding point between success and failure, or more realistically, loss of your ship.

There was no doubt in anyone's mind that if the Soviets had a SPADS, Commander Bruce Stewart and *Jackfish* would be rated ten plus.

Although it was obvious to the skipper that Dave wanted to question the target, a U.S. submarine of the *Jackfish* class, the executive officer marched off smartly to obtain the requested data.

Bruce would have preferred to get this important piece of the tactical puzzle personally. However, he realized that he needed the full support of his most capable executive officer.

The chiming of the highly polished brass clock inlayed into the outboard bulkhead of the wardroom made Bruce realize it was now thirty minutes until the twenty-first day of December commenced. Time was traveling too rapidly.

"Let's get on with it, Nat. Time, tide, and the execution of this mission wait for no one."

The captain continued to provide Nat with tactical information for plotting.

"Lay out the standard track and speed outbound from Groton, Connecticut, down the Thames River and across Block Island Sound. Use noon tomorrow as the underway time.

"Thence past Montauk Point, turning south southeast into international waters heading towards Point Charlie. We then will put *Jackfish* into her natural habitat—under the water."

After he reviewed the chart, Bruce continued, "I want to travel at an average speed of advance of thirty knots on a ship's course to touch the northeast portion of the sixty-mile circle drawn around Bermuda.

"We will continue at this speed of advance toward Point Bravo until we meet the three-hundred- nautical-mile circle drawn around Point Bravo."

Bruce took a sip of coffee and then continued, "Compute the time *Jackfish* will arrive at this latest position. Give me the best time and the worst time accounting for contingencies such as reduced visibility while operating on the surface across the sound in shallow water before submerging.

"The rest of the plan will be developed after we get the data from Dave."

Nat acknowledged the directives and immediately immersed himself into the exacting task of ensuring compliance.

He thought to himself, to make an average speed of advance, or SOA, of thirty knots would require flank speed of up to forty knots. This would allow time for the slower speeds needed for such evolutions as taking the submarine to periscope depth for communications periods, housekeeping chores, and the possibility, always to be reckoned with, of an interaction with a Soviet submarine.

Hard driving the ship under these conditions of maximum speed was not consistent with Bruce's way of operating his most capable ship and superb engineering plant.

He was recognized throughout the Submarine Force as an exceptionally well qualified nuclear engineer who thoroughly understood the integrated complexities of the nuclear reactor and associated systems, main propulsion plant, and ancillary equipment. This included the zero defect quality control that went into developing and constructing his wonderful submarine.

He also realized that these submarines were expensive platforms constructed for an operational life expectancy of at least thirty years.

As the capital ship in the U.S. Navy, these submersibles were the linchpins in carrying out the United States maritime strategy in fulfillment of our president's national objectives and interests.

Bruce took special pride in the "care and feeding" of *Jackfish*, driving his submarine hard only when absolutely necessary, but yet operating it at its designed war fighting potential to successfully complete all assigned missions.

Nat and Dave both had their tasks to complete in developing the detailed navigation plan following the directions provided by their leader.

Bruce took this opportunity to leave the wardroom and evaluate the progress taking place throughout the rest of the ship to ensure *Jackfish* would make the underway commitment.

As he entered the sonar room, he saw sonar man chief Keller and five of his expert sonar men "head down and tail up." They all were engrossed in technical manuals following the detailed check- off lists as they energized, checked, tweaked a little on the calibration knobs, and observed the installed oscilloscopes.

Then they rechecked the meter settings to ensure they were correct as required by the system technical and operating manuals. The sophisticated data displays on some panels made the space look like an advanced downtown arcade with space age machines.

"Good evening, Captain," said Keller when he noticed that his captain was observing his men at work. No big problems yet. I expect to have everything on the line and ready to support the mission prior to underway."

"Thanks, Chief. As always, I will rely heavily on your eyes and ears." He paused, and then continued. "This is a big one, friend and shipmate."

Chief Keller had been with Stewart long enough and under the most dangerous situations and understood the message his captain was sending him.

Bruce knew that it would be the expertise of these men that would make the difference between success and failure. The target would have the same advanced sonar system they did except that *Jackfish* had the mod six installed. This system modification upgrade gave *Jackfish* a slight margin of superiority.

However, *Jackfish* would have to travel at high speed en route to and then into the area of interest looking for the target. The faster a submerged ship moved through water the more radiated noise it generated.

The target would be operating at slow speeds generating minimum radiated noise into the water. This scenario gave the *Tigerfish* the advantage of finding the *Jackfish* at a longer distance and also made the target harder to locate.

Sonar man Keller had been with the captain for three years and had proven that he could pull contact detection and classification out of just a few noises amongst much ocean environmental background interference. Hopefully, his team would not fail on this possible one-way voyage.

Bruce threw Keller an understanding nod as he exited his space.

His next stop was to the after part of the ship to the engineering spaces to see how Tom, his engineer officer, and his nuclear trained engineers were progressing in readying the start up of the nuclear reactor plants and propulsion equipment.

As he passed through the crew's dinette en route to the engineering area, Bruce was surprised to see his old shipmate Chief Machinist Mate Wayne Douglas as he was drawing a cup of coffee.

Douglas had served with Bruce on his last ship for over two years before going to a well deserved tour of shore duty in the Repair Department on the Groton Submarine Base.

Stewart was instrumental in making this happen and the chief and his family of three always thought the highest of him.

He hurried over to the chief and shook his hand strongly as sincere friends do.

"What are you doing onboard *Jackfish* at this time of the night, Chief? You should be home wrapping Christmas presents with Nadine. As you know, Christmas is only four days away."

Chief Douglas replied with a proud smile on his face. "Well, Captain, you are going to have to put up with me some more. I volunteered because if you are getting underway on short notice like this and you need replacement crew members to support your trip, it must be important. The successful completion of this mission will, in the long run, also benefit my family. So I just want to add my help in any way possible."

Wayne then continued, "Captain, your number one fan club members, Nadine and my youngsters, fully understand and would rather have me here with you than home with them for Christmas."

"By the way, Nadine asked me to wish you a Merry Christmas and God speed."

Bruce gave his reunited shipmate a pat on the shoulder, rapidly turned, and headed aft.

Chief Douglas observed the slight tears forming in the corners of his adopted captain's eyes and realized that he had made the correct choice of where to spend this Christmas.

As the captain proceeded into the engineering spaces of *Jackfish*, he admired the tremendous engineering accomplishments of Admiral Rickover and his Naval Reactor's staff in their design of such a magnificent undersea warship.

It was apropos that Bruce also reflected at this time back to his Naval War College days and his study of Admiral Alfred Thayer Mahan. A passage from Mahan almost a century past seemed applicable to the young commanding officer at this moment. "The true aim of the War College is to promote not the mechanics of naval material, but how to use the material in the conduct of war."

The genius of engineering developed the weapon and the genius of naval warfare provided him the philosophy for the use of the weapon.

Now it was up to him not to disappoint the two naval wise men of the twentieth century.

Tom was hunched over the workbench in the forward part of the engine room talking with his engineering duty officer. They were reviewing in detail

Mission Complete

the check lists, valve lineup sheets, and the rest of the myriad of paperwork required as prerequisites before taking a nuclear reactor plant critical and lighting off the mechanical components of the associated engineering and propulsion plant.

"Evening, Engineer. Looks as if you have had a busy night."

"Yes sir." The dark-ring eyed engineer officer continued, "But I have a good handle on the scope of the problems and have them fully covered."

After awhile in the job, the engineer officer of a nuclear attack submarine usually appeared at least five years older than his true age. This was particularly applicable to Tom, who had never relaxed for the eight months of their last deployment.

With the minimal amount of time in port with his family, he hadn't had sufficient time to recharge his physical system back to normal. His wrinkled forehead looked even more pronounced with the newly added pressures caused by this untimely, unscheduled underway.

"Besides the normal underway routines, I want to have number four condensate pump replaced. The shaft is out of line and I'm afraid it could bind and fail while underway. The squadron engineer has a replacement condensate pump and we will make the transfer about four o'clock in the morning. Six high-pressure steam traps are being lapped in by ship's force personnel now and we will replace the packing material in them before installation. This should give us a good tight steam system."

Tom continued his status report to the captain. "The Submarine Base personnel are giving us good support and will provide us tonight the lubricating oil necessary to top off all of our systems."

The people-conscious commanding officer asked, "Tom, do you have enough engineers aboard to handle the workload?"

Bruce knew that he had transferred to his engineer some of his non-quantitative philosophy in handling the Navy's most important commodity—its people. This was reaffirmed when Tom replied, "Half of the department is in now. The rest will arrive at zero five hundred. After about a two hour turnover of information/ status of the plant and work in progress, I have scheduled tonight's workers to depart the ship and get some time with their family. This also will give them time to get organized on the beach before putting out to sea. All will return no later than eleven-thirty in the morning."

Bruce was proud of his protégé and expected great things from him in the future.

Moving out of the engineering spaces to the forward part of the ship, Bruce observed some of the crew members starting to report back aboard, ditty bags in hand ready for sea.

Many of the crew made it a normal routine to spend their last night in port aboard the ship to ensure they do not miss ship movement, and also to pitch in and help their shipmates if needed.

Ray, the ship's duty officer and weapons officer, was sitting in front of the fire control display panels in the attack center.

The conversation he was having with his leading fire control technician and leading petty officer of his torpedo division centered on the remaining work to be accomplished by the weapon's department before the ship got underway.

Bruce waited patiently, unobserved until the meticulous weapons officer completed his work conference.

He was proud of the detailed knowledge and management skills this young officer displayed.

It's amazing, thought the captain, *just how intense the responsibility that is placed upon a young officer in nuclear submarine duty is.*

In the civilian sector, his contemporaries would have at least four echelons to pass through before being permitted to make the decisions that Ray was making here on the spot. Also, his contemporaries' salaries would be at least double to compensate for this responsibility.

Proud and dedicated service to our country was certainly a wonderful thing.

"Excuse me, Captain. I was just reviewing some last minute details with my troops," Ray stated apologetically to his boss.

"Keep up the good work, weps. I need to discuss some items with you if you have the time."

Ray knew that he always had the time for the captain. "Yes sir."

Stewart wanted to ensure that Ray would be ready to receive the three Mark 56X nuclear capable torpedoes starting at zero seven thirty in the morning, and support the landing and installation of the repaired Type Twenty Four periscope and the loading of food and supplies into the ship.

All three significant evolutions were to occur at the same time.

Good coordination between ship's personnel assigned to *Jackfish* and the Submarine Base sailors would be especially crucial to complete these tasks on time and without incident.

"Ray, I want to ensure that space is available in the torpedo stowage racks

Mission Complete

behind the torpedo tubes to nest the three Mark 56X torpedoes. As soon as possible after underway, I want the final checks made and then the torpedoes loaded into the torpedo tubes."

The captain continued, "By the way, I want a technical manual for this weapon. I will personally inspect each torpedo to become familiar with the newest and most capable torpedo in the Submarine Force."

Ray acknowledged this odd directive.

What Ray didn't know was that his captain would covertly activate the combination system in the nuclear portion of the torpedo before the torpedoes were tube loaded. This activation would give him the option of making the torpedoes detonate as a nuclear explosion device if needed in the not- to-distant future.

Ray also was notified that one officer and twelve enlisted personnel would be reporting to *Jackfish* as replacement crew members.

"Ensure that the duty chief petty officer sets up bunks and lockers for them. Also, ensure that their emergency data records are current and that the squadron has a copy of the updated data."

"Thank you, Ray. I will be in the wardroom with Nat and Dave completing the navigation and tactical plan."

Bruce departed the attack center en route to the wardroom.

As he approached the wardroom to review the work of his executive officer and navigator, a thought suddenly came to him from his study so many years ago of Carl von Clausewitz's classic book, *On War*: "An army's efficiency gains life and spirit for enthusiasm for the cause for which it fights, but such enthusiasm is not indispensable."

He wonderd why the memory disc of his computer mind happened to display this output at this time.

He hoped that he could hold the enthusiasm of his crew until the completion of the mission.

By following the verbal orders from his superiors in Washington, Bruce was astute enough to know that he was driving a wedge ever so slowly between himself, his executive officer, and his officers.

Entering the wardroom after his one hour information gathering tour of the ship, he observed Dave completing the verification of the navigator's track data with his desktop mini processor.

Dave reported to Bruce. "Captain. Nat has completed laying out the track to our intended destination. I have verified the track and see no unforeseen problems. *Jackfish* will arrive at the point designated northwest of Point Bravo on the twenty-third of December at zero-zero-thirty in the morning."

Bruce mentally calculated the times and concurred with Dave and Nat.

He then slowly and clearly provided the tactical plan for the mission to his two comrades.

"We will have forty-seven hours to cautiously enter the outer search area, get acclimated to the environment, give the sonar team time to get organized into an alert combat profile, and then thoroughly search the area slowly and cautiously."

The three officers took a sip of coffee and digested the information being provided.

"We will then press closer to the one-hundred-and-twenty-nautical mile second area and repeat the procedure until contact is made."

Bruce continued, "If no contact is generated, *Jackfish* will move into the sixty nautical mile area around Point Bravo until contact is made. Then we will maneuver our ship closer for a good firing solution."

Bruce thought, *Then a loud explosion will signal the end of the threat to the future free world and the United States.* Remorsefully, his thoughts rapidly shifted to the destruction of an American submarine crew and his best friend.

What would be disclosed to the families and friends of the crew of *Tigerfish*? Would his crew ever know what really happened and why?

Dave and Nat were as baffled as before.

Dave had previously been directed to get data from the SPADS for a target of *Jackfish* class. They both knew that the only ship that met this classification was the *Tigerfish*.

This could not possibly be just an exercise, he thought, *or we would not have been rousted away from home before Christmas. But why a United States submarine?*

They both were getting tenser as a result of not being given the details of the operation, particularly Dave.

The question ever pressing on Bruce's mind was what if he had assumed incorrectly and the threat submarine was not located were he thought it was. He must develop a logical search plan and hopefully be able to allocate enough time for this possibility before the Christmas Eve deadline.

The basic principle of making a torpedo attack—essentially detect, localize/classify, approach, and then attack—had been preached to Bruce in officers' basic submarine school many years ago. The steps were later reinforced in Prospective Commanding Officer's (PCO) school.

Successful completion of this PCO school and a three month intense training program directly under Admiral Rickover were prerequisites before being awarded command of a nuclear submarine.

It seemed so simple to make torpedo attacks and practice the principles in the attack training center at the Submarine School in Groton, Connecticut. There the enemy were little models of ships or man-made reproductions of submerged submarine sounds.

It added more realism to the problem when the target would shoot back real torpedoes. Also, a whole new degree of reality was added when the man behind the eyeballs looking out his periscope at you had a wife and family like you and was fighting for what he considerd to be the best way of life.

Bruce evaluated the two crucial items needed now for underway planning from the output data Dave had retrieved from the SPADS. The items were time to search each area on a step-in basis and the range for the target to detect *Jackfish*.

Unfortunately, the target would be moving or patrolling on station at a much slower speed while *Jackfish* would be closing the anticipated target location at a higher rate of speed. The faster the submerged speed, the more radiated noise was put into the water by the submarine and the greater potential for detection by the enemy sonar.

Bruce thought that hopefully *Tigerfish* would not be alerted and would be casual in their operations. This would provide some margin in favor of *Jackfish*.

A long shot was the fact that the Soviet submarines did not have any sonar equipment similar to that of the *Jackfish* class. Thus, the Soviet submarine officer monitoring in the *Tigerfish* sonar room could possible not interpret the noise signal being generated by *Jackfish* as that of a submarine closing in for the kill.

Also, there was the possibility the captive American sonar operators in *Tigerfish* would covertly put a noise source into the water when they heard *Jackfish* approaching. This would provide an accurate true bearing to the target, allowing *Jackfish* to generate a high probability torpedo kill solution before the Soviets knew they were under attack.

The captain continued the discussion with his two supporting officers. "The rest of the data will be analyzed after the ship is underway. Then the final decisions will be made regarding the tactics to be used for the mission."

Nat and Dave continued to feel left out of the planning and thought process associated with this mission. They knew it was dangerous and that they could possibly not return from it. Yet they would have no say in their fate.

Dave, a very proud individual whose inputs to tactics and strategic planning of previous operations had been significant to the success of these missions, felt especially slighted. He was the next in command and would ascend to the top position of responsibility in *Jackfish* should an emergency happen to Bruce.

In the past, the captain had make it a practice to always discuss in detail the operation, tactics to be carried out, and his own personal or sometimes fatherly philosophy on the conduct of the mission.

This was not happening now. It added mysticism or just irritation to the knowledgeable and professional executive officer.

After all, thought Dave, *I will be transferred from* Jackfish *in two months to get my own command, and I certainly feel competent in my chosen field.*

Bruce looked at the navigation chart. Nat had, as usual, done a superb job.

Dave handed the captain the movement report used to inform higher authority the track that *Jackfish* would use for the forthcoming operation.

This movement report allowed the Submarine Force Headquarters in Norfolk, Virginia, to plot the submarine's position at all times. This procedure prevented any possible submarine interferences or collisions and let the boss know the location of all friendly submarines at sea.

The report was a formatted form containing the significant data that had been extracted from the proposed track laid out by Nat.

The top half of the form was in narrative form in short data dump paragraphs that provided overall status for significant events.

The bottom half provided specific details such as course, speed, and time to achieve certain goals.

The duty radio man knocked on the wardroom door and entered carrying a clipboard containing a priority message.

"Excuse me, Captain, a priority weather message, sir."

Bruce acknowledged the report and started to read the latest weather predictions for the area and the twenty-four hour forecast.

"Great, this was all we need!" The Captain exhibited a damning expression that was out of character. "The northeast winds are to increase to twenty-five knots with gusts to thirty-five knots with heavy snow causing limited visibility. This is fine for Santa Claus, but not for us."

Bruce took a copy of the message, placed his initials on the message master copy, and handed the clipboard back to the deliverer.

"Dave. On this trip we must ensure that the ship is exceptionally well battened down and stowed for rough seas. We just don't have time to fall back and regroup from a casualty."

Mission Complete

The same thoughts had gone through Dave's mind and he acknowledged, "Yes sir, I agree and will take care of it."

Bruce studied the movement report as if he were studying for a final examination at the Naval Reactor School under the tutelage of Admiral Rickover.

The admiral was a tough taskmaster and had been a pioneer in the development of *Jackfish*, the ship that enabled the United States to maintain a slight edge of superiority over the Soviets.

He recalled his elation when the admiral had walked by his study room at Naval Reactors Office just prior to his graduation from the Washington, D.C. school. The door had opened, the admiral had partially entered, and bellowed, or rather scowled, into the room, "Stewart, I don't know how you managed to stand first in the class. I was ready to throw you out the first week."

Bruce knew that for the admiral to walk to his study room and talk to him meant a real compliment. After all, the "kindly old gentleman" couldn't destroy the image he had worked so hard to develop over many decades.

The top half of the formatted movement report read: "...Five hours to turning point at Montauk Point/Block Island. Then another four hours at flank speed on the surface at twenty knots to reach Point Charlie. This point is the diving location at the hundred fathom curve. Sunset will be seventeen forty nine on the twenty-first of December."

Bruce commented, "With us making flank speed in the reduced visibility and high seas, a limited amount of the ship will be out of the water. This will make it difficult for the Soviet AGI spy ship to pick us up visually or on radar. This means not making any electronics transmissions, including not using our radar for navigation or for contact detection."

When the time came, he would have to evaluate how badly the ship was taking a beating from the high seas and strong wind while traveling at flank speed. Most likely he would have to slow the ship to prevent damage to the ship and possibly to personnel in the ship.

Bruce most probably would shift the officer of the deck from the bridge to the control room with lookouts manning the periscopes.

"Dave, I want to start to rig the ship for dive as we turn east heading across the Block Island Sound, with the exception of rigging the main ballast tank vents for dive."

Rigging the ship for dive or surface required placing critical valves, circuits, and switches throughout the ship into the proper position to support the evolution. The rigging was a two man process. A qualified enlisted man would accomplish the initial positioning of the valve, switch, breaker, or other designated component on the "rig for dive/surfacing" list. Subsequent to the initial positioning, a final check to ensure the item was in the proper position was always conducted by a qualified officer.

The ballast tanks wrapped around the hull of the submarine and were used for submerging and surfacing the submarine. The bottom and top of each ballast tank were opened. Hydraulic pressure operating vent valves sealed the opening in the top of the tanks.

When the submarine was on the surface, high pressure air was used to push the water out of the bottom of the ballast tanks and the submarine would now be in the positive buoyant condition.

To submerge or dive the submarine, the vent valves in the top of the ballast tanks were hydraulically opened by operating control valves at the ballast control panel in the control room. This operation allowed the air cushion in the tanks to be replaced with sea water.

The submarine would now be in the negative buoyant condition and submerged.

When you didn't want to dive the submarine, such as in restricted and shallow water, the hydraulics used to operate the main ballast tank vent valves were locked in the shut position, or not rigged for dive.

Not rigging the main ballast tank vents for dive was a safety insurance policy to make sure no one accidentally opened the vent valves and caused the submarine to inadvertently submerge in shallow water.

Dave knew that to rig the ship for dive was a time consuming procedure, normally taking five hours. The evolution today would take even more time with the crew discomfort caused by the rough seas.

Traveling at high speed and not using the ship's radar in reduced visibility and high seas was in direct violation of the International Rules of the Road. The captain realized that he would be held totally at fault should an incident occur.

Making decisions like this, taking into account the necessity of the tactical situation to avoid the Soviet AGI and not lose valuable time, was the responsibility that came with command at sea.

Nat added, "With the expected weather conditions, reduced visibility, and the rough seas, it could take up to an additional four hours to reach Point Charlie and submerge the ship."

Bruce continued to review the navigational data.

Mission Complete

"*Jackfish* will operate at a depth of three hundred feet at twenty knots for the next hour. The water depth then will rapidly deepen to greater than eight hundred fathoms or forty-eight hundred feet. Then we will increase the ship's speed to flank, and the submerged depth of two thousand feet through the remainder of the transit. Our speed of advance (SOA) of thirty knots will be maintained from the diving point. The total distance to travel to our destination is eight-hundred-and-twenty-eight nautical miles. Once past one hundred nautical miles southeast of Point Charlie, the water depth never will shallow less than twelve hundred fathoms."

Stewards mate first class Bococo, the leading steward aboard *Jackfish*, quietly entered the wardroom with a fresh pot of steaming coffee.

He had served with Bruce for three years on his last ship and had reenlisted for an additional four years to get duty on *Jackfish*.

Bococo carried the pot to the table and professionally filled his captain's mug to the top.

"Captain, could I get you a sandwich or something else?"

It appeared that this dedicated man had long ago elected himself to ensure that his devoted and loyal leader was well taken care of.

"No thank you, Bococo."

Bococo then departed the area as quietly and nonassumingly as he had entered.

As thoughts came to his mind, Bruce would direct action to his executive officer and navigator.

"Dave, we must check out all systems thoroughly. We have operated the ship hard for eight months with not much time in port to do much corrective maintenance. This mission cannot support risk of a possible machinery derangement or an electrical or electronics system problem. Ensure that our replacement torpedo man comes from the SUBASE torpedo shop and has some knowledge on the workings of the Mark 56X torpedo."

Bruce wanted the top expertise in the maintenance and readiness operations of the newly developed Mark 56X torpedo onboard his ship for this trip.

Stewart had read the evaluation reports on the new weapon and knew how to tactically employ it; however, he would feel more comfortable with someone who worked on the team conducting the torpedo final operational evaluation.

This evaluation included actual shooting the torpedo during tests in the non nuclear mode of operation.

With the navigation data calculated by Nat in his one hand, Bruce slowly followed the proposed track on the chart with his index finger. He was scrutinizing the depth of water under the submerged highway *Jackfish* would follow during the outbound voyage.

He also examined the area on either side of the track, or on the shoulders of the highway.

Once *Jackfish* turned south of Montauk Point, the ship would proceed on course one-six-five degrees true to Point Charlie. It would take nine hours since underway to arrive at this position—at time 212100, meaning twenty one hundred (nine o'clock p.m.) on the twenty-first of December.

After a sip of his freshly brewed coffee, he continued his meticulous double check of the navigator.

"Course one-three-eight degrees true from Point Charlie to the tangent of the pre-drawn sixty-nautical-mile circle around Bermuda. At 221600, nineteen hours after departing Point Charlie, *Jackfish* will arrive at this position. Data checks."

The meticulous scrutinizing of the navigation track was time consuming, especially if a long voyage was planned. However, Bruce considered this procedure to be an insurance policy for his submerged operations.

This review ensured that the proposed track did not pass over any shallow or shoal water or uncharted pinnacle that could cause an underwater collision with his ship.

This procedure was one of the many lessons that had been driven home to him as a student in the force commander's prospective commanding officer's school in Groton, Connecticut.

A training method used effectively at the school was for students to analyze case studies of actual submarine casualties.

It was during one of these sessions that his group analyzed for lessons learned from the submerged collision of the United States nuclear attack submarine *Sharkfish* with a pinnacle or underwater mountain in the Northern Pacific Ocean.

Bruce stopped the review of the outstretched chart on the wardroom table as he rethought the details of this disastrous, needless, and unfortunate incident.

Sharkfisk had been traveling at a depth of eighteen hundred feet at a speed of twenty-eight knots. The submarine was proceeding as directed by higher authority to intercept a Soviet surface action group (SAG) made up of three surface combatants, a Mod *Kashin* and two *Kresta* 11's.

Both classes of Soviet ships were heavily armed with the latest air, surface, and underwater ordnance and electronic detection and classification equipment.

The Soviet SAG was escorting two U.S. fishing vessels under gunpoint toward the Russian port of Vladivostok. The Reds had falsely accused the American fishermen of being in the Russian contiguous fishing zone disguised as fishing vessels.

The Soviets insisted CIA agents manned the two ships and were attempting to covertly intercept sensitive intelligence data on the Soviet's forthcoming submarine launched missile firings. These evaluation firings were to be from their newly developed fleet ballistic missile submarine, the first of the *Hurricane* class.

Much pro United States support had been printed in the international press. However, the Soviets rebutted the charges in a professional manner. They justified their actions based on the assumption that if the United States government was truthful in their counter charge that the Americans were not CIA agents, the superpower would have responded with the show of force.

Actually, United States State Representatives were waiting for the *Sharkfish* to be in a position of forceful tactical advantage. An ultimatum then would be issued to the Soviets. At this time, the United States would back up its words with accurate high-speed torpedoes if necessary.

The Soviets attempted to bait the United States to send a show of force with aircraft. These planes would be easy targets for the Soviet's newly developed advanced surface-to-air missiles installed on the surface combatants.

Timely information from the Central Intelligence Agency saved us from falling into this well-baited trap.

The navigation team of *Sharkfish* had laid out a safe track. However, an urgent message was received in the early morning changing the position of the SAG. This change of position required a new track to be laid out on the navigation chart by the quartermaster of the watch to intercept the SAG as originally scheduled.

The quartermaster was very junior with not much experience in standing this watch by himself. The officer of the deck, or conning officer, also with minimal experience, reviewed the chart in the somewhat darkened attack center.

Since this was the early morning, all lights in the attack center were dimmed and red in color. This darkened condition allowed the submarine operators to maintain "night vision" should it be necessary to take the ship to periscope depth in an emergency.

The captain and the navigator, both sleeping at the time, were not informed of this tactical change.

Being a newly qualified submarine officer who had just recently received his coveted gold dolphins, the young officer failed to take the extra prudence that was learned by more senior officers with more submerged operating time in submarines.

A course change was ordered by the conning officer to carry out the ship's mission and the speed was ordered to be increased to thirty-four knots.

The conning officer then directed the messenger of the watch to notify the captain and the navigator of the course and speed changes and the rationale for the changes.

As the captain of *Sharkfish* reached the control room in a gallop, dressed only in his skivvies, the six thousand ton mass of steel increasing speed towards thirty-four knots met a mass of stationary rock, a submerged pinnacle. This collision obstacle was made by God many thousand years ago in such a manner that it would not be disturbed for many thousand years to come.

Fortunately for the *Sharkfish,* only one compartment was breached. It rapidly flooded.

The ship was barely able to surface using its last ditch emergency high pressure blow system. This system, to be used in extreme emergency conditions, was coupled with the gas generating and bubble system located in the ship's main ballast tanks.

This was a one-shot emergency "hope, faith, and pray" system where gas stowed in high pressure cylinders in the ballast tanks was released under four thousand pounds of pressure to mix with the salt water in the ballast tanks.

This chemical reaction rapidly caused tremendous expanding gas bubbles to be generated. The bubbles pushed the negative buoyant water out of the ballast tanks and thus developed significant positive buoyancy for the entire ship.

This emergency system was the saving grace in getting the broken ship to the surface. This modification had been inspired by the loss of the United States nuclear submarines *Thresher* and *Scorpion* many years ago.

As fate would have it, the North Pacific Ocean weather was not kind to the damaged *Sharkfisk* and its shattered crew. It took fourteen hours for assistance to arrive at the wind beating ocean area.

Mission Complete

Twenty-three brave submariners were dead, plus many more casualties.

A scarce resource in the arsenal of the United States Navy required a major shipyard overhaul lasting thirty months at a price tag of eighty-nine million dollars.

The Board of Inquiry directed the commanding officer to be relieved of his command and be issued a punitive letter of reprimand. His conning officer/officer of the deck was disqualified from submarine duty and also issued a letter of reprimand. The executive officer and navigator, for not ensuring the proper training was conducted and not ensuring that operating procedures were followed, were issued punitive letters of reprimand.

This period of less than total vigilance cost lives, dollars, and the end of the successful careers of four officers.

In addition, the United States was embarrassed in the eyes of the international community for allowing two of our ships operating on the high seas plus their crews to be highjacked by the Soviets without taking any action.

The crews of the fishing vessels were tried under the Soviet judicial system and are still in prison somewhere in the Soviet Union.

Bruce had a cold flash come over him with beads of perspiration forming on his brow as he envisioned the significance of a similar miscue with *Jackfish* having to abort this mission.

The *Jackfish* commanding officer pressed on more intensely than before with his scrutinizing of the proposed track.

"Course one-five-three true is the next direction *Jackfish* will point her bow en route to the three-hundred-nautical-mile circle from Point Bravo. Eight hours and thirty minutes will be required to travel the measured distance of two-hundred-and-fifty-eight nautical miles."

Too much was at stake. Bruce repeated the complete procedure as Dave and Nat observed.

The finesse the captain showed in manipulating the mini computer and following the laid out track was astonishing. Dave thought as he looked at the captain, *His mind and hands were not those of an engineer trained submariner, but resembled more those of a heart surgeon conducting a delicate heart operation coupled with the genius of a computer-like brain.*

Bruce then transcribed the pertinent data into his green pocket notebook, looked up at Dave, and started speaking. "Dave. We have the easy part done now. Let's analyze the data dump from the SPADS and develop our tactical plan of operation."

"Yes sir, Captain."

Dave assembled the data on the table.

Bruce stretched his legs, moved to the coffee pot, and poured a cup of the submariner's lifeblood for the three partially fatigued officers.

As he sipped his coffee, he was glad that Bococo had anticipated their needs and provided a fresh pot of really good tasting coffee.

A quick glance at the clock showed that the twenty-first of December had only twenty-three hours remaining.

Dave presented his SPADs data to Nat and the captain.

"The SPAD shows that there is a little over thirty-five-thousand-and-three-hundred-square-nautical miles to search in the outer semicircle. This reduces to eight-thousand-and-eight-hundred-square-nautical miles for the next arced area. In the sixty mile area on the northwest semicircle from Point Bravo there are fourteen-hundred-square-nautical miles to search."

Within twenty minutes the trio had computed the search plan and the tactical approach to use for this mission.

Bruce looked at his two assistants, then pointed to the outstretched chart and stated, "This area at Point Bravo is the most likely location for our target submarine. Estimate the target to arrive at this location about eighten hundred on the twenty-fourth of December and remain below the layer."

The captain continued, "The target should then go to periscope depth about twenty two hundred. We have until no later than twenty three forty five to locate, attack, and sink the enemy submarine."

Bruce thought, *This is assuming that sufficient time will be available!*

If his basic assumptions were not correct, this superb captain would fail the orders of his superiors for the first time in his shining career. And, the world as we know it would be changed dramatically.

This tasking, under the worst conditions possible, placed a tremendous burden on the shoulders of this young and talented officer.

The question that had passed through Bruce's thought process more than once tonight was whether he could cope with this amount of responsibility and pressure.

He put a heavy navy-colored scarf around his neck prior to raising his large lapel bridge coat around his ears. "I am leaving the ship for the few remaining hours of the night, Dave. I will be back about seven-thirty in the morning."

The time was two a.m., so this was to be a short trip.

The captain spent a few minutes talking with the topside security watch prior to walking across the slick brow en route to his buggy at the head of the pier.

His eyes were bloodshot with heavy dark bags under the lower lids. He noticed his fatigued body as he sloshed through the snow. Much was passing through his mind.

Bruce had adapted his nuclear engineer thought process to the care of his automobile. He understood the importance of preventive maintenance, constant check and verification, and solving small problems before they erupted into major problems of severe and untimely consequences.

On the first turn of the key, the "old mariner" turned over and purred like a well contented kitten.

His home was only fifteen minutes driving time from the submarine base pier. This early morning, though, it seemed as if he drove for hours before reaching his destination.

Bruce reflected much on his past and some on the future during this drive home. On the average, in the last ten years he had been at sea away from his family at least seven months a year.

Ann and his family fully supported him and accepted the separations and the future unknowns. All this sacrifice by the family was based on him being happy doing what he enjoyed and did best.

The possibility of his ship not returning was never discussed, but was on Ann's mind nevertheless.

The salary was sufficient, but his wife had done without much of what Bruce felt he owed her.

Many of his friends in industry had constantly called him to leave the Navy and join them in the civilian nuclear power industry.

Oh, how an eight-to-five job appealed to him now! Especially since it would mean no half-year deployments away from his family, no relocation of the family every two to three years, and double his current salary.

Maybe he was just getting old, or was just over stressed.

Bruce was in fact depressed. He continually told himself that he would stay in the Navy as long as he was having fun. When the time came that it was no longer fun, he would retire and make money. Maybe now was the time?

As he slowly drove up to his home, it looked like a World War II blackout was in effect in the neighborhood. The only light lit was the light on his front door.

All was quiet in the Stewart house as Bruce made his way into the kitchen and popped the cap on a cold beer. He was not a drinker, but he did enjoy a cold beer at times, especially when he was spun up and needed time to come back to ground level.

Since the rooster would crow earlier than usual this morning, Bruce decided to shave and shower now. He could then spend more time with Ann and the wee ones in the last remaining hours before departing to sea.

He slowly pulled the sharp razor over his strong face of Indian heritage with the expertise of a professional barber from the old country.

With the can of beer consumed, he now thoroughly relaxed in a steaming shower, and attempted to clear the depressing—or maybe self-pitying—thoughts out of his mind.

This was the wrong time to have confusing ideas clutter up his thought process. He would have to be at one hundred percent output—error free—to carry out the forthcoming mission.

His family, his crew, his ship, and all the people of the United States and the free world depended on his clear thoughts and correct decisions.

As he finished drying his broad shoulders, the door to the bathroom opened.

Ann stood there with a thin white gown covering her gorgeous body. Her shoulders were partially exposed and the front of the gown was draped just right to reveal her strong firm breasts. Bruce was certain that his bride would never be able to carry a pencil under her breasts.

Ann gave a sexy smile, as she knew that she had her sailor husband's undivided attention, and then dropped her robe completely. She was dressed in the clothes that God had provided her at birth.

She then looked Bruce in the eyes and asked the long standing mating call between the two. "Want to bogie, big guy?"

Arm in arm, the two nude forms disappeared down the hallway as they proceeded in the direction of the master bedroom.

/3/ THE MISSION

Although the exterior of his automobile looked like it had participated in a demolition derby and barely won, it was mechanically sound and guaranteed to keep its passengers warm.

Commander Stewart stepped from his heated sanctuary in sight of the *Jackfish* moor. His ears immediately signaled to him that the chill factor was well down into the minus numbers.

This was the wrong day to get his ship underway to challenge the wind-swept Thames River.

The commander had had a more difficult time than usual this morning. He had an early breakfast with his wife Ann, son Doug, and daughters Lynn and Kay. Breakfast was very quiet between the professional submariner and his wife. The youngsters kept talking and playing games. They did not understand that their father was to leave in a few hours.

Bruce had told his crew and family last night that the underway period would be indefinite. This meant the return date either was not known or could not be divulged for reasons of secrecy.

Everyone associated with the *Jackfish* family knew their loved ones would not be there to celebrate Christmas, most likely not New Year's, and that they would possibly miss Easter as well. Submariners accept this, as do the hardy dependents of the men who spend much of their lives underwater.

Bruce and Ann were able to read each other's thoughts through their eyes. They understood these times and after sixteen years of marriage had an unwritten, unspoken language of their own.

Bruce kissed his bride and the children goodbye. He paused for a few minutes to admire the beautiful Christmas tree with all the fancy decorated presents stacked under the brightly flashing evergreen. No tears were shed, but Ann's eyes reddened as her husband started through the door.

Bruce retraced his initial steps back to his automobile, opened the door, and placed the ignition keys under the driver's seat. Ann knew this hiding location should she receive any news her tiger was de-clawed and would not return.

The major activities on the pier were centered on three separate groups engrossed in their specific tasks. Heavy clothed *Jackfish* sailors wearing double woolen mittens and insulated boots were topside the submarine supporting each evolution.

The captain thought as he walked down this longer than usual pier, *Eighty-eight hours remain and counting down. Will that be enough time? Will we see another peaceful Christmas?*

"Good morning, Captain. The troops are mighty cold, but with any luck, we'll have these torpedoes loaded in two more hours," reported chief torpedo man Bradley.

The report broke Bruce's deep thoughts. "I certainly appreciate your early start, Chief." He followed with a smile on his face, "Have you rigged the torpedoes to sing Christmas carols for us?"

Bradley smiled and continued his supervisory role. His responsibility now was to ensure that the two remaining Mark 56X nuclear tipped torpedoes received his loving and tender care during the torpedo transfer from the pier, through the air, and into the submarine.

The chief torpedo man knew of Bruce's reputation and that of *Jackfish* and had volunteered to go aboard as a replacement crew member during this forthcoming trip. His request was disapproved.

Two sleek and deadly sophisticated twenty-one inch diameter by nineteen feet in length Mark 56X torpedoes were resting on the torpedo low bed trolley on the pier waiting transfer to the submarine. The third torpedo had already been transferred to the ship and was halfway through the topside torpedo loading hatch.

The ship's torpedo loading party, under Lieutenant Ray Jones' expert supervision, was topside on the ship, gently guiding and controlling the torpedo with wire mesh in haul lines en route to a safe stowage in the submarine torpedo room.

This torpedo loading scene topside reminded Bruce of a stubborn donkey halfway into the stable and not really sure if he wanted to go in all the way.

Ray's torpedo men would subsequently perform pre-load and final checks on the torpedoes. Each torpedo then would be loaded into a torpedo tube and be ready for shooting when the need arised.

Mission Complete

Prior to tube loading, Bruce planned to covertly set the combination to the nuclear activator option in each special nuclear capable Mark 56X torpedo. This would allow him, if needed, to use the torpedo as a nuclear weapon against the enemy submarine.

He would prefer to use the non-nuclear conventional TNT warhead since it would decrease the probability for damage to *Jackfish*. However, it was mandatory that the target be sunk at any cost.

The nuclear explosion would result in a greater probability of success. It would also increase the probability for damage to *Jackfish*.

Bruce realized it had been over fifty years since a nuclear weapon had been used to kill people. He now more clearly appreciated how President Truman felt when he gave the order to drop two atomic bombs on Japanese cities to hasten the end to World War II. Truman had lived with this decision for the rest of his life.

Stewart greeted his crew members as they passed him on the pier en route to *Jackfish*, their unexpected new home for Christmas. Each sailor carried his at-sea baggage. Not a sad face was observed but rather broad proud smiles as if to say, "We're the best sailors sailing with the top captain on the best ship."

The captain talked to many of the chilled Submarine Base support sailors on the pier, much as a politician saying goodbye to his staff during his last days in office.

As he worked his way toward the brow of the ship, he observed another crane suspending the repaired type twenty-four periscope high in the windy sky.

Crew members grappled with tag lines guiding the end of the forty-six feet in length by eleven inch cylindrical barrel into the periscope bearing housing atop the sail area of the ship.

He felt proud of the United States sailors and what they could do in an emergency. The initial time estimate given to repair the bent periscope by its manufacturer had been at least three weeks. The time would start after the periscope was shipped and received in the repair factory.

The Submarine Base repair department, knowing that *Jackfish* did not have the luxury of three weeks in port, took on the repair challenge.

Working around the clock for five days with expert sailor artificers, Bruce's one-of-a-kind prototype periscope was now fully operational.

After installation, the periscope would need to be laser aligned. This would insure the maximum potential was reached from the complicated optical mechanisms that provided for the visual transmission from object to the eyeball of the observer.

Also the communications intercept, electronics intercept, and photographic equipment would need to be installed into the periscope and tested prior to going to sea.

These tactical capabilities all are available to the user when the periscope head just breaks the surface of the water, leaving the submarine in a covert position. This results in minimum potential exposure for being detected by visual or satellite means. All of these periscope attributes in *Jackfish* must be in perfect operational condition to maximize the advantage against the enemy.

Bruce smiled as he waved to his crew, which was lined up like a chain gang, loading food into the ship. The men were passing the food boxes from the parked trucks on the pier hand to hand to the submarine topside access hatch. This hatch provided a clear access to the refrigeration and chill boxes and food stowage area below decks.

Cardboard boxes and other debris were removed topside to reduce any clutter in the ship and allow the food to be immediately stowed and the ship readied for going to sea.

"*Jackfish* arriving" blared on the ship's 1MC general announcing system alerted the crew to the fact that their leader had arrived.

Bruce scrambled rapidly down the vertical ladder into the bowels of the ship. He proceeded to the wardroom to meet with his key officers. He paused just long enough at his cabin door to toss his cap, gloves, and bridge coat on top of his narrow bunk.

Bococo handed the captain some freshly brewed hot coffee while the duty officer provided a detailed report of the ship's current status and the readiness of the ship to get underway.

His executive officer and navigator listened and provided amplifying information as the briefing progressed.

Dave and Nat were dressed for at-sea operations wearing navy blue coveralls; coveted gold dolphins, the symbol of an officer qualified for submarine duty; and collar rank devices.

Both had stayed aboard the ship last night to complete the myriad of details required prior to getting underway. It was obvious by the dark bags under their eyes that neither had used any of the few available hours to sleep.

Bruce directed his navigator, "Nat. Prepare the ship's movement report from the data we developed last night. I want to give it to the squadron commander when he comes onboard the ship this morning."

The movement report would provide higher authority with the exact

Mission Complete

location of the *Jackfish*, by depth, course and speed, from underway Groton, Connecticut, until the ship returned back to port.

The captain, satisfied with the underway preparations, finished his coffee with another sticky bun and headed for his cabin to get ready to lead his warriors into battle. There was still much to be accomplished. He expected Commodore Bill Walter onboard in about two hours.

After changing into his at-sea attire, Bruce sat at his desk and wrote two long letters to Ann and the children. One letter would be given to Bill Walter with instructions and the other would leave the ship with the last mail to be posted that day.

Bill's letter was a "what if" and was to be delivered to Ann only if *Jackfish* did not make the return trip.

As he sat at his desk, he reflected on his studies of Mahan and his classic book *Influence of Sea Power Upon History*. In this naval classic, Mahan described the English captains during the disastrous battle of Toulon.

He vividly recalled that Mahan's lesson from this battle was the danger of disgraceful failure of men who had neglected to keep themselves prepared, not only in knowledge of their profession, but in the sentiment of what war requires.

He resolved never to be so documented in history as a repeat performer. Bruce now felt reasonable sure of himself; however, not with the same total self-confidence he had prior to previous highly classified secret missions.

It was apparent that his executive officer and the other officers were not showing the same enthusiasm and "gung ho" spirit they previously had displayed preparing for other dangerous and demanding operations.

A winning team was being divided because of the rigid order from the commander in chief to Bruce not to discuss the details of the mission with anyone onboard the *Jackfish*.

Bruce vividly remembered the disastrous results of a divided team in the wardroom. As a junior officer, the nuclear attack submarine he was attached to had been on a highly classified special operation. The same wardroom, with the exception of the commanding officer, had completed an extremely successful mission the year before.

Members of the force commander's staff had intimidated the new commanding officer before the mission started to the point where he was reluctant to be aggressive to maximize the results of the operation.

The only good result of this situation was as a lesson learned not to be repeated.

Unfortunately, Bruce now found himself in the same position, not as a junior officer, but as the captain.

Unconsciously, he spun the three tumbler combination lock to his desk safe, opened the door, and checked his loaded thirty-eight caliber Smith and Wesson pistol. The weapon came onboard *Jackfish* the day Bruce took command.

After studying the classified report documenting the capture of the *USS Pueblo* by the North Koreans in 1968 and the torture inflicted upon her commanding officer and crew, Bruce vowed he would take the route of Captain John Cromwell rather than ever be taken prisoner.

Captain Cromwell, a senior submarine officer fighting the Pacific war against the Japanese, was extremely knowledgeable about the details of the United States future war plans and also our secret communications intercept system.

This intercept system was crucial in allowing the United States to gain some margin of superiority over the Japanese while we grew our forces to be able to inflict major damage on the enemy.

Cromwell elected to go down with the scuttled battle-damaged American submarine *Sculpin*, east of Truk Island in 1943, rather than be taken as a POW.

The question flashed in Bruce's mind whether he would have to use the gun against his crew to accomplish his mission.

He returned the pistol to the safe, shut the door to the safe, and spun the combination dial mechanism of the lock. Hopefully, he would not have to go into the safe again.

As he sat in a relaxed position, his mind churned continuously in an attempt to put into perspective the incredible mission briefing he had received last night.

Impossible—unbelievable—but true!

He rethought every word that had been spoken by Vice Admirals Dale and Hasting and by Warren Andrews.

Bruce would never forget that session because of the total shock that it delivered to him physically, mentally, and psychologically.

Maybe the impact would not have been so tremendous had it not been for the impact of the opening statement by Vice Admiral Hasting: "The *Tigerfish* was not lost at sea as previously thought."

After a slight pause for the audience to regain composure, the Admiral had continued. "The submarine was pirated and is currently threatening the security of the United States and world peace. Captain Mike Morello, the ship's commanding officer, and most of the *Tigerfish*'s crew are alive."

Hasting then described in the following scenario the events that had happened. On the morning of the nineteenth of December, Lieutenant Michael Hodges, the electrical division officer of the *Tigerfish*, delivered a sealed package to the Office of the National Security Council (NSC) in Washington, D.C.

The package was to be opened only by Donald Lindsey, the chairman of the NSC.

Mike was smuggled into Florida by the terrorists before *Tigerfish* put out to sea from Cuba. He then was put on an airplane at Key West with routing to Washington, D.C.

His directives were that if he communicated with anyone else, his commanding officer and other shipmates remaining aboard *Tigerfish* would be assassinated. Through his ordeal during the last month since captivity, this young officer was convinced the terrorists were not making idle gestures or threats.

Access was made available to Lindsey and in the company of Admiral Justin David, the chief of naval operations, the sealed envelope was opened. Both Lindsey and David read the contents of the envelope simultaneously.

They then starred at each other in total disbelief. Impossible!

At the meeting last night Vice Admiral Hasting had then emphasized, "It was a ransom on the United States government and the life we in this country have enjoyed for over two hundred years. The letter was addressed to the president of the United States and laid out the following demands:
$100 billion dollars with 50 billion in U.S. dollars and 50 billion in gold bullion; two Trident D-5 missiles with competent technicians to be transferred with the missiles; all intercontinental ballistic missiles are to be deactivated; all submarine-launched ballistic missile submarines (*Poseidon* and *Trident*) are to be surfaced prior to 2359 hours, the twenty-fourth of December, and then commence a surface transient back to home port."

The ransom note had continued. "Acknowledgment that the above demands will be met must be transmitted on frequency 4548 megahertz between 1600 and 2359 hours, December 24, 1989. Once this acknowledgment message is received, further instructions will follow."

The admiral's voice weakened, and slightly quivering, he continued. "If the demands are not met, nuclear tipped submarine launched Axehandle cruise missiles will be launched against Norfolk, Virginia; Washington,

D.C.; New York; and Groton, Connecticut, at exactly midnight, December 24, 1989."

The letter was signed "Merry Christmas from the Leaders of the New World."

At this point in the presentation, the admiral lost some of his composure. Perspiration was visible on his wrinkled forehead.

He sat down, wiped his brow with his handkerchief, and nervously sipped a cup of coffee.

Silence prevailed.

Bruce knew that the real significance of the ultimatum was the elimination of the United States Triad, the "hammer" that had been responsible for world peace for the last fifty years.

He understood the synergistic effect of the TRIAD, options available to the NCA, considerations in targeting, how it is done, capabilities and creditability, and the future of the TRIAD as it related to the Unites States basic defense posture.

He respected what the founders of the TRIAD had done in the late 1950's and early 1960's. They had developed the system with the philosophy of possible employment of strategic nuclear forces to the undertaking of deterrence. Each element of the TRIAD brought strength to the Strategic Integrated Operational Plan (SIOP), which, when integrated with the other elements, resulted in a credible strategic nuclear deterrence at the upper end of the warfare spectrum.

The units that made up our TRIAD consisted of the submarine launched ballistic missiles (SSBNs), land based intercontinental ballistic missiles (ICBMs), and the B-1 land based bombers.

Proper targeting also contributed to deterrence because the enemy knew that, if deterrence should fail, the United States had a plan for the actual employment of our nuclear weapons based on sound national planning factors.

When Vice Admiral Hasting remarked, "Without an effective TRIAD to maintain deterrence, the political military balance of power throughout the world would shift under the iron fist of the Soviet bear. NATO would crumble to the demands of the Soviet Union or be victim to the Communist military supremacy. Cuba would rise to be the super power of the North and South American continents."

Bruce just nodded agreement with disgust.

The main question passing through his mind was how we could get into such a checkmate situation in the world political arena.

Mission Complete

He knew that the *Tigerfish* carried ten Axehandle submerged launched cruise missiles, as did the *Jackfish*. Each missile was MIRV'ed to carry four warheads, each with forty kilotons of destructive power. Each warhead could be individually targeted within fifty miles of the target area. This would equate to forty warheads.

He recalled, as a comparison, that the atomic bombs that had destroyed Nagasaki and Hiroshima to cause the end of World War II were just twenty kilotons each.

Hasting continued, "Each missile has a cruising range of fifteen hundred nautical miles at a speed of nine hundred nautical miles each hour. The missile has an accuracy of one hundred feet." As if briefing an uninitiated audience, the admiral detailed for effect, "An Axehandle missile launched from the Philadelphia Veterans Stadium, the home of the Philadelphia Eagles, has the accuracy and endurance to land within the thirty- to fifty-yard line of the Chicago Bears football stadium in Chicago."

He then looked around the room as if to shift the responsibility, then stated, "The missile is low flying with no defense against it. Radar detection of the Axehandle missile is extremely difficult because of the small radar cross section. There will be approximately one hour and twenty minutes from launch to detonation on target, with no warning or alert time at the impact point. It is driven by a power plant consisting of a cruise turbo fan engine with a solid fuel booster. When the missile reaches the predetermined range, it then climbs at ninety degrees to two thousand feet before detonation. This allows the full impact of the mirv'ed warheads to be realized. There is enough destructive power in each warhead to put every major city on the East Coast of the United States, as well as other cities within fourteen hundred nautical miles of the eastern seacoast, in harm's way!"

Warren Andrews added, "Evacuation of the targeted cities, if ordered in anticipation of the attack, would be disastrous. Panic and looting would be ramped with the toll in lives being tremendous. Also, as we all know, evacuation plans have not been developed and civil defense shelters are nonexistent."

Andrews continued. "Also, we must not alert the terrorists to the fact that anything unusual is happening as that might prompt them to launch early."

Bruce remembered that when he was a young officer the administration had decided the cost was too high to develop a sufficient nuclear defense for the home front, so they had avoided the issue. Instead, resources were devoted to develop the TRIAD and deterrence.

He also knew the Soviets had devoted significant resources to civil defense and the protection of civilians and the total infrastructure of the Motherland against nuclear attack.

During the first coffee break, Bruce questioned the selection of Lieutenant Hodges to deliver the message.

Hasting responded, "From the information we got from the lieutenant, there were two bachelor officers on the *Tigerfish*. The Soviet-Cuban terrorists didn't want a married officer to deliver the message since they knew we would have to give the messenger a new identity and forbid him to ever talk to any of his family. This was necessary to keep the fate of the *Tigerfish* concealed forever."

The admiral continued, "These bums were certainty correct. They thought out the plan well. The other bachelor officer was very religious and they figured that he would confess to a priest and divulge the whole caper. That left Hodges to be the messenger."

Although this was not the time for thoughts of merriment, Bruce did get a chuckle to himself. He knew Mike well and knew he was a real hell raiser and ladies' man on the beach. His claim to fame was his newly purchased forty thousand dollar Porsche automobile. The automobile was located in the facility on the Submarine Base where bachelor officers put vehicles for safe storage when their ship deployed for extended at-sea periods.

Bruce wondered what the attendants at the storage garage would do with the vehicle since Mike could never reveal his true identity and claim his pride and joy.

Captain Bob Beck unrolled his charts and laid them on the table to be visible to all present. Beck delayed his presentation to allow each to study the charts.

Circles had been drawn around the center of each targeted city known to be at ground zero. The first circle radius was twenty-five miles with other circles extending out at fifty and then seventy-five miles.

This chart with all the circles was a terrifying sight to Bruce, especially since he immediately recalled friends in each of the circled areas, the most important being his wife's family in the Newport News, Virginia, area and his sister and her family, and of course Ann and his family in Groton, Connecticut. Friends, close relatives, and family all could be located within the center of ground zero's path of destruction.

Captain Beck pointed his telescopic pointer to the Norfolk, Virginia, area on the chart. He discussed in detail what he expected the terrorist's operational plan to be for maximizing damage. This area was a tremendously important military complex. He pointed to the specific locations on the large scale chart simultaneously as he spoke.

"I estimate that in this area, one warhead will be targeted for the Norfolk Naval Shipyard, one for the Norfolk Naval Base complex, and the third across Hampton Roads seaway at the Newport News area. This last warhead alone will take out the Newport News Shipbuilding Corporation, Langley Air Force Base, NASA, Fort Monroe, and other military facilities.

"The fourth warhead will hit the Virginia Beach area taking out the Little Creek Amphibious Base and the Oceana Naval Air Station, just to name a few of the key military installations in that sector."

Beck continued. "This one missile, carrying four warheads, would totally wipe out a significant part of our Naval Force, repair and construction capability, in addition to the largest military complex on the east coast."

During the pause after this shocking scenario, Hasting added, "One aircraft carrier is located in each of the shipyards in this target area for repair. This includes the newest and largest nuclear aircraft carrier ever built in the United States, just completing construction at Newport News Shipbuilding Corporation. All these valuable assets would be destroyed."

Bruce mentally recalled the current order of battle for the United States Naval Forces. The results indicated that counting the ships in port at Norfolk, this destruction would equate to almost twenty-five percent of our aircraft carrier force destroyed.

Beck continued.

"The total loss of naval combatants in the Norfolk-Virginia Beach-Newport News area would be over thirty percent of our already sparse Naval Force. This does not include loss of Air Force, Army, and Marine Corps assets. Also significant is the tremendous loss of our military command and control infrastructure that is desperately needed to conduct large scale warfare. This attack would dwarf Pearl Harbor in total devastation of material assets as well as personnel losses!"

Hasting allowed time for the audience to digest these statistics.

He then solemnly reported, "Our analyst estimates there would be at least three hundred thousand casualties in this area with at least one hundred thousand deaths."

It was apparent that the civilian member of this briefing team, Warren Andrews, had never had to accept the responsibility for lives or been trained in the art of warfare where hard decisions must be made—decisions necessary to meet an objective knowing that men would bleed and die.

The minimum facial color he had had at the beginning of the briefing had changed into a snow white appearance.

Observing Andrews's lack of composure, Admiral Hasting took the lead and left the table, poured a cup of coffee, and lit a cigarette.

His dark eyes penetrated Bruce's eyes and in a quiet voice, almost as if he were speaking father to son, remarked, "Bruce, we need you, son. This Christmas you will be the world's savior. Hopefully, with God's guidance and your expertise, this nasty business will be taken care of and the world will be stable again."

Beck continued his briefing as he pointed to the Washington, D.C. area on the chart.

With his head tilted downward, eyes slightly closed, he stated with a distinguished tremor in his voice, "The first twenty-five mile radius is drawn with its center at the White house—ground zero."

The Assistant Secretary of State regained some of his composer and added, "When we briefed the president, he was quite taken back and directed that ground zero be changed to the Washington Monument."

Although Bruce admired and respected the president, he realized he had absolutely no understanding of the total destructive power of a nuclear weapon.

The brief continued with a description of the significant targets within each of the destructive circles.

Not much would be left of the nation's capital and the Baltimore-Washington complex.

At least eight hundred thousand casualties and approximately five hundred thousand deaths would occur as a result of the second missile, with its four individually targeted nuclear warheads.

Andrews, observing that he had gotten a few smiles from his last statement about changing the location of ground zero, chimed in, "The president would have just enough time to turn out the lights before the missile warhead detonated."

No humoring smiles this time, only ten glaring and questioning eyes met those of the speaker.

Although the remaining briefing was not necessary for Bruce to fully comprehend the severity of the situation, Bob Beck continued his gloom and doom presentation for the New York and Groton areas.

Bruce later found out that the president had personally directed that the complete data dump be given. This way, there would be no doubt that Bruce fully understood the challenge ahead of him. And more so, the consequences of him failing the mission.

Should Bruce and the *Jackfish* fail to accomplish the mission, the foundations of the government, the military, and the financial structure of the United States would be destroyed.

In addition, millions of civilians would be killed. This destruction would amass from just four of the Axehandle missiles. *Tigerfish* would still have six missiles remaining.

Beck folded his charts marked distinctly TOP SECRET-LIMITED EYES ONLY while Admiral Hasting continued his brief.

"While the National Security Council was in emergency session discussing the alternatives to the ultimatum, Rear Admiral Bill Willis, the senior watch officer of the National Military Command Center interrupted to report an urgent message. He told us that the *USS Forbes (FF443)*, while transiting in area latitude twenty-three point seven degrees north and longitude seventy-two point one west, about six hundred and twenty nautical miles southwest of Bermuda, gained sonar contact on an unidentified nuclear submarine.

"The frigate evaluated the contact as a submarine of the *Jackfish* class. However, the submarine would not acknowledge any recognition signals sent by the United States surface ship."

The admiral reported that the *Forbes* had attempted the standard "Uncle Joe" procedure using the frigate's underwater sonar communications system to obtain the identification of the submarine.

No response had been received from the contact.

The frigate's commanding officer had requested that the command center confirm if any of our submarines were using or transiting through the area. He planned to maintain contact while waiting instructions from higher authority.

As the brief continued, Hasting described that one of our newest and most sophisticated maritime air patrol antisubmarine airplanes, a P3D Orion, was conducting a routine operational patrol near this location. Naval Air Station, Bermuda, vectored the aircraft to the position of the *Forbes* to assist in a coordinated air surface holding operation on the submarine contact.

Shortly thereafter, a partial unclassified FLASH message was received from the frigate reporting, "UNDER TORPEDO ATT— "

Nothing more was heard from the *Forbes*, although they continued to attempt to regain communications contact.

"Within ten minutes of the partial message reception," continued the admiral, "the P3 reported that while en route to the holding area, he observed the frigate explode, break into two parts, and sink in less than three minutes. Some survivors were in the water."

Bruce quickly recorded in his green pocket notebook the latitude, longitude, and time when the *Forbes* was sunk.

This valuable data would be the starting location, a positive *Tigerfish* datum, when he developed the tactical plan for carrying out his mission.

The sinking of the *Forbes* led credence to the story told by Mike Hodges.

There was no doubt they were dealing with radical fanatics who would do anything to achieve their goals.

Hasting interrupted with other bits of valuable information. "On the twelfth, thirteenth, and fourteenth of November, a United States satellite picked up a large container ship patrolling about five miles seaward of the Cuban port of Baracoa. We sent in a high flying reconnaissance patrol flight to gain better photographs. The ship was being maneuvered by using four sea going tug boats. No visible self propulsion was evident. The ship entered the Cuban harbor on the fifteenth of November. While in port, much activity was observed in the proximity of the ship. Increased security was established.

"Later on the fifteenth of November, a Soviet cruiser entered the Cuban harbor and moored alongside the container ship. The cruiser was flying an admiral's flag. A large set of shore power cables were led from the cruiser to the container ship, and also what appeared to be portable water hoses. Heavy security was established on the pier, on both ships, and in the surrounding water. Heavy tarps were installed across all the brows and on the access doors from the cruiser to the container ship.

"Later, Hodges confirmed that an Axehandle missile, a nuclear torpedo, and a conventional non nuclear torpedo were transferred to the cruiser for transporting to the Soviet Union. Hodges also confirmed that a Soviet naval admiral was aboard the cruiser and in charge of the operation in port.

"The cruiser and the container ship got underway on the fifteenth of December. The container ship proceeded to sea about five miles and then stopped. About another hour the container ship returned to port. Minimum security was now established around the port.

"We believe this container ship was a holding area for the *Tigerfish*.

"The timeline for the sinking of the *Forbes* lines up with the *Tigerfish* underway from Barcoa Harbor on the fifteenth of December. The submarine then transited west from the harbor and then north in the Straits of Florida."

Vice Admiral Dale took this opportunity to provide the conditions aboard the captive submarine.

Mission Complete

"Bruce, I know that the captain of the *Tigerfish*, Mike Morrello, in addition to being your brother- in-law, is like a brother to you. If there were any other way, I would not put you into this position."

Bruce nodded understanding as Dale continued.

"*Tigerfish* is still being operated by its crew who are in bondage, confined by leg and arm chains. They are being inhumanely treated, under continuous attack with severe brutality and torturing under the guns of the terrorists. A highly trained partial crew of Soviet nuclear submarine officers ensures that the *Tigerfish* crew does not sabotage the ship.

"Prior to Hodges leaving the ship, three enlisted and one officer crew members were murdered and some others disfigured. Subsequent to *Tigerfish* getting underway from Cuba, thirty enlisted men were assassinated. They mean business!"

"Admiral, if something must be done, I'm sure that Mike would have wanted me to be the one. I appreciate the confidence that you have in me, my crew, and the *Jackfish*."

Hasting continued his scenario of events leading up to this meeting.

"Immediately after getting the *Forbes* sinking report, an emergency session was set up with the president, the chairman, and all members of the joints chief of staff, the secretary of state, and the secretary of defense.

"It was not difficult to arrive at the options available for the president.

"The first, to conduct a preemptive first strike against the Soviet Union with our strategic nuclear forces.

"This option is not reasonable with the current international arena diplomatic climate. The Soviets were carrying out too good of a ploy of negotiating in 'good faith' at the Geneva Arms Conference for nuclear disarmament. Also, the credibility of the United States would be shattered since our commitment for deterrence was never to release a first strike, but to ensure that our adversaries know we will counter strike if attacked.

"Another option available is to honor the ultimatum. We all know this would reduce the United States to a second rate nation. The bipolar superpowers then become Cuba in the western hemisphere and the Soviet Union the dictator in the eastern hemisphere."

Hasting looked directly at Bruce and when they both had eye contact, stated, "The remaining option was to seek out and sink the *Tigerfish*."

Bruce now realized why he was being included in this briefing.

"All possible options were analyzed with consequences evaluated against risk and uncertainty. The president then made the final decision.

"You are directed to get *Jackfish* underway as soon as possible, but no later than noon tomorrow. Then have the ship proceed to the best evaluated location of the *Tigerfish*. Finally, *Tigerfish* must be destroyed prior to 2345, December 24.

"The president would not accept any other commanding officer.

"Also, the president directed that no outside staffing or rudder orders by any Washington brass would be tolerated."

Hasting stated for effect, "The president's words were, 'I have complete faith in Bruce to accomplish this tasking against insurmountable odds. He has never failed me before. He has always brought home the bacon.'

"The rest of the tasking, should you fail to locate the target, is to report by unclassified FLASH message on a special frequency that will be guarded worldwide by all United States communications stations. The president would then acknowledge the terrorist ultimatum to advert a nuclear attack against the United States.

"If the mission is accomplished, your message will read 'MISSION COMPLETE.'

"Prior to concluding the emergency meeting in Washington," Hasting stated in a voice that added credence to the importance of the mission, "the president authorized your use of nuclear weapons if required to satisfactorily complete the mission."

Bruce thought back to his studies of risk and uncertainty and the definition of the two components of risk: The probability of occurrence failure and consequences of failure, measured against some standard.

This definition meant more to him now when the standard being measured was the destiny of the United States.

Now he wished he had received a written operational order for this mission, especially since there was the possibility of shooting a nuclear torpedo.

Reemphasizing the critical state of affairs facing the country, Andrew informed the group that Contingency Plan XRAY now was in effect.

The questioning look on Bill Walter's face led Andrews to further explain the plan.

"Press releases have been disseminated from the White House with notification the president and the first lady will depart Washington the afternoon of December twenty-third to spend Christmas with their family in the Midwest."

Andrews continued, "Additionally, top level executives, some select cabinet members necessary for the reconstitution of our government, and high level military echelon listed on the relocation team will covertly depart Washington before the close of business on Christmas Eve. A few persons in the other target areas have been directed to depart the potential destruction area."

This specific list had only the top AA priority persons, thus no visible signs of an evacuation would be apparent.

Bill was quite surprised that such a contingency plan existed. He wished he had been included in the select few.

The group also was advised that the National Emergency Airborne Command Post, or NEACP, would go airborne at sixteen hundred on the twenty-fourth of December. All present knew that the reconstitution of our government via this command aircraft would be possible should nuclear missiles be launched.

This plan was put into operation as a contingency should the *Tigerfish* not follow the schedule in their ultimatum and launch early or in the event of a possible communications foul up.

Not to be discounted was the possibility the *Jackfish* would not achieve success.

Since he and *Jackfish* were now tasked, Bruce felt no restraints about getting as much information as possible from this group of high priced messengers of ill tidings.

"By whom, why, and how was the *Tigerfish* pirated?" was his initial question to the admiral.

Vice Admiral Hasting provided the answer to the "who" question first. He spoke in a strong voice that reflected hate and vengeance.

"It is obvious that this was a well-thought-out and equally well executed plan by a combined Soviet/Cuban team of professional bastards. The team was extremely knowledgeable about nuclear submarine in-port operations in the Mediterranean Sea. They had rehearsed the takeover operation to perfection, and completed their objective flawlessly."

The answer to the "why" became more obvious as Warren Andrew discussed the major political decisions made by the previous pacifistic and extremely liberal presidential administration.

"Cuba had escalated above just being a surrogate country of the Soviet Union. A power play, in conjunction with the Russians, was in progress to reduce the United States from being a super power state."

Andrews then provided a pessimistic scenario of the existing political and military conditions in Cuba and Central America.

"Castro's country now has the highest estimated annual defense expenditure in Central America, the Caribbean, and South America at about $800 million. A fair proportion of this is Soviet aid. This expenditure has tripled since the beginning of the 1980s.

"Cuba's military forces are the most powerful in the western hemisphere behind the United States. Modern Soviet jet aircraft form the backbone of their air force. Their navy has acquired a submarine force of over twenty long-range Soviet *Foxtrot* torpedo shooting submarines.

"In addition, they possess a force of fast attack Soviet *OSA* and *KOMAR* missile boats capable of shooting torpedoes as well as surface-to-surface and surface-to-air missiles, and their SAM sites located throughout Cuba form a formidable defense of the homeland."

The Assistant Secretary of State continued his brief more dynamically.

"Nicaragua and El Salvador signed a defense and economic alliance with Cuba known as the Nicaragua-El Salvador-Cuba (NEC) Alliance without any protest from the United States government. Cuban controlled Communistic puppet governments then were installed in both countries.

"The Honduras pro-Western government was then at the point of abdication. They did not have the resources to battle the rebel terrorists being supplied and supported by the NEC Alliance.

"During this Communist infusion into Central America, the United States' liberal government refused to take any positive or aggressive moves to support the elected officials of our neighbors, or to protect the provisions of the Monroe Doctrine."

Bruce very vividly recalled that in the United States at this time liberal human rights issues, increased give-away programs, and reduced defense spending were the headline stealers of the day.

Unfortunately, this atmosphere was supported by our spineless administration. Also affecting the issues were a multitude of influential lobbyists, some with more of an eye on their own interests than to their country's security.

Andrews continued his saga of the despair of our country.

"As a show of force, an NEC Alliance sea and air security zone was established. This security zone severely limited our sea lines of communications in this area. Shipping out of the Gulf ports through both the Yucatan Channel to and from the Panama Canal and through the Straits of Florida to the eastern seaboard and European ports were threatened continuously. The United States limited their action to verbal protests."

Mission Complete

Andrews then directed his comments to the Soviet Union part of the plan.

"NATO was weakened by its member countries being threatened by the Soviet Union's control over the output of the natural gas line. Russia controlled the 'valve' and throttled down on the gas supply at times to prove their unilateral control of this natural resource.

"The course was plotted and the time was near when the Soviets would easily take control of Western Europe by diplomatic means. A little of Teddy Roosevelt's 'big stick' diplomacy would be all that was needed to sever the weakened and leaderless NATO countries.

"Coupled with the Soviets taking over Europe, Cuba then would escalate to a super power and be the leader of the Western Hemisphere."

As he continued, it was obvious that Andrews was pleased with the vast improvement in our countries' diplomatic and military posture throughout the world.

"Fortunately, an upsurge of nationalism was generated in our country. A strong and dynamic president and cabinet were installed. The general populous applauded increased military spending and a buildup of our military forces. The natural transformation of Communism to our side of the ocean would now be forcible opposed by the United States."

After a slight pause, Andrews then continued to his conclusion. "The Soviet/Cuban world conquest plan was now in jeopardy. Thus, the terrorist decision was made to use the *Tigerfish* ultimatum as the lever to accomplish their goals."

"Captain, I have the movement report data for your review."

Nat's knock on the captain's stateroom door and the navigator's report broke Bruce's deep trance.

Bruce took his green notebook out of his pocket and checked the information carefully line by line.

This report detailed the *Jackfish*'s track from port to its operating area. Expected courses, speeds, and depths with associated times were provided.

Nat stood by as his work was scrutinized. He was an expert at his job and did not expect any errors.

The normal procedure was to transmit the movement report by message to the submarine force commander in Norfolk, Virginia. The admiral's staff would then compare it to all other submarine movements to ensure no possible submerged interference, and then approve the movement.

This time, the report would be given to his squadron commander. Bill would telephone the information direct to Vice Admiral Dale, the commander of the submarine force, U.S. Atlantic Fleet, by the red telephone.

This system of telephonic encrypting and scrambling circuits was used for highly classified information. Transmitting information in this mode prevented any compromise or covert interception by unfriendly intelligence agencies.

As an example, the primary task of the Soviet AGI ship located just three miles off Montauk Point, Connecticut, was to intercept any data on submarine movements and any other submarine operating related information.

This AGI was stationed on the track of any submarine outbound from the Submarine Base at Groton, Connecticut.

There was no doubt that the *Jackfish* movement plan would be approved.

COMSUBLANT controlled submarine movements through the ocean similar to a major railroad network control center. Underwater major tracks or highways allowed submerged submarines to travel in different directions through the ocean with controlled intersections where the submerged highways in the ocean meet and intersect.

Submarines are assigned different operating depths or operating depth separations at these intersections to prevent mutual interference.

Bruce knew that Vice Admiral Dale would resemble the state trooper regulating traffic on a highway to permit VIP's to pass without interference.

All other submarine movements on the submerged highways would be diverted to allow *Jackfish* to be the VIP. It was mandatory that his ship get to the expected operating area of the *Tigerfish* unimpeded.

"Correct as usual, Nat," Bruce said with a smile. "I will give this movement report direct to the squadron commander when he comes aboard. It will be telephoned to the Norfolk, Virginia, Headquarters instead of being sent by message."

"Thank you, sir."

Nat departed the stateroom thinking that another usual operating procedure had been changed.

He would feel better if his captain provided more information about this mission. It seemed as if he had a complex puzzle to put together; however, his intuition told him that some of the pieces to the puzzle were missing. How true this was!

With an automatic response that had been formed through habit, Bruce reached over and pushed a call button mounted in his stateroom bulkhead. This response sounded a buzzer in the wardroom pantry and alerted the stewards mate that the captain was summoning him.

Mission Complete

In less than one minute, his buzzer response was acknowledged.

Bococo gave a slight knock on the door, slowly opened it, and with a "Good morning, Captain," placed a large mug of black coffee on the corner of his desk.

"Thank you, Bococo."

Dave entered the captain's stateroom carrying the message clipboard. "Only two messages of significance, Captain. One weather and an intelligence summary giving the latest location of the potential interfering Soviet AGI."

Dave smiled as he reported, "We also have the standard Christmas greeting message from the Boss, but that doesn't apply to us this year."

"No let up in this miserable northeastern snow storm. The outbound transit is going to be a rough one, Dave," Bruce grumbled disgustedly as he read the latest weather prediction. "This will cost us at least five valuable hours, probably more."

As Bruce read the second message, he thought that the Soviets were covering the New London submarine operating area in first class. Their newest AGI, the *Balzan*, was on station right on the planned track of the *Jackfish*.

He had every Soviet ship's characteristics memorized and stored in his computerized mind.

The *Balzan* was three hundred and forty-five feet in length, displaced four thousand tons and was armed with SA-N-5 Grail SAM missiles and 30 MM Gatling guns.

He hoped her one hundred and eighty men and women crew would be thoroughly seasick from the heavy seas they were now encountering.

"The crew has been mustered, Captain, including the replacement men. No absentees and all ready to go to sea."

The able exec reported his directions to the department heads to start getting the ship battened down and well stowed prior to underway.

"Recommend we station the maneuvering watch at eleven-thirty."

"A heavy meal will be served at ten-thirty and continue until we secure the underway detail. Think the weather will only allow a sandwich and soup dinner tonight. With the expected heavy seas, only the hearty will be available for that."

"Concur, Dave. Thank you."

Bruce handed Dave the message board. "Ask Tom to give me an update of the engineering status as soon as he has an opportunity."

The captain entered the torpedo room and observed the last Mark 56X torpedo being strapped into the torpedo loading skid.

The torpedo loading hatch was shut and a torpedo man was tightly dogging down the twenty-five inch diameter hatch. This boundary ensured that the 13,000 pounds per square inch pressure of sea water that occurred with the *Jackfish* at test depth remained outside the ship.

The operator was taking a final tug on the hand wheel that drives the barrel locking device. This mechanism ensured the hatch stayed shut during all conditions, even during depth charge attacks.

Bruce smiled as he thought of the submariners' old wives' tale: The man who dogs the hatch last always attempted to take an additional twist for each of his children. Looks like this operator had two children.

"All torpedoes have been loaded onboard, Captain," reported his weapons officer. "We also have the latest technical manual for the new torpedo although it is not in final form nor approved by NAVORD."

Ray introduced to the captain torpedo man first class Greg Mitchell. "He is attached to the Submarine Base Torpedo Shop and volunteered to sail with *Jackfish*."

Bruce knew of Mitchell's torpedo expertise and was pleased that his squadron commander had fulfilled his request and embarked someone knowledgeable on the operation of the new torpedo.

"Welcome aboard *Jackfish*, Mitchell, and thank you for giving up your holiday." Stewart said as he shook Greg's hand.

By reaping the benefit of Mitchell's recent operational experience with the Mark 56X torpedo coupled with the in-depth information he was able to obtain from the preliminary technical manual, Bruce felt confident that he could master the operational characteristics of the weapon by the time it would be needed for an attack.

"Let me borrow the torpedo technical manual now, Ray. I want to glance at it for a few minutes before we get underway."

Bruce had only a short time to read the procedure for setting the combination to the nuclear weapon option. He wanted to be ready when he got the combinations from Bill Walter.

The combinations had to be set prior to tube loading the deadly torpedoes.

While departing the torpedo room, Ray reported the periscope had been landed in the submarine. Wiring of the electronics was progressing well. "Expect it to be fully operational by eleven hundred, Captain."

Bruce made a mental note to ensure a well deserved letter of commendation got written for those responsible for the timely repair.

Mission Complete

Ray continued, "Also, all provisions are struck below decks and final stowage was in progress. Completion of the prerequisites for sailing are on schedule."

All problems had been anticipated and corrective action taken, just as Bruce and his crew had done routinely in the past.

"Ray, let me know if any unforeseen circumstances threaten our noon underway. Also, give your boys a well done for their superb job of loading the torpedoes this morning. I appreciate the can-do spirit, particularly working in freezing weather."

Ray acknowledged the good words from his boss and observed with a smile as the captain departed his space.

The weapons officer felt fortunate to be working for this man. In addition to the outstanding fitness reports he had received ensuring his promotion, Ray was serving his apprenticeship under the best of the best. An aspiring young submarine officer could ask for no more.

Bruce turned to the section of the torpedo technical manual that detailed the nuclear interlock system.

He read from the manual slowly. Two sequential operations had to be performed for the nuclear weapon to be able to accept a detonation signal.

To prevent someone from randomly dialing the correct combination, a special non-reproduction key had to be inserted into the access hole in the side of the nuclear interlock section of the torpedo. The correct three numbers would be dialed and the key removed.

The weapon now was ready to receive the nuclear option signal. This signal would be generated from the attack center only on the command of the submarine's commanding officer.

Bruce continued to read the procedure from the technical manual. Another safety device was on the front of the firing panel in the attack center. This device was a nuclear detonation option switch installed under a spring loaded plastic cover. This feature prevented inadvertent activation of the nuclear warhead when the conventional explosive mode was planned.

Bruce now realized all he had to do was to get the keys and combinations from Bill Walter and then covertly set the nuclear option into the nuclear tipped weapons.

The first two events would be easy. He would have to think some more on the last.

"SQUADRON EIGHT ARRIVING" echoed on the ship's 1MC general announcing system throughout the ship, alerting the crew to the arrival of Bill Walter.

As Bruce approached the access ladder into *Jackfish*, Bill Walter's feet hit the deck as he entered the torpedo room.

The ship's duty officer waited to greet him.

"Good morning, Commodore."

"Welcome aboard," echoed the ship's duty officer and Bruce.

Bill smiled. The expression on his face relayed the message that he knew Bruce and his duty officer were just being polite to their senior and had more to do than greet him.

The commodore rubbed his hands vigorously to regain some warmth and circulation as the two officers proceeded to Bruce's stateroom. Bococo was waiting with two cups of well-received black and hot coffee.

"Thank you, Bococo. One of these days I am going to steal you away from the *Jackfish* and get you up to my Headquarters." Bill knew that Bococo would never leave Bruce's service.

Bruce handed Bill an envelope boldly marked TOP SECRET on the front and back. "This is my movement report. It routes *Jackfish* to the area I anticipate *Tigerfish* will be operating."

His letter to Ann also was given to his boss with instructions.

Bill jokingly laughed and reassured Bruce that he would return the letter to him when *Jackfish* returned after Christmas. His gut feeling told him that this letter was not too bad an idea just in case.

Bill removed three large numbered keys from his inner coat pocket and placed them on Bruce's desk. "As you can see, each key has a numbered tag attached."

From his other pocket, he withdrew three envelopes. Each had a serial number written on the outside.

Bill held up one of the envelopes and showed Bruce. The number on each tag matched a number on one of the envelopes. The combination to the nuclear option activator for each torpedo was enclosed in the envelopes.

The squadron commander pushed the pile of envelopes and keys towards Bruce and remarked, "God knows, we hope you won't need to use this option, but the consequences would be worst."

Walter stood up, finished his coffee with a large gulp, and struggled to put on his heavy bridge coat.

"One last item, Bruce. Don't disconnect your telephone line connection to the pier until you have received a call from Washington, D.C. It should come in at about eleven-thirty."

After a strong, longer than normal handshake, Bill headed for the door.

Mission Complete

"Good hunting, skipper. We'll be anxiously awaiting your Christmas message."

Bill departed the ship as rapidly as he had arrived.

"Good morning, Captain. Do you have a few minutes for an engineering status report?"

It was obvious from his unshaven and more than usually tired face that Tom had been up since he came onboard the *Jackfish* last night.

Bruce stated sympathetically, "Come in and sit down, Tom. You look awful, Engineer. Don't wear yourself out before we get underway."

Bruce also had been a chief engineer of a nuclear submarine at one time and could personally relate to the strain and pressure the responsibilities of the job put on an officer.

"We're in pretty good shape now. We had a few unanticipated problems earlier this morning I thought needed my immediate attention."

The engineer continued, "The pressurizer level indicator for number two nuclear reactor would not pass the final check. We had to enter the reactor compartment and realign the system. The problem was corrected on the first try so I didn't call you to report the problem."

After a pause and sip of his coffee, Tom continued, "Everything is checking out perfectly with number one plant. The final reactor startup checks now have been completed on both units."

The captain fully understood the engineering terminology being discussed. His in-depth knowledge of engineering principles and good engineering judgment was superb.

These traits, coupled with his superb tour of duty previously as an engineer officer, were instrumental in his being selected personally by Admiral Rickover to be the first commanding officer of *Jackfish*.

This ship boasted a new design and the most advanced reactors and engineering plant of any naval combatant in the world.

With its two three hundred megawatt S-14-W pressurized water reactors, modern state of the art steam turbines, driving one shaft at forty thousand combined shaft horsepower, the *Jackfish* had been clocked at forty knots submerged.

The ship was acclaimed the gold medal winner of all underwater warriors and far superior in all aspects to any submarine constructed by any country.

Tom directed his question to his captain. "Request permission to take both reactors critical at ten-thirty."

"We will be generating our own ship's power and ready to remove the shore power cables from the pier by eleven-thirty."

"I will rotate the watch standers for chow between ten-thirty and noon so all maneuvering watch personnel will be on station prior to underway."

"Permission granted, Tom."

"Also, Engineer, ensure that your spaces are stowed prior to leaving the mouth of the Thames River. This is going to be a rough trip all the way out to the diving point."

The leading stewards mate interrupted the captain with his announcement that lunch was being served in the wardroom.

"Please start without me, Bococo. I will be in shortly. Need to complete a few things now."

Bruce needed this opportunity to configure the Mark 56X torpedo interlock system.

As he entered the torpedo room, he could see two torpedo men putting away the special tools used to complete the final torpedo pre-load checks before the torpedoes were tube loaded.

He approached the men and opened the dialogue. "You men did a good job bringing these torpedoes aboard this morning."

A glance at his watch, then continued, "This will be the best time to get your lunch before tube loading the torpedoes. I don't want you to miss what may be the best and possibly your only meal today."

Both men were looking forward with great anticipation to this meal so not much encouragement was needed.

As they departed, Bruce rapidly started his covert task of setting the weapon interlock devices. He departed the torpedo room in ten minutes with his task completed.

Being sneaky was not one of his best traits and he felt uneasy about his actions.

He placed the three keys and combination envelopes into his stateroom safe.

After washing his hands and face, Bruce took his seat at the head of the wardroom table. This was the same seat he had occupied as the ship's captain for almost four years.

After lunch, coffee was interrupted when the below decks security watch knocked on the wardroom door, entered, and stood at attention. "Excuse me, Captain. You have a long distance telephone call in your stateroom."

All heads turned in the direction of the captain as he excused himself and departed the wardroom.

The volume and intensity of buzzing with conjecture about the telephone call increased as he departed the wardroom en route to his stateroom.

Mission Complete

"Good morning, Commander Stewart speaking, sir."

Bruce had a good idea who was calling and this was confirmed when the person on the other end responded, "This is the White House. Please remain on the telephone for the president."

"Hello, Bruce. I wanted to wish you and Ann a Merry Christmas and let you know that we'll be thinking of you. The First Lady and I will be leaving town for a few days. Hope your bear hunt over the holidays goes well. We're looking forward to having both of you to dinner at the White House after Christmas. I want to talk to you about your hunt."

After a slight pause, the president added in a solemn voice, "Good luck, son."

"Thank you, Mr. President, for the thoughtful call. Ann and I look forward to our meeting after the holidays. Have an enjoyable visit and hurry back to Washington."

The conversation was over. Although short and cryptic, Bruce understood his commander in chief's message.

He wondered if the president detected his unsure sense of confidence.

Dave entered Bruce's stateroom and reported, "Three Mark 56X nuclear tipped torpedoes are loaded into the torpedo tubes and the torpedo room is secured for sea. The ship is now providing its own electrical power and the engineers have started to remove the shore power cables from the pier."

After an acknowledgment from the captain, Dave continued. "Permission to station the maneuvering watch, Captain?"

Thirty minutes remained until *Jackfish* severed her remaining umbilical cord with the pier—the mooring lines—and put out to sea.

The 1MC general announcing system echoed throughout the ship, "STATION THE MANEUVERING WATCH."

/4/ PIRATES AT WORK

The maneuvering watch was stationed and there was only thirty minutes remaining until *Jackfish* got underway.

Bruce went to his stateroom to get dressed in his Arctic clothing to brave the blistering cold on the bridge of his submarine.

The outbound transit from the pier to open water would usually be about six hours. As required by U.S. Navy Regulations, the commanding officer had to remain on the bridge while the submarine was in restricted or confined waters.

He took care of his personal requirements, then dressed in his Arctic clothes which included insulated boots and headgear.

Remaining prerequisites before getting *Jackfish* underway included the last mail delivery off the ship, testing the main engines, dumping trash and garbage in the containers at the head of the pier, removing the personnel brow from the ship to the pier, readying the anchor for letting go, removing the ship's telephone connected to the pier, and, lastly, singling up all mooring lines.

Bruce would go to the bridge when the mooring lines were singled up or about five minutes before underway.

As he relaxed for a few minutes in his stateroom, a cold sweat came over him and his coffee mug started to shake. Although he disliked thinking thoughts like this, he realized much luck and God's help would be needed to successfully complete this mission.

If only I had been allowed to bring Dave and Nat into my confidence, Bruce thought. *At least it would reduce some of my burden and give me the backup that has proven successful in previous missions.*

He realized that orders are orders and he was not about to defy those of the highest level, especially those coming directly from his commander in chief, the president.

His mind churned in an attempt to put into perspective and to actually believe the incredible mission brief he had received last night.

As he sat, he rethought every word spoken by Admirals Hasting and Dale.

The captain shuttered as he relived those striking words: "*Tigerfish* was not lost at sea but has been pirated with Captain Tom Morello and most of the crew still alive."

The "how" was most shocking and totally unbelievable. However, the more the story evolved, the more possible it became.

Admiral Hasting had recited an episode that was related to him by Lieutenant Mike Hodges when the junior officer delivered the terrorist's ultimatum to Washington.

Mike was onboard *Tigerfish* when the Soviet/Cuban pirates took over the ship. The admiral prefaced his remarks by saying, "Mike stated that this was the best scenario that the *Tigerfish* crew could piece together as to how the take-over actually occurred."

It was obvious that this was a well-thought-out, rehearsed, and executed plan made by by well-trained Soviet/Cuban pirates.

The spider started to spin its web the evening of October twenty-third while the *Tigerfish* was anchored in Piraeus Bay, Greece. This was the last night of a well-deserved five-day port visit for the hard working *Tigerfish* crew.

The submarine had been at sea submerged for the previous month conducting close surveillance operations against the Soviet surface ships and submarines during a period of high international and diplomatic tension.

This was one of the many incidents the Soviets were involved in attempting to pressure the United States to condone the Soviet aggressive actions on the high sea.

This particular incident was precipitated when the Soviets tried to board a small American registered cruise ship that they accused of taking photographs of their military operations. The United States Sixth Fleet in the Mediterranean Sea went to top alert and moved all United States combatant surface ships and submarines to sea.

This show of force and resolve was a message to the Soviets that there was no doubt in anyone's mind that action would be taken if required.

Tigerfish was submerged, undetected in close proximity to the Soviet forces. The crew was at battle stations ready to inflict serious damage to the aggressors if ordered to do so by higher authority.

The Soviets backed down when their bluff was called and a serious international conflict was eliminated.

The wind in the Greek bay this time in October was cold. Raindrops were falling at just the correct rate to make the *Tigerfish* topside security watch, Petty Officer Blake, uncomfortable.

The time was approaching midnight with just thirty minutes remaining of his four-hour topside security watch. Hot coffee and some sticky buns, then a few hours sleep before reveille were paramount thoughts in the petty officer's mind.

The maneuvering watch would be stationed early to support an underway at zero six hundred.

Blake's pleasant thoughts were interrupted by the presence of an approaching overcrowded small boat. In the boat was a coxswain, a dark skinned man giving orders in broken English. Three passengers were huddled in the rear of the boat.

One of the passengers was dressed in a wrinkled suit. The other two men were wearing sports clothes and wind breaker waist jackets.

Two of the three passengers carried a sea bag. The one in the suit, the tallest of the three, had a large suitcase in one hand and an executive type briefcase in the other.

The dark man wore heavy foul weather gear that partially covered his face. He was standing in the bow of the boat, well braced to counter the rolling sea, and appeared to be in charge of the operation.

The boat was maneuvered expertly in close proximity to the submarine, its engine then throttled and the boat coasted toward the *Tigerfish*.

Blake was startled as the man steering the boat bellowed at him from four feet away, thus breaking his trance. "Hey—you there, catcha dis rope and tie my boat to your side. These official people wanta come ona your boat."

Almost simultaneously, a one-half-inch line was unfurling through the air in the direction of Blake. The young sailor caught the line, pulled the boat alongside, and made the line fast to the topside deck cleat.

The boat now was positioned in proximity to the personnel access brow. This brow provided a walkway to the topside of the curved black hull of the *Tigerfish* from the small boat.

The tallest of the three men moved hastily across the brow. Looking the

Mission Complete

young petty officer in the eyes, he stated in an authoritative voice, "Permission to come aboard?"

The other two followed, balancing their bulky sea bags as they attempted to synchronize the rolls of the two vessels to reduce the hazard. Although the sea was not too rough, enough chopping sea and swells in the bay were present to make the crossing somewhat precarious.

Once aboard *Tigerfish*, the last of the embarked men untied the line holding the small boat to the *Tigerfish*. The boat disappeared into the dark night as quickly and quietly as it had appeared.

The leader of the group removed a piece of paper from his briefcase, while almost simultaneously withdrawing his wallet to display a Unites States military identification card.

"We're ordered as crew members for the *Tigerfish*. Here are copies of our orders."

Blake didn't realize at the time that these were excellent forgeries of military identification cards and authorization orders for reporting aboard the *Tigerfish*.

The orders showed them to be Naval Reserve personnel. One was Lieutenant Tracy Smith. The other two were petty officers third class Wayne Lynn and Billy Russell.

"We are assigned to your ship for two months." Tracy continued. "This is long enough for the ship to complete its nine month Mediterranean Sea deployment and transit the Atlantic Ocean back to Groton, Connecticut."

The chilled topside watch called below decks on the ship's 1MC general announcing system for the duty chief petty officer to come topside.

Blake introduced the duty chief of the *Tigerfish* to the three new crew members. The group then proceeded smartly below decks to get settled in prior to the forthcoming underway in the early morning.

Blake then logged the identification data of the new arrivals into the topside security log.

Lieutenant (junior grade) David Newton, the ship's duty officer, welcomed his new officer shipmate and proceeded to arrange accommodations in the wardroom stateroom area.

Part of his indoctrination for the new officer was to show him the location of the wardroom and the coffee pot. Next was the location and operation of the head or toilet.

On departing, he gave Tracy a copy of the Plan of the Day (POD) and remarked to Tracy, "The POD is the Bible for the ship's daily activities. The executive officer is a stickler for following it verbatim." Dave pointed to the copy of the POD and stated, "As you can see, all significant events are sequenced for the coming day with associated times."

Tracy looked impressed as if he were learning something new.

Dave didn't know that this officer had had command of a first rate Soviet nuclear attack submarine when Dave was still a midshipman at the United States Naval Academy.

"Of significance, Tracy," Dave said as he pointed to the POD, "is that all hands reveille is to occur at zero five hundred to meet the scheduled underway at zero six hundred."

They both said goodnight and shook hands.

Dave proceeded about his duties of ensuring the safety of the ship and its personnel.

In addition, he ensured that the time sensitive items needed to support the underway were in fact proceeding on schedule.

Shortly afterwards, the *Tigerfish* captain, Commander Tom Morello, his executive officer, Dick Varley, and three junior officers entered the ship's attack center.

The group had just returned from a liberty ashore. None were intoxicated, but all had had a few drinks to keep warm during the boat ride from the liberty boat landing ashore to the submarine anchored eight hundred yards from the shore.

Dave knew they would be tired as the five of them started out mid-morning to visit Athens. Their plan was to spend the last in-port day shopping and then visiting and taking pictures of the historic Acropolis.

It was evident to Dave that the rain had intensified since he last conducted his hourly inspection of the topside area of the ship. The five drenched and cold officers standing in front of him attested to this fact.

Following one step behind his fast moving captain, Dave provided a brief account of the day's events including the status of preparations for getting the ship underway as scheduled.

He didn't discuss the three new reservists at this time. This information could wait until morning.

His more detailed status to the executive officer included a report that a new reservist officer had reported aboard and was bedded down for the night.

The hour of zero five hundred came earlier than normal after a night of shore leave. Wake up knocks were heard on the wardroom stateroom doors and lights were turned on throughout the berthing areas of the ship.

The general announcing system echoed throughout the ship, "REVEILLEE, UP ALL HANDS."

The smell of breakfast was evident in the wardroom and the crew's dinette area.

The majority of the crew awakened at zero five hundred. However, the unsung heroes, the junior mess men and duty cook, were up at four o'clock to ensure that a well-cooked breakfast was available for their shipmates.

The crew hastily ate their bill of fare consisting of eggs, steak, potatoes, juice, milk, and sticky buns freshly baked. The sticky buns were advertised as "no-cal." Some of the chow hounds' waists were evidence that this was just another sea story.

At zero five thirty, just as scheduled in the POD, the ship's 1MC general announcing system echoed throughout the ship, "STATION THE MANEUVERING WATCH."

All personnel moved quickly to their assigned maneuvering watch stations. Sirens and alarms were tested. The steering system was tested in its three different modes of operation to ensure the backup and emergency modes were available.

Communications were tested and all the myriad of tasks accomplished to ensure the ship and crew were ready to answer all demands of the officer of the deck while moving this massive vehicle through and under the water.

Captain Tom Morello, dressed in heavy foul weather gear and wearing warm headgear, insulated boots, and a double set of mittens, worked his way through the watertight door between the wardroom compartment and the control room. He then headed towards the navigation plotting table to discuss with the navigator the forthcoming transient.

"Looks like a good morning for getting underway, Dave," Tom stated to his navigator as he looked at the outbound track from Piraeus Bay, Greece, to the location where the *Tigerfish* would submerge into its natural habitat.

"Yes sir, Captain. Don't expect any heavy seas or bad weather, except it won't be like San Diego weather on the bridge."

The executive officer entered into the control room and reported to Tom. "The ship is ready to get underway."

Dick Varley made it a matter of routine to thoroughly inspect the ship prior to underway.

He was responsible for ensuring proper stowage to prevent any flying objects during rough weather or when maneuvering the ship at steep angles. Also, it was his job to ensure that the equipment, as well as the personnel, especially after a hard night on liberty, were ready to respond. Complacency had no place in the operation of a complex nuclear submarine.

Five minutes before underway time, Tom gave permission to the officer of the deck on the bridge to test the main engines.

The ship surged slightly in the reverse direction and then forward as the engineering officer of the watch in the maneuvering room, the heart of operations for the control of the engineering spaces, directed the main engine throttles slightly opened to gulp the high pressure steam.

This testing ensured the steam flow path was clear and the equipment components were all functional as prescribed.

"Main engines tested. Ready to answer all bells" was reported from the engineering officer of the watch in the maneuvering room to the officer of the deck on the bridge.

Time for underway was fast approaching.

Tom ordered the officer on the bridge to heave in the anchor to short stay.

He then continued to review the track and agreed on the plan of action on moving *Tigerfish* from Greece to Naples Bay, Italy, some seven hundred and twenty nautical miles away.

"Captain up," Tom bellowed as he made his way up through the access hatch to the bridge cockpit.

"Good morning, Captain. Ready to get underway in all respects."

At exactly zero six hundred, *Tigerfish* was underway.

The officer of the deck, OOD, slowly backed the ship while the anchor was being hauled into its faired underbody cavity near the stern of the ship.

Slowly backing the ship prevented the anchor chain from fouling the finely tuned blades of the single propeller.

A nick on one of the blades of this special propeller would cause cavitation, the nemesis of a submarine. This popping of bubbles off the rapidly turning propeller would make the submarine detectable at long distances by opposing submarines. In combat, cavitation could result in the loss of ship and crew to a hostile torpedo.

The report, "BRIDGE-ENGINE ROOM, THE ANCHOR IS HOUSED," broke the early morning stillness.

Ship's course was set at zero seven five degrees true with a speed of one third.

The maneuvering watch was secured and the order given to "Rig ship for dive." *Tigerfish* was brought up to half speed as ordered by the OOD.

The sleek curvature hull sliced through the clear warm water en route to

Mission Complete

Naples. The ship would submerge in three hours into the Aegean Sea with a depth of water greater than one thousand meters.

While listening to the briefing, Bruce recalled his study of Thucydides and the Peloponnesian War which had taken place in this same location four hundred years B.C. He concluded that the treachery and trickery of the Spartans against the Athenians during this thirty-five year war was minimal compared to that of the Soviet/Cuban team of bastards setting up to pirate the *Tigerfish*.

Once things settled down to normal after the early morning underway, Lieutenant Tracy Smith entered the executive officer's stateroom and shut the door.

"Commander Varly, here is my identification card from the Office of Naval Intelligence (ONI). I am here with my two other agents, Russell and Lynn, to gather information on drug smuggling operations from United States submarines outbound from the Mediterranean Sea to the states."

Dick smiled as he motioned Tracy to sit down. "So the reservist act is just a cover story?"

"I feel quite confident about my crew. However, we will certainly assist your operation in any way possible."

"Thank you, sir. There are some things I need to make this investigation complete." Tracy paused, then stated, "I desire to have my enlistees mingle with the crew and try to pick up information as to whether there were any smuggling operations planned or actually in progress. This includes having access to all areas of the ship, in particular the engineering spaces."

The executive officer nodded to the affirmative and Tracy continued.

"It is essential that my agent assistants, now acting petty officers, be assigned topside security watch under instruction to the regular *Tigerfish* watch the last night in Naples. This would be the time any drugs, if it did happen, would be smuggled aboard to be transported to the states."

Dick assured Tracy that he would make this happen and would provide full cooperation to the ONI for their investigation.

Tracy then reiterated, "No one is to be briefed on this operation, except the captain of course. Not even the submarine commodore in Naples."

After reaching an agreement on the conduct of the clandestine operation, Tracy and Dick went into the captain's stateroom and briefed Tom on the complete operation.

When Tom and his exec, Dick Varley, entered the wardroom, Dave had the navigation charts laid out on the table.

The intended track to Naples was plotted and Dave used his finger as a pointer while he briefed the details of the voyage.

"We will submerge at this point in the Aegean Sea, then head on course one-nine-five for eighty-five miles to the thousand meter curve off Kithira Island. We'll need to slow and get to the surface in a hurry here as it shoals up rapidly."

Tom interrupted the navigator's presentation. "Exec, what's the latest intelligence report tell about Soviet warships anchored at Kithira?"

Varley responded, "The best we have, Captain, is that all their ships are underway participating in a big exercise. This will certainly make it easier for us to dash pass this well-used Soviet anchorage on the surface and not have to worry about their routine harassment."

The navigator again pointed to the chart and continued the briefing.

"After the forty mile surface run past Kithira, *Tigerfish* will submerge on course two-eight-five degrees true and then travel three-hundred-and-eighty nautical miles submerged across the Ionian Sea."

Dave took a sip of coffee and then continued, "After surfacing, we make passage through the Strait of Messina on course zero-zero-five degrees true."

The briefing concluded with a description of the ship's route across the Tyrrhenian Sea to a point south of the Isle of Capri and then to the Gulf of Naples for anchorage.

The ideal location was to moor at one of the piers in the Naples Harbor. This eased loading any stores or other supplies.

Crew liberty ashore also was easier from a pier location in the harbor. Being able to moor inside the harbor was dictated by the political climate at the time between the United States and Italy.

When the submarine had to anchor outside of the harbor, getting the liberty party ashore and back depended on the whims of the liberty boat crews from one of the larger U.S. ships anchored in the same location.

A good showing by the submarine against the other U.S. surface combatants during at-sea exercises prior to coming to Naples for liberty always ended up with few liberty boats stopping at your submarine to pick up your liberty party.

The arrival of *Tigerfish* in Naples was scheduled for ten hundred on the twenty-sixth of October using a speed of advance of a little over fourteen knots for the transit.

Being able to operate at this reduced speed provided quite a relaxed change for the crew from the previous high speed tension-filled maneuvering

Mission Complete

required to conduct the many sensitive and dangerous missions over the last nine months.

Dave completed his navigation track briefing and looked at the other officers for comments.

Tom responded, "Looks good, gentlemen. We want to maximize these scheduled ups and downs when we change our submarine depth to give our two newest officers ample opportunities to complete their practical factors needed for submarine qualification."

Tom continued, "I want both officers ready for final qualification upon our arrival in Groton, Connecticut."

Dick had already coordinated with the engineer officer to optimize the engineering plant casualty drill schedule to coincide with the navigation requirements to take the ship to periscope depth.

This was the first opportunity in many months for any dedicated crew training. The ship's operations, as they should, had first priority.

Time was set aside for ship's as well as engineering casualty drills and an accelerated training program set up for the engineering personnel.

Much to Tom's dislike, the Atlantic fleet commander scheduled a two-day exhaustive operational reactor safeguards examination prior to *Tigerfish*'s arrival in the states.

Upon arrival at the mouth of the Thames River at the channel entrance to Groton, Connecticut, before any leave or liberty for the crew, the ship would pick up the team of experts from the fleet commander's staff. *Tigerfish* then would reverse course and proceed outbound to sea, conducting the examination in the deep water of the Atlantic Ocean. This was an annual examination given to all nuclear submarine crews.

A failure or poor showing on this examination seldom occured; however, it was not tolerated or condoned by higher authority and could in some cases take the brilliance off a commanding officer's successful career.

Seeing your home port so close, but yet so far away after a nine-month cruise was not conducive to good morale.

Tom and his crew knew that a poor showing during this examination could tarnish the ship's great achievements during her long deployment and certainly put a black cloud over the heroes' return.

Tigerfish had done well in all the previous operational reactors examinations and Tom was confident his crew would again meet the challenge.

The crew and ship had been driven hard during this deployment and had accomplished each mission beyond expectation.

The effects of operating under constant pressure and stress were evident in all three of the senior officers. Dark rings circled their eyes and the wrinkled foreheads were more likened to men much older.

During these operations, the unknown was always present and constant vigilance was a must. In this intense cold war environment, one error in judgment could result in a collision with an enemy ship or possible grounding of a submarine on the ever-shifting volcanos making up the floor of the Aegean Sea.

Immense embarrassment to the United States in the international arena could be the outcome with the possibility of severe ship damage with a resultant degradation of operational readiness or, worst case, the loss of ship and crew.

Dick Varley interrupted the deep thoughts of his captain and handed him a thick patrol report for his review. "Our last patrol report is finished, Captain, and ready for your signature. The Mediterranean Sea report will be complete prior our arrival in Naples so you can brief the admiral."

"Well done, Exec. Thank you."

As Tom started to leave the wardroom, he turned to the two officers and said with a smile, "Let's ensure a good movie is shown tomorrow night. We might even need a double feature. I get the feeling that the anxiety of homeward bound channel fever is already spreading throughout the crew!"

Tracy Smith sat in the wardroom watching the evening movie and munching popcorn with his newly acquired, but temporary, officer shipmates.

The Russian didn't fully appreciate the humor in the flick, but faked an outward laugh in unison with the other officers in the wardroom.

In reality, the audience displayed more laughter than was warranted.

Heading home did have a way of adding lightheartedness to weary men.

Tomorrow morning the ship would anchor off the Naples harbor. Two days later *Tigerfish* would start the final leg of the homeward voyage.

Inwardly, Tracy despised these professional men for wasting this valuable time with such frivolous activities. On Tracy's Soviet submarine, this time would be devoted studying Marxist doctrine under the tutelage of the embarked communist party commissar officer.

Tracy's mind wandered back to the rigorous training program for those Soviet and Cuban submariners selected for the distinction of being part of this coup of the century.

The first lecture, basic indoctrination, made a lasting impression, one that he would have rather missed.

The head instructor at the formal training school, in rimmed glasses with his hair plastered down, pointed to a cut away diagram of the United States submarine *Tigerfish* as he lectured to the professional and well-trained pirates.

This academia probably never had been near water except to take a bath.

Now he was presenting the subject as if talking to a group of young sea cadets, rather than to a select group of warriors who had spent most of their adult life operating submarines around the world.

"The internal hull configuration of *Tigerfish* consists of a forward compartment, reactor compartment, and an engineering space."

The instructor stopped his presentation and looked at his students to ensure that they were following his presentation. He then continued. "A high pressure bulkhead and a watertight door for access separate each adjacent compartment. The locking device for the watertight door is a high leverage wheel operating system of spur gears and drive shafts that expand into the breech door locking assembly. The integral bulkhead is capable of withstanding the crush depth pressure of the ship, 60,000 pounds per square inch."

The short stocky academia again scanned the audience to see if this handpicked group of top Soviet submariners fully understood his basic statements. Proud of himself for his accomplishments to date, he continued.

"All the propulsion and its ancillary equipment, electrical switchboards, and distribution system, the reactor controls and the maneuvering area where watch standers control the reactors and provide the propulsion demands of the officer of the deck are located in the engineering spaces."

Tracy, as well as the other men, were anxious and getting frustrated with such a trite offering. This was the last of this type of presentation.

Tracy vigorously complained to the top officer of the school about the poor quality and quantity of the subject material and of the instructor.

This head instructor never returned to the classroom.

The pace accelerated with twelve- to fourteen-hour study days being the norm for the rest of the training program. No one complained. There was always the light at the end of the tunnel, the capture of the *Tigerfish* and glory for the Motherland.

For Tracy, it meant the long awaited revenge for his father that drove him the hardest of the group.

It didn't have to be dwelled upon by his superiors that access to and control of the engineering spaces in *Tigerfish* was the linchpin of the operation.

One alerted *Tigerfish* watch stander in the space could easily jam shut the locking mechanism for the watertight door. This would prevent access for the pirates into the engineering spaces and abort the takeover.

The contingency plan, should this occur, would be to use captured U.S. personnel in the forward part of the submarine as hostages to be tortured until Tracy's demands were met and the access door opened to the engineering room.

This delay, should it occur, could waste valuable time with the possibility of an alerting signal being transmitted by *Tigerfish* to other United States forces in the area.

The Soviet team leader, with a vengeance to fulfill, was not accustomed to failure and did not intend to start now.

Billy Russell and Wayne Lynn were actually seasoned officers in the Soviet submarine force, well trained and experienced in the operation of nuclear powered submarines.

Russell had recently completed a successful tour as Tracy's chief engineering officer on a fast attack Soviet nuclear submarine. Of course, he was highly recommended for this takeover assignment by his previous boss, Tracy.

During the short transit from Piraeus Bay, Greece, to Naples, Italy, both Soviet engineers were frequent visitors in the *Tigerfish* engineering spaces. Some of the United States crew members jokingly referred to them as assistant watch standers.

The Soviet imposters observed the normal routine of all watch station personnel and operators in *Tigerfish* and mentally recorded their normal location, at precise times, during the watch cycle.

The location of the electrical distribution panels and the fuse holders for the engineering alarm and communications systems were confirmed. It was mandatory that these components be silenced just prior to the coup to prevent any warnings.

Both Lynn and Russell were thoroughly knowledgeable with the details of the ship's blueprints and reactor operating manuals.

This knowledge, coupled with the many months of study in the full scale *Tigerfish* engine room mockup in Russia, made them well qualified when it came to the operation of these reactors and propulsion plant.

However, this time spent at sea on the ship was extremely valuable for gaining actual as built familiarization of the spaces and individual operators.

The operation order for this crucial event had Russell and Lynn positioned as point men in the engineering spaces.

Mission Complete

Each of the Soviets would have concealed tranquilizer guns under their lightweight foul weather jackets.

The top priority of the takeover of *Tigerfish* was to ensure the access door to the engineering spaces was available for passage of the pirates.

The second priority was to take out as many watch standers as possible and that the reactors remain in operation throughout the takeover. It was of extreme importance to prevent an alerted watch stander from "scramming" or shutting down the reactors.

During the two day visit in Naples, Russell and Lynn completed their final prep session.

Tracy would receive their readiness report prior to *Tigerfish* underway.

The Soviet leader played his game of charades expertly during the voyage from Piraeus Bay to Naples. He was able to gain the full confidence of the executive officer and the complete crew of *Tigerfish*.

His plan was coming together nicely.

The last night in Naples, Wayne Lynn was assigned the 2200-0200 Topside Security watch under Instruction. Billy Russell was assigned the 0200-0600 watch.

These watch assignments provided the pirates complete coverage throughout the night as a contingency to ensure their well-thought-out devious plan worked as rehearsed.

At zero one hundred, Lynn was able to convince the regularly assigned topside watch stander, Seaman Kelley, to go below decks for coffee and to get first crack at the freshly baked pastries.

Lynn, although under instruction as the watch stander, convinced Kelley that he would maintain a taut topside security watch.

Once Kelly's head disappeared below the deck level of the topside twenty-five inch access hatch into the bowels of the ship, Lynn flashed a predetermined signal with his flashlight.

Almost immediately, the silhouette of a small boat approached out of the darkness without running lights in operation.

As the boat rested alongside *Tigerfish* without a tending line, six "newly reported" men rapidly boarded the submarine by leaping across the open area between the boat and the sleek submarine topside.

There was no stumbling during this regimented evolution as each man gave the performance of a well-trained gymnast with agility, speed, and strength.

These were not run-of-the-mill sailors. Sea bags were tossed from the small boat to the grasping hands of the six men topside on the submarine.

Lynn resembled a coach in an overtime basketball game as he coaxed and directed the movements of the boarders to speed up the transfer.

The contents of the sea bags were later identified as handguns, gas canisters, gas masks, and leg and arm irons.

Fake identification ID cards and forged orders from the chief of naval personnel to report to *Tigerfish* were handed to Lynn.

On long deployments of submarines to the Mediterranean Sea, there is a paucity of mail deliveries to the ships, coupled with infrequent port visits. Therefore, it is not uncommon for personnel to report to the submarine well in advance of the ship receiving any written notification from the chief of naval personnel.

It was obvious the six night boarders were expert in their mission and fully understood all the characteristics of this submarine. They rapidly and professionally passed through the ship's topside access hatch, lowering the bags to each other as they moved.

Once inside the *Tigerfish*, the new Soviet/Cuban arrivals dispersed to their preassigned locations in the ship to wait for plan execution.

Lynn was making the entry into the topside security log about the newly reported personnel when Kelley returned. He was balancing a tray with two cups of coffee and delicious smelling bear claws pastries.

The fake topside watch assured Kelley he had verified the military issued identification cards and orders for the newly reported men.

Phase two of the operation was accomplished as scheduled.

It was to be learned later that these six, plus the previous three new arrivals to the submarine in Piraeus Bay, were the nucleus of the team that pirated *Tigerfish*.

Tracy Smith knew the operations of the submarine well—essentially that the ship would get underway at fifteen hundred, then proceed outbound on the surface from Naples Bay while rigging ship for dive.

The ship would submerge about ninteen thirty, proceed to transit the Strait of Gibraltar outbound, and thence commence the long awaited trip home to love ones in Groton, Connecticut.

The takeover plan had the pirates taking over the ship after all preparations were made for submerging the ship and after the last required ship-to-shore radio transmission had been made.

Tigerfish was originally scheduled to depart port early in the morning;

however, the submarine admiral in Naples wanted Tom to attend lunch with the Sixth Fleet commander and other high ranking admirals from different warfare specialties.

After lunch, Tom would brief some of his significant classified operations conducted against the Soviets while he was assigned to operate in the Mediterranean Sea.

Normal routine was taking place in the *Tigerfish*. After lunch, the executive officer ordered the ship rigged for dive.

The rig for dive would be accomplished with the exception of the ventilation system, the upper bridge access hatch, and the main vents for the ballast tanks. These would be rigged just prior to submerging the submarine.

All crewmen not involved in the ensuing evolutions of rigging the ship for dive or on watch standing duties were catching up on the rest lost during the two-day visit to Naples.

Tracy Smith's new team members took this opportunity to better familiarize themselves with the ship and to ensure that their part of the plot was executed without a flaw.

Tracy sat in the wardroom drinking coffee and reading the Plan of the Day.

"Underway at fifteen hundred, evening meal is to be served at eighteen hundred, dive the ship at nineteen thirty, and movie call at twenty thirty."

He smiled, as he knew the POD was incorrect. There would be no movie call tonight, nor any night in the future for these dumb capitalistic sailors.

The Soviet leader was very proud of himself. The plan was progressing on schedule just the way they had rehearsed every detail of it for five long months. His personal long-awaited revenge was close approaching.

Tracy had been brought up in a long line military family in Moscow. His father, one of the first commanding officers of a Soviet nuclear submarine, was on his way to becoming a leader of their rapidly growing elite nuclear navy.

Destiny was changed when his father's ship collided with an United States aircraft carrier in the North Sea during a period of international tension. The Soviet sub sank with all hands lost.

At the time of the accident, Tracy had just graduated with top honors from the Soviet Naval Academy. He was a distinguished student in all subjects, including speaking English. He spoke this language better than most members of the United States attaché in Moscow.

Subsequent to graduation, he reported to a nuclear attack submarine as a junior officer.

Lieutenant Tracy Smith had just completed his first assignment as the commanding officer of the newest nuclear attack submarine in the Soviet fleet. He excelled in all operations assigned to his ship.

He was beside himself when informed of his assignment as the leader of the group to pirate the *Tigerfish*.

Subsequent to the takeover, he would be the new captain of the American submarine. The opportunity to avenge his father's murder had finally arrived!

"*TIGERFISH* ARRIVING" echoed over the ship's 1MC general announcing system.

This was followed by the announcement, "STATION THE MANEUVERING WATCH."

Cheers and shouts were heard throughout the ship.

Each crew member knew the next stop would be Groton, Connecticut. Home at last!

Tom came below decks, talked briefly with his exec, changed clothes, and headed for the bridge. He was in a good mood.

The briefings for the Sixth Fleet commander and his staff were well received. The admiral responsible for the submarine operations in the Mediterranean Sea provided innuendoes to Tom that his ship would be recommended for a navy unit commendation for its secret operations in the Med area. A legion of merit medal for Tom and many personal awards for the crew also would be recommended.

"Captain up" was heard on the bridge at the same time the captain's head entered the cockpit area.

"Good afternoon, Bob. Ready to go home?"

Lieutenant Bob Ramsey, the ship's officer of the deck, replied with a smile, "Yes sir, Captain. Ship's ready to get underway. All hands onboard."

Tigerfish headed southwesterly on the surface at full speed toward the designated diving position.

Tom gave directions to Bob, "Once the ship is clear of all ship traffic in the congested sea lanes around Naples Bay, follow the track laid out by the navigator. I want to be on station ready to submerge the ship right after evening meal."

"Yes sir, Captain."

"Laying below," Tom yelled as he worked his way down the access ladder like a cat. His twenty years ascending and descending the stainless steel ladders in seven different submarines made him somewhat of an expert.

The captain made a quick tour of his ship, then hit the sack fully clothed

Mission Complete

for a fast nap before dinner. The night was to be a long one as it always was on leaving port.

The exacting details of first making the ship ready to submerge and then safely guiding it to thousands of feet underwater required his utmost attention. This period from fully surfaced through the transition to a submerged condition was the most dangerous time in the life of a submarine. Command vigilance was a must during this crucial time.

The engineering spaces were fully manned. The same number of engineers were required on watch stations whether the submarine was on the surface or submerged, as long as the reactor was in a critical mode of operation providing propulsion to the ship.

The surface steaming watch was stationed in the forward part of the ship.

In this mode, only a minimal number of men were required to ensure safety of the ship and provide navigational support to the officer of the deck stationed on the bridge who was directing the movement of the *Tigerfish*.

Four men were stationed in the control room.

In addition, a roving watch stander ascertained the security and ship safety in the forward spaces.

Another watch stander was stationed in the torpedo room to safeguard the nuclear missiles and torpedoes.

An operator manned the operating gear in the sonar room, and another monitored the equipment in the communications room.

One cook was busy preparing evening meal while three mess men assisted in setting up for the meal.

The lights were dimmed throughout the rest of the ship with not much activity evident, except for those personnel rigging the ship for dive. These sailors were necessary to ensure the multitude of switches, valves, and electrical breakers were in the proper position for safely submerging the ship.

The captain was awaken with the report from the ballast control panel operator. "Captain, the ship is rigged for dive."

"Very well, Chief," Tom replied and then shut his eyes for another fifteen minutes shut eye before evening meal.

Tracy and one of his pirates were in the control room with the rest of his team in their designated positions waiting the take over signal as rehearsed.

The future captain of the *Tigerfish* keyed the 1MC general announcing system microphone twice. This was the predetermined signal to start the planned operation.

Russell and Lynn were positioned in the engineering spaces waiting for the signal to put their part of the plan into operation.

Fuses were rapidly removed from the ship's alarm system and communications system making the systems inoperative for crew warnings.

The re-circulation ventilation fans for the chief's and crew's berthing areas were turned to the off position. This allowed the maximum damaging effect from the pirate's gas canisters.

The master valves to the ship's personnel emergency air breathing system were shut.

Even if some of the crew in the gas-filled compartments had time and presence of mind to put on their emergency air breathing masks, the masks would be useless without a supply of breathing air.

The team of experts moved swiftly throughout the submarine, executing each assigned task with precision.

One pirate took out the cook and his three mess cooks in the crew's dinette with his well-aimed tranquilizer gun. He then moved to stand guard at the watertight door separating the engineering space with the forward part of the ship.

Two Soviet sailors wearing gas masks discharged gas canisters into the crew's berthing area.

Another exploded the canisters in the sleeping quarters for the chief petty officers.

The doors to each area were locked and a terrorist guard stationed at the door.

Another terrorist used his tranquilizer gun to rapidly silence and put into a deep sleep the sonar watch stander and the single operator in the communication room.

Two intruders rapidly moved through the wardroom area shooting each officer with tranquilizer bullets as they slept or were at their desks.

Tom was the first to be put out of action.

The security watch in the torpedo room and two wanderers who were up and about the forward part of the ship were likewise subdued.

Another pair of pirates entered the control room and nodded to their leader.

Tracy acknowledged then silenced the ballast control panel operator and the helmsman with tranquilizer bullets.

His Soviet crew took over these watch stations exactly as they had prepared for during the previous months in training.

Tracy looked at his watch as he proceeded to the bridge access hatch. Exactly ten minutes to complete the takeover. Just as scheduled.

Mission Complete

"Request permission to come up?" the agile Soviet submariner yelled in a deep voice as he started to ascend the ladder from the control room to the bridge cockpit area.

"Permission granted," responded the unaware officer of the deck.

After a few minutes of idle conversation on the bridge, and at the opportune time, Tracy expertly silenced both the OOD and his lookout with tranquilizer bullets.

He then ordered the ship to one-third speed by positioning the engine order annunciator on the bridge. The engine room responded with the ship quivering as it slowed from full speed.

Tracy's flashing light signal into the darkness brought a fishing vessel into view. This was the same fishing vessel that had been following close abeam the *Tigerfish* for the last half hour.

Once alongside, the fishing vessel placed a portable brow between their ship and the *Tigerfish*.

Men dressed in foreign uniforms, wearing holstered hand guns and automatic weapons over their shoulders rapidly boarded the submarine. Each carried large sea bags with some carrying bags containing high explosives.

The torpedo room access hatch flopped open and the new arrivals, eighteen total, scurried down the access ladder into the submarine. The last man expertly shut and dogged the hatch.

The fishing vessel broke free and drifted off into the darkness.

Phase III of the mission was completed on schedule.

The two unconscious *Tigerfish* men on the bridge were lowered into the control room and one of the pirates relieved Tracy as the new officer of the deck. Full speed was again ordered on the engine order annunciator.

The rest of the terrorist group moved quickly throughout the ship, carrying out preassigned duties. They proceeded to their designated locations and put leg and arm irons on the sleeping *Tigerfish* crew.

After all the *Tigerfish* personnel in the forward part of the ship were in irons, the ship's ventilation system was returned to normal.

Armed guards took their stations, lights were turned on and the pirates waited the crew's return to their new world of bondage.

The tranquilizer bullets had been developed to subdue their human targets for four to six hours.

If the *Tigerfish* crew had realized what was in the future, they would rather have stayed subdued.

The takeover of the forward part of the ship had gone as planned. The harder part and that which would require swiftness and an element of surprise to be successful would be overtaking the watch standers in the engineering spaces.

Allowing just one gallant *Tigerfish* operator time to damage the critical electronic panels that control the reactors could possibly abort the complete mission.

This phase had been rehearsed the most and the final approval for the mission had not been provided until the team demonstrated to its superiors that it could consistently achieve the objective without any flaws.

During training, professional Soviet submariners played the roles of Americans in an exact scale model of the *Tigerfish* engineering space.

All possible scenarios were developed and played out by both sides with senior Soviet officers critiquing each exercise.

Each event was videotaped, then played back during the critique of the exercise until perfection was achieved. The final examination was soon to be executed.

Lynn and Russell were making their last observations in the engineering spaces. No surprises would be accepted.

They heard Tracy's double keying of the 1MC general announcing system and knew the operation had started in the forward part of the ship. If all went as planned, in less than eleven minutes the ship would slow to one-third speed to allow their comrade shipmates to board the *Tigerfish*.

Both Lynn and Russell were in the lower level engine room between the main condensers. Lynn pretended to observe the vacuum gages while Russell, on his hands and knees, was looking into the bilge area under the deck plates.

They felt the ship shake as it started to slow from full speed.

Russell looked at his watch, glanced up at Lynn, and stated in a whisper, "On schedule, Comrade."

Lynn nodded, smiled, and then moved to his location in the upper level engine room to carry out his assignment. They both knew that in ten minutes Tracy would enter the maneuvering room area ready to execute the takeover.

Between the two, five *Tigerfish* watch standers outside of the maneuvering room area had to be subdued. The control for the reactors then had to be shifted to local control exactly on time so as not to alert the watch standers in the maneuvering room. Shifting control of the reactors prevented the normal reactor control operator on station at the reactor control panel in the maneuvering room from scramming or shutting down the reactors and taking away all propulsion power for the ship.

Mission Complete

If this were to happen, the controlling mechanism for the reactors would be inoperative and it would take four to five hours to restore the system to normal operation.

Tracy entered the maneuvering room on schedule and started to talk with the engineering officer of the watch (EOOW). He asked some basic questions while waiting for Russell and Lynn to take their positions on either side of the area.

Three replacement Soviet nuclear watch standers were positioned forward of the maneuvering room out of sight, awaiting their signal to take over the operational controls.

Another pirate was passing through the lower level engine room and ancillary areas putting leg and arm irons on the watch standers that had been subdued by Russell and Lynn.

Tracy nodded to his two assistants.

Then in rapid succession the three *Tigerfish* operators and the engineering officer of the watch (EOOW) were quickly subdued. The Soviets took over operation of the engineering spaces just as planned.

Billy Russell, now the chief engineer officer of *Tigerfish*, called the reactor compartment tunnel on the ship's inter-space telephone.

Five Soviet submariners entered the engineering spaces and assumed their new watch standing duties.

Tracy, smiling with pride bubbling over, shook the hands of Russell and Lynn as he provided congratulations to them for a job well done. He then proceeded forward to take over the responsibilities as captain of his new command.

Phase IV of the plan was completed.

The next three phases included transmitting a distress signal to a United States ship, coupled with setting off explosive charges simulating a sunken submarine. *Tigerfish* then would transit submerged from the "submarine sunk" location through the Strait of Gibraltar out of the Mediterranean Sea and into the Atlantic Ocean. Then the submarine would pick up three Soviets from a trawler off the coast of Africa and thence proceed southwesterly undetected to Cuba.

Bruce's deep thought process was broken hearing the report from the officer of the deck. "Captain—officer of the deck. Ready to get underway in all respects with the exception of singling up mooring lines."

This request from the *Jackfish* officer of the deck indicated that only five minutes remained until the start of the most demanding and dangerous mission Bruce and the *Jackfish* had ever undertaken.

"Officer of the deck—captain. Very well."

The officer of the deck continued, "Request permission to single up all mooring lines."

"Permission granted to single up all mooring lines," replied Bruce.

/5/ UNDERWAY

Bruce departed his stateroom and proceeded to the bridge. He stopped momentarily at the navigator's table in the control room to review the navigation chart that showed the outbound track *Jackfish* would take to get into the open ocean. The captain had memorized this transit from the many times he had made the trip over the last fifteen years.

He rapidly moved up the twelve foot stainless steel ladder to the bridge cockpit.

"Captain up."

"Yes sir, Captain," responded Lieutenant Jim Smith, the officer of the deck.

"Ready to get the ship underway, Captain."

"Very well, Jim. Get the ship underway."

Jim commenced to give a series of orders to his telephone talker who was in close proximity to the OOD in the bridge cockpit.

The talker repeated each order back to the OOD verbatim and then gave the order over his sound powered telephone headset to the applicable recipient of the specific order.

"Cast off all mooring lines except number one line."

"Heave around on number one line with the capstan."

The bow of the ship moved slowly towards the pier and the stern moved away from the pier towards the middle of the slip.

When *Jackfish* was in the middle of the slip, Jim ordered,"Back one third."

The submarine now started to back slowly into the Thames River.

"Cast off number one line. Rig the capstan and the topside cleats for sea."

Both the capstan and topside cleats were repositioned into the hull to make them flush. This new faired position of the capstan and cleats eliminated flow noise from being generated when the submarine was operating submerged.

Bruce saluted and then waved goodbye to Bill Walter who was standing on the pier and to the Submarine Base personnel who were on the pier wishing them a successful voyage.

These were the sailors who had worked all night to ensure the *Jackfish* made the underway commitment.

They didn't know what the submarine's mission was; however, it was obvious that it was of the highest priority.

Jim directed his telephone talker, "All stop. Ahead one third. Right fifteen degrees rudder. Steer course one-eight-zero degrees true."

The officer of the deck continued, "Take in the colors. All personnel topside lay below."

"Ahead two thirds."

Ice started to form on the Arctic face masks worn by Jim, the captain, the telephone talker, and the lookout as the freezing wind blew across the bridge cockpit. Water was washing across the bow of the submarine and part way up the sail area.

Although the *Jackfish* was still in the protected waters of the Thames River, the ship started to roll with the effects of the gusting wind.

This present weather condition was just a preview of the forthcoming trip.

As the ship passed under the railroad bridge connecting Groton with New London, Connecticut, a group of *Jackfish* dependents could be seen waving from the parking lot close to the water's edge on the port side of the ship. This welcome committee was the standard ritual that many of the dependents followed when *Jackfish* departed port and when the ship returned from being at sea.

Looking through binoculars you could see one of the dependents dressed as Santa Claus. Three people dressed as elves were holding a large banner with the words "MERRY XMAS—HURRY HOME" printed on it.

Jackfish passed Electric Boat Company, the premier submarine shipbuilder. No one was visible in the shipyard as they also were having a holiday stand down period.

The lighthouse at Race Rock was rapidly approaching on the port side of *Jackfish*.

Throughout this area and in the race many white floats could be seen in the water. These floats were lobster pot locators and each had a heavy line attached to it from the lobster pot on the bottom of the river/sound.

Mission Complete

The ship would have to pass through the rapid currents of the race to depart the Thames River and enter the waters of Block Island Sound.

The officer of the deck ordered, "Left full rudder. Ahead standard. Steer course zero-nine-zero degrees true."

Jim had to bellow orders to his telephone talker to ensure the orders were heard over the gusting winds.

The current was running so swiftly through the race that the submarine had to crab to be able to maintain the ordered course.

The windswept water was licking its way up the sail area and splashed through the bridge cockpit area.

This trip normally would be a five hour transient from the Groton Submarine Base through Block Island Sound to the turning point of the submarine at Montauk Point. At this location at Montack Point, the submarine entered the waters of the Atlantic Ocean. This estimated transient time assumed that *Jackfish* could continue to fight the elements and made the projected ship's speed through the water.

More realistically, this leg of the trip today would probably take an additional two hours for a total of seven hours.

"Captain—executive officer. Request permission to rig the ship for dive with the exception of the ballast tank vent valves, bridge, anchor, and ventilation system."

"Executive officer—captain. Permission granted."

The captain directed his officer of the deck, "Jim, increase speed slowly. I want to go as fast as possible without undue hazard to the ship or crew."

Jim acknowledged the captain's order and commenced to increase the ship's speed in small increments.

"Control—bridge. Send two safety lines to the bridge."

These personal safety lines would secure the officer of the deck and the captain into the bridge cockpit area to prevent them from being washed overboard.

Bruce recalled that a short time ago the commanding officer of one of our nuclear attack submarines in the Pacific had been washed overboard from the bridge and lost at sea. The ill-fated captain had just reported onboard his submarine and this trip was his initial trial at sea as commanding officer. He was entering the bridge cockpit from below and didn't realize how rough the San Francisco Bay really was at this location under the Golden Gate Bridge.

A tremendous mountain of green water had passed rapidly from the stern of the ship up into the bridge cockpit. Time was not available for the captain to secure himself into his safety hardness before he was swept overboard.

The officer of the deck, who was secured in the bridge cockpit area by his safety harness, suffered many cuts and bruises and a broken arm.

Bruce directed his officer of the deck, "Jim, send the lookout and the telephone talker below. The captain continued, "The lookout can operate the periscope and conduct lookout responsibilities below decks in the control room." After clearing away some caked ice from his face mask, Bruce remarked, "The gusting winds and horizontal rain are reducing the effectiveness of the lookout on the bridge anyway."

The lookout and telephone talker both smiled and hurried down the access ladder into the warmth of the ship. Both hoped it would not take too long for them to thaw out.

Dave called the bridge to have Bruce pick up the hand telephone.

"Captain, I observed through the periscope some bad news when we were hit with a pooping and following sea revealing the stern of the submarine and the propeller area." Dave continued after a slight delay, "It appeared that we picked up two or three white lobster pot locator floats and they are wrapped around the propeller shaft. We are probably dragging the lobster pots."

This was an unsatisfactory condition since lobster pots could nick the blades of the fine-tuned *Jackfish* propeller and cause cavitation and noise to be generated into the water.

The results of this noise generation would ruin the *Jackfish*'s stealth and announce her presence. Any noise generated from the *Jackfish* would be a certain invitation for disaster when the "locate and attack phase" of this mission commenced.

Bruce rapidly made the decision and provided it to Dave.

"After the ship submerges and is in water greater than depth three hundred feet, we will remove the entanglement from the propeller shaft using our ship's divers." Bruce continued, "Dave, brief the diver team leader and the other two scuba divers what our plan of action will be to correct our potential noise problem."

After wiping the cold salty spray out of his eyes, Bruce continued. "We will submerge to a depth of one hundred fifty feet to perform the diving operation when the depth of water is greater than three hundred feet. The propeller shaft will be locked and the retractable maneuvering motor will be lowered."

The maneuvering motor allowed *Jackfish* to make maximum speed of three knots.

Mission Complete

The divers would pass through and be tethered to the after escape trunk. The team leader would be in charge of the overall operation and direct the operation of the MMS (manned maneuverable sled).

The captain continued, "Ensure the battery is fully charged for the MMS, the spare oxygen bottles are full, and the underwater lights fully operational."

Dave acknowledged each order from his leader.

"Test all the functions of the local MMS control panel in the engine room and the remote console in the control room."

"We should be able to submerge about four but closer to five hours after we make our turn past Montauk Point heading into the Atlantic Ocean."

After a short pause, Bruce stated, "The plan also will need to factor in the location of the Soviet AGI on station near *Jackfish*'s outbound track. We will try to triangulate the bearings of the AGI's radar signal with our ECM (electronics countermeasure) receiver equipment as soon as we can pick up a good electronics signal."

It was obvious that more details had to be factored into this hazardous plan to clear the lobster pot lines from the propeller shaft.

The follow-on discussions would wait until the captain left the bridge after departing restricted water and securing the maneuvering watch.

The underwater manned maneuverable sled (MMS) was a battery operated vehicle capable of making five knots under water fully loaded. One operator lies on the sled and controls the sled's movements. Space was available for two other divers to be pulled by the sled.

The sled contained replacement oxygen bottles in case the job exceeded the time planned and the diver had to remain under water longer to complete the task. Also, there was a quick gulp oxygen feature that the diver could use in an emergency should he have a problem with his breathing system. Tool storage was also provided.

The divers had communications available directly with the submarine with a specially designed underwater communications system.

A pressure regulator was installed in the MMS to keep the sled neutrally buoyant at the operating depth selected by the sled operator.

The width of the system was twenty-three inches to allow egress and ingress from the standard twenty-five inch submarine hatch. The MMS was stored in the shore power access trunk in the engine room during the ready to get underway process.

To open the upper escape trunk hatch when underwater to deploy the MMS, the shore power access trunk was flooded at the same time the escape trunk was equalized with sea water pressure.

The MMS tethered a hose to each of the swimmers with a circulating water heating system capability to ensure the divers' all-cover suits remain heated.

The three *Jackfish* divers had used the MMS system expertly in a highly dangerous operational scenario during the submarine's last deployment.

A United States reconnaissance airplane had had a mechanical problem while flying an intelligence gathering mission over the Soviet mainland. The pilot ejected and the plane crashed into the ocean within the twelve-mile territorial limit of the Soviet Union near the Murmansk area of the Barents Sea.

Higher authority ordered *Jackfish* to enter the crash site area undetected and retrieve selected highly classified pieces of equipment from the damaged aircraft. After retrieval of the equipment, the downed airplane was to be destroyed by demolition explosive charges.

The mission was carried out as directed.

Soviet warships patrolled the crash site area to search for the wreckage while awaiting the arrival of their salvage ships. The Russian intention was to retrieve the damaged plane and obtain the United States government's latest stealth technology used for gathering intelligence.

A timed demolition charge gave *Jackfish* time to evacuate the area of interest. The underwater explosion of the reconnaissance plane made it clear to the Soviets that their potential prize would not be available.

Jackfish arrived at the Montauk Point turning position two hours behind schedule at nineteen hundred.

Jim ordered, "Helm—bridge. Right fifteen degrees rudder. Steady on course one-six-five degrees true." His orders were acknowledged by the operator in the control room.

As the submarine turned into the wind and ragging sea, Jim and Bruce held on to the bridge cockpit with all their strength. The submarine started rocking up to twenty degrees either side as the bow of the submarine dived into the ever increasingly rough ocean.

As the captain departed from the bridge, he directed the officer of the deck.

"Secure the maneuvering watch. Station the underway watch, section one. Rig the control room for red."

The officer of the deck repeated back each order verbatim.

When the control room was rigged for red at night, only dimmed red lights were used for illumination. Using dimmed red lighting ensured that the

Mission Complete

operators in the attack center and control room maintained their night vision should there be a necessity to look through the periscope.

When in the control room, Bruce called the bridge. "Officer of the deck—captain. Direct the weapons officer to ready all war shot torpedoes."

As a safety precaution, all war shot torpedoes were electronically blocked to prevent them from being inadvertently activated when the submarine was in restricted waters.

After the submarine departed from restricted waters, the torpedoes were made ready to shoot in the war shot mode.

"Officer of the deck—captain. Secure the anchor for sea."

When the submarine was in restricted waters, the anchor was partially lowered from its housing in the engine room. In an emergency, the anchor and anchor chain would be let go in a rapid manner and dropped to the ocean bottom.

This safety precaution was used should the submarine lose propulsion power and steering capability and the ship was required to stop to prevent a collision or grounding.

"Control—officer of the deck. Raise the electronics countermeasures (ECM) mast and man the electronics search and detection equipment. The primary target is the radar or any other electronic signal from the Soviet AGI that should be located on our outbound track."

Should *Jackfish* detect any Soviet signals, the attack panel operator would triangulate the signals and determine the distance and location of the AGI.

The Soviet ship would be operating with all its navigation lights energized.

Jackfish had its decks awashed because of the rough sea. This condition made the submarine a very small target to pick up visually or with radar.

With the two *Jackfish* periscopes in the raised position, the lookouts would see well over the horizon. This allowed the good guys to see the AGI's navigation lights before being spotted themselves.

"Captain—navigator. If *Jackfish* could maintain the current speed of twenty knots as planned, we will arrive at Point Charlie, the designated diving point, at twenty three hundred. This will put us two hours behind schedule."

"Very well, Navigator."

"Officer of the deck—captain. Secure the bridge and lay below. Ensure that both periscopes are manned by lookouts in the control room."

When the officer of the deck cleared the bridge cockpit area and relocated his responsibilities into the control room, he was then titled conning officer and the station was called "conn."

The ocean was too rough to hazard a man on the bridge. Green water now was being washed over the cockpit area.

Not having the bridge manned with an OOD and proper lookouts, making the speed *Jackfish* was making through the high wind and rainy condition, running at night without any navigational lights energized, and not activating the ship's radar would jeopardize the career of the captain should an incident occur with another ship.

To operate under these conditions was the decision that Bruce had to make as the commanding officer to ensure *Jackfish* was not detected by the Soviet AGI and the mission was not compromised.

Bruce sat in his stateroom and removed his water-drenched clothing. He observed the three-by-five brass plaque on his desk. The words on the plaque read, "O God, Thy Sea is So Big and My Ship is So Small."

How true these words were at the present time.

The original plaque had been on the desk of the captain of a U.S. fast attack nuclear submarine in the late fifties and early sixties. Admiral Rickover saw the plaque during one of his trips at sea aboard the submarine. The admiral had borrowed the plaque and had it duplicated.

A prerequisite for an officer to command a U.S. nuclear submarine was to satisfactorily complete a three-month prospective commanding officer (PCO) training course in Washington, D.C. This course was taught in Admiral Rickover's office building and the admiral was personally involved with "hands-on" the course output.

As recognition for successful completion of this program, the admiral would present each graduate one of the plaques with a brass plate on the backside with the graduate's name and rank engraved on it. This plaque remained a treasured keepsake for each recipient.

"Captain—conn. The ship is rigged for dive."

"Very well. Thank you," responded the captain to the rig-for-dive report.

Bruce reviewed the navigation chart with his navigator.

Nat informed the captain, "Our current position is forty nautical miles from Point Charlie, our diving point. The time is twenty two hundred. At this speed, *Jackfish* will arrive at the one hundred fathom curve at zero one hundred the twenty-second of December."

The navigator continued, "This means we will be four valuable hours behind schedule as it stands, not including any time we may lose evading the AGI and for the diving operation to clear the propeller shaft of the lobster pot lines."

Mission Complete

Bruce acknowledged Nat's status report. The frown on the captain's face clearly expressed his displeasure about being four hours late already.

Dave entered the control room and reported to Bruce.

"Captain, I toured the ship and all compartments are battened down well for the rough weather. No major problems. Many of the crew are seasick but that should abate when we submerge into calmer waters."

"Very well, Dave. Thank you. Dave, I want you to start prerequisites for our diving operation to clear the shaft. Use the check-off sheets and ensure that our three divers are ready in all respects." Bruce continued, "We must regard the safety of the divers; however, we must complete the operation as fast as possible. Anticipate submerging in three hours at the hundred fathom curve at Point Charlie. This will give us more water under the keel to counter the rough sea."

"Conn—captain. I am going to tour the ship."

Bruce directed his conning officer, "Be alert to detect the radar and any other electronic emissions from the Soviet AGI with the ECM equipment and also visually through the periscope." He continued, "When the AGI is detected, steer a course to have the bearing of the target move from our bow to stern while maintaining the same signal intensity from the contact. This maneuver should keep the AGI from closing our position."

Dave started completing the diving operation prerequisites with the senior diver assisting.

The first step was to energize the diving suit hot water circulating system. This system was used until the heating system was hooked into the tether of the MMS.

"Conn—ECM operator. Have an electronic signal intensity five on the bearing of one-zero-zero degrees true. Bearing remains steady. Estimate the range to the signal source to be about four thousand yards. Signal is being transmitted from a Soviet shipboard radar."

The conning officer responded, "Very well. This is the Soviet AGI we have been expecting. Maintain contact and provide continuous reports."

The conning officer then directed the helsman, "Right fifteen degrees rudder. Steady on course one-nine-zero degrees true."

Bruce rushed to the control room and was provided the details of the current tactical situation by the conning officer.

The lookout reported, "Dim white lights bearing one-zero-zero degrees true. A red navigation light is showing on the same bearing. The contact range is about four thousand yards."

The ECM operator continued to report the status of the ECM electronics signal. "Intensity remains the same and the bearing of the signal is drifting left."

This provided the information ascertaining that the AGI would pass down the port side of *Jackfish* at a range no closer than four thousand yards.

"Lookouts-conn. The lookout on number two periscope will maintain contact on the AGI. Continuous reports are required. Report when you lose contact with the red navigation light. Lookout on number one periscope continue to search through three hundred and sixty degrees."

The navigator set up the tracking console in the attack center to generate a best-target solution of course, speed, and range to the AGI.

Continuous bearings from number two periscope, the ECM signal intensity and bearing, and the red navigation light bearing were the inputs used to generate the rough target solution.

The red navigational light was on the port side of the AGI and had an arc from relative bearing zero-zero-zero, or dead ahead, through the arc of one hundred degrees, or ten degrees abaft the port beam of the AGI.

When the red light disappeared from sight, the *Jackfish* would be greater than ninety degrees abaft of the AGI's beam with the AGI increasing the distance from *Jackfish*.

Reports of the visual observation continued to show the AGI drawing down our port side.

The conning officer reported to the captain, "Bearing now zero-nine-four degrees true."

Bruce directed the conning officer, "Change ship's course slowly back to base course one-six-five degrees true when the bearing to the AGI decreases to zero-seven-five degrees true."

"Conn-navigator. Take a depth sounding with the fathometer in the single ping mode with minimum output intensity to verify our navigation position."

The reverberation of one ping of the fathometer was heard in the control room with the conning officer reported, "Depth sixty fathoms."

With the sea so rough only a minimal amount of the hull of *Jackfish* was out of the water. This resulted in a very small probability for the Soviets to gain a radar contact on the submarine.

Also, the lookouts topside on the AGI were probably seasick and trying to get shelter from the weather rather than look for another ship. As a result, it was an easy task for *Jackfish* to evade the AGI.

The executive officer reported to Bruce, "Ship is rigged for dive."

Mission Complete

Nat then reported, "We have twenty miles to Point Charlie, our dive position. Should arrive at zero one hundred. It is now midnight."

Nat continued, "We are currently four hours behind our intended track. Assuming all goes well, we should be able to remove the fouled lines from the shaft in two hours and be ready for deep diving and flank speed. If assumptions are correct, we then will continue the transient six hours later than projected on course one-three-eight degrees true."

Bruce acknowledged as he sipped his coffee, "Very well, Nat."

The captain of *Jackfish* received the status report for diver operations from Dave. "All prerequisites are completed for the diving operation. The divers are standing by in the engine room."

At zero zero forty-five, the conning officer directed the helmsman to slow the ship to two-thirds speed.

The chief of the watch took a fathometer sounding and then reported to the conning officer, "Depth one hundred fathoms and increasing in depth."

Jim reported to the captain the current status of the ship readiness to submerge.

"Very well, Jim. Dive the ship. Make your depth one hundred and fifty feet."

"Trim the ship to be able to maintain depth control with only three knots speed by the retractable maneuvering motor."

"Maneuvering room-conn. Rig out the maneuvering motor. Put it on relative course zero-zero-zero. Standby to energize the motor."

The engineering officer of the watch (EOOW) in the maneuvering room acknowledged the order.

Jim orderd the diving officer, "Dive the ship. Make your depth sixty feet."

Two blasts of the diving alarm klaxon were heard as the diving officer announced over the 1MC general announcing system, "DIVE. DIVE."

Jim directed the chief of the watch, "Lower the ECM mast and secure the ECM operator."

"Lower number one periscope."

Jim continued to give orders while he monitored outside the submarine with number two periscope. He reported, "Forward ballast tank vent valves are open."

Looking aft out of the periscope, Jim announced, "After ballast tank vents are open."

When the vent valves in the top of the ballast tanks were opened, air escaped through the vent valves under pressure of the sea water entering the open grates in the bottom of the ballast tanks.

This event changed the submarine from a positive buoyant condition to that of being in a negative buoyant condition. A plume of air water mixture from the open ballast tank vents gushed up into the air about fifty feet as the submarine started to submerge.

"Diving officer—conn. Make your depth one hundred and fifty feet. Trim ship to maintain order depth at ship's speed three knots."

The diving officer repeated his orders back verbatim to the conning officer and then directed the planes men to the correct amount of attitude, or bubble, to maintain the ship's downward angle as it glided through the ocean towards ordered depth of one hundred and fifty feet.

Speed was slowly decreased as the diving officer directed the ballast panel operator to pump water overboard out of the variable ballast tanks.

The responsibility of the diving officer was to pump enough water overboard from the variable ballast tanks so that the ship could be maintained at ordered depth with a small ordered down bubble, or attitude, at the ordered speed of three knots.

Once this condition was achieved and as directed by the conning officer, the engineering officer of the watch would shift propulsion to the retractable maneuverable motor.

The main engines would be disengaged from the reduction gear. The propulsion shaft then would be mechanically locked, the first prerequisite for putting divers into the water to work in close proximity to the propellers.

As the diving officer was finalizing his trim so that the ship would be able to maintain ordered depth at minimal ship's speed, the conning officer ordered the auxiliary man of the watch to energize the ship's atmospheric control equipment.

The atmospheric control equipment in the submarine consisted of two oxygen generators, two hydrogen burners, and two carbon dioxide scrubbers plus banks of oxygen tanks under pressure. The oxygen tanks were located in the main ballast tanks outside the pressure hull of the submarine.

When fully charged, the external oxygen tanks contained oxygen at 3000 pounds per square inch (psi) pressure. The tanks had a capacity to provide oxygen to the total *Jackfish* crew for one week without charging the tanks with either of the oxygen generators.

The auxiliary man adjusted the oxygen bleed from the oxygen tanks into the ship to be at that value computed by the ship's diving officer to sustain the crew at maximum efficiency.

In normal operation, one of the two oxygen generators was put into

Mission Complete

service when the ship submerged. The oxygen generator discharged into the oxygen tanks to maintain a constant pressure, or float, while bleeding oxygen into the submarine.

The auxiliary man on watch recorded gage readings hourly of each one of the atmospheric control equipment to ascertain the environmental condition in the ship. He made adjustments to the atmospheric control equipment as necessary to keep all the readings within required specifications.

The hydrogen burners and carbon dioxide scrubbers eliminated unwanted air pollutants. The installed atmospheric equipment functioned to maintain the ship's atmosphere at an optimum condition.

The diving officer reported to the conning officer, "At ordered depth. Ship is trimmed satisfactorily at speed three knots."

"Very well, diving officer."

"Captain-conn. The ship is trimmed for three knots. Request permission to disengage the main shaft and energize the retractable motor."

"Very well, conn. Permission granted."

The wave effects of the rough sea were being felt in *Jackfish* at one hundred and fifty feet below the ocean surface. The ship was changing depth twenty to thirty feet up and down coinciding with the ocean wave action on the surface. This wave action would certainly add hazard to the forthcoming MMS diving operations.

Bruce directed the conning officer, "Energize the MMS support consoles and test out all the equipment. Have the executive officer direct the divers to ready their equipment and standby to commence diving operations."

Jim acknowledged the orders from the commanding officer.

The electronics technician energized the MMS remote console in the control room and commenced the pre-dive checkout of the unit.

The color TV screen in the control room was energized and all the high intensity external lights focused on the stern area of the submarine were observed to be in operation.

Communications were tested satisfactorily at the control room with the engine room and with the divers at the MMS station.

The operations officer got permission from the conning officer to raise the Mk Twenty-Four periscope ten feet. He then took his station at the periscope lower-level platform. This configuration put the periscope in the partially raised position and with its laser intensity lights allowed full visibility outside the ship in the area of the stern and propeller.

In addition to visual observation through the periscope, this view of the after area of the submarine also was transmitted to the remote TV station in the control room.

Dave reported to the conning officer from the engine room MMS station. "MMS control console checks have been completed satisfactorily. Divers are dressed in their heated suits and ready to exit the ship."

"Executive officer—captain. Have the divers exit the ship and commence defouling the propeller."

The divers exited the ship through the engine room access hatch and the escape trunk while tethered to the MMS. The lead diver steered the MMS to the propeller area of *Jackfish*.

The divers realized the present danger due to the large wave action on the surface being mirrored at their operating depth.

Eyes of all the observers in the control room and engine room were welded on the divers as their tethered lines attached to the MMS tossed them around.

The fouled lobster pot lines were slowly extracted and cut from around the propeller shaft.

As the divers completed the task of removing the lobster pot lines from the propeller shaft, one of the diver's tethered line got fouled around one of the blades of the propeller. The tethered line from the MMS to the diver was ruptured, causing the diver to lose the heating to his suit.

The second diver was able to grab the diver in jeopardy and headed him back to the MMS.

The MMS driver maneuvered the vehicle to the *Jackfish* access and escape trunks.

The crew monitor in the engine room, using reach rod controls, had opened the topside hatches to both the escape trunk and the access trunk.

The injured diver had stopped all movement and his eyes had shut.

The diving team rapidly got the MMS and the unconscious diver into the access trunks. The other two divers entered, closed the topside hatches, and rapidly operated the two isolation valves in the trunk to drain the water into the lower level engine room.

"Conn—engine room. All divers and their equipment are in the ship. The propeller shaft is clear."

"Engine room—conn. Very well."

"Engage and test the main shaft," continued the conning officer.

The main shaft was engaged and the propeller was tested while the sonar operators listened and observed the noise recorders to ascertain the condition of the propeller.

Mission Complete

Sonar reported to conn. "Propeller tested satisfactorily. No noise generated. Will continue to observe the propeller area for noise generation as we increase the speed of the ship."

"EOOW—conn. Secure the maneuvering motor. Train the motor to relative bearing zero-zero-zero and retract the motor."

The hospital corpsman anxiously awaited the opening of the lower access hatch to be able to extract the stricken diver. All hoped and prayed that the obvious was not correct and that the diver was not dead.

Oxygen was rapidly administered to the diver with portable oxygen bottles as two of the crew removed his wet suit. Blankets and hot water bottles were applied to the diver in an attempt to raise his body temperature.

After twenty minutes of medical emergency recovery procedures were completed, the hospital corpsman pronounced the diver to be dead.

Stewart knew the family of his stricken crew member. He was married and had two small children.

The captain had met his family and Petty Officer Jackson's parents at the awards ceremony when Stewart presented the petty officer with the Meritorious Service Medal for his courageous accomplishments during the demolition of the damaged United States reconnaissance plane.

Bruce pushed the actuator on the microphone of the 1 MC general announcing system in the control room. "This is the captain speaking."

There was a short pause while Stewart picked the correct words.

"I regret to inform you that our shipmate and friend, Petty Officer Billy Jackson, has just passed away. He served the *Jackfish* and his country with honor and with distinction at all times. He will be sorely missed. Please join me in a minute of silence and prayer in respect of our fallen shipmate."

The captain then recited the verse of the "Navy Hymn" dedicated to the Submarine Service.

"Lord God, our power ever more,
Whose arm doth reach the ocean floor,
Dive with our men beneath the sea,
Traverse the depths protectively.
O hear us when we pray, and keep
Them safe from peril in the deep."

Petty Officer Jackson's corpse was placed into a body bag after all egresses to his body were sealed. The body bag was put into the freeze box to preserve the corpse. After return to port, the petty officer would have a proper military funeral with all the military honors he had earned.

Stewart would wait until his head cleared and the shock of losing Petty Officer Jackson dissipated before he wrote Jackson's wife about her husband's death.

On the ship's return to port, Bruce would send a classified message to Commodore Walter giving the details of Jackson's death.

He also would ask Walter to notify his wife Ann so that she could be prepared to provide support for the soon-to-be-stricken wife of Jackson when the *Jackfish* returned to Groton.

Bruce's wife Ann was the "commanding officer" when the *Jackfish* was at sea. She assumed the responsibility of providing assistance when it was needed by the dependents and kept the *Jackfish* family together as a close-knit group.

Assuming this responsibility was one of the many tasks under the unwritten "position description" of the wife of the commanding officer of a nuclear attack submarine.

Bruce also would request that the ambulance to remove the corpse not be sent to the pier until all *Jackfish* dependents had departed.

/6/ AT-SEA OPERATIONS

"Conn—captain. Take a sounding with the fathometer. Make your course one-three-eight degrees true, speed twenty knots and depth three hundred feet."

"Very well, Captain."

The conning officer repeated the orders back verbatim and reported, "Sounding one thousand feet."

"Diving officer—conn. Make your depth three hundred feet, ten degrees down bubble, and increase speed to twenty knots."

The submarine quivered as the propeller shaft started to accelerate. The bow of *Jackfish* rolled down heading toward the ordered depth.

At this time in a dive, you get the feeling of a hawk nosing over and increasing speed as it heads towards a prey.

As the ship increased speed, the sonar operator reported. "Conn—sonar. No ship's noise detected as we increased speed. Indication is that we did not do any damage to the propeller blades."

Stewart thought, *Jackson's life was not expended in vain. Jackfish is at least on even footing with the Tigerfish.*

The captain gave tactical directions to the conning officer. "Conn. Take a sounding every thirty minutes. In one hour, at time zero five hundred, increase depth to two thousand feet and increase speed to forty knots. Night orders will be provided shortly with additional tactical directives."

The captain's night orders are directives to the conning officer, engineering officer of the watch, and selected watch standers on how to operate the ship while the captain is sleeping.

Course, depth, and speed changes, the time interval for taking soundings and clearing baffles, when to take the ship to periscope depth, and changes to the engineering plant status are some orders that are included in night orders. Also, significant events for the next day are usually included.

On this mission, the navigator also would include for the complete day the "open window" time periods for both Soviet and United States orbiting photographic satellites. This was the period when the satellites would be in an orbit that would not make possible the detection of *Jackfish* while the submarine was operating at periscope depth.

Should a Soviet satellite detect *Jackfish*, a signal would be sent from the enemy satellite to the USSR station monitoring the Soviet satellite program. The station would notify all Soviet ships and submarines of the contact.

This message would certainly alert *Tigerfish* that a United States nuclear submarine was approaching its position.

"Nat, please include in the night orders the requirement for each watch section to station the section tracking party and check out all equipment and systems. Use the input from the sonar contact generator to provide a simulated submarine target input signal for tracking purposes."

Each of the three watch sections stood a six hour on watch with twelve hours off watch. When the section tracking party was stationed, additional personnel were added to each section to allow the section to track a surface or submarine contact on a round-the-clock basis.

Ths use of section tracking had been required previously on many occasions when *Jackfish* maintained contact on a submerged adversary for many weeks at a time.

The fire control attack console was manned by an operator from the watch section. The console received bearing inputs from sonar and visual bearings through the periscope if the contact was a surface combatant and *Jackfish* was at periscope depth.

The attack center plotter also was manned by an operator from the watch section. The plotter received contact bearings from sonar while also providing a continuous plot of his own ship's movements.

A combined recorder and telephone talker recorded all data for use by the operators and also for historical use in generating the patrol report.

Own ship was maneuvered to develop changes in bearing to the contact. The changes in bearing thus enabled the plotter and the console operator to develop speed and course of the target.

A change in depth to below the gradient was made to determine the contact's approximate operating depth.

This depth determination was obtained by observing the sonar signal strength of the detected contact with *Jackfish* taking a position above and then below the gradient. The contact would be located at the depth where the larger sonar signal strength was observed.

Best course was determined by maneuvering *Jackfish* to either side of the contact bearing. The course of *Jackfish* where the sonar contact signal faded would indicate the baffle area of the target and best course of the target, plus or minus twenty degrees.

In addition, Nat and Dave were both command tactical officers in charge of a section and responsible for the correct tactical decisions during the absence of the captain from the attack center.

During long periods of continuous contact with an adversary submarine, Nat and Dave also were responsible for ensuring that the ship's patrol report narrative provided the details of the operation and that the generated track of *Jackfish* and the annotated track of the target were maintained up to date.

"Nat, I want you to observe and critique the section tracking party for one section and Dave the other. I will randomly observe the performance of the teams during the tracking process."

The navigator usually wrote the night orders for the captain. Bruce then would add any additional directives and sign the book for distribution to the conning officer, engineering officer of the watch, and all other watch standers.

Each reader would initial the night orders when they had read the directives.

Nat and Bruce leaned over the navigation chart to refresh themselves as to the future tactical plan.

Dave entered the scene and reported to Bruce. "Captain, have walked through the ship and all is normal."

Both Dave and Bruce routinely walked through or toured the ship at staggered hours of the day and night when the ship was underway to ascertain the status of the ship and watch standers.

Also, this availability of the captain and executive officer provided an excellent opportunity for the crew members to talk with the leaders of the ship on an informal basis.

Bruce's heart was heavy with sorrow. He was fatigued and only half into the navigation and tactical review with Dave and Nat.

However, he realized he must put Petty Officer Jackson's death behind him now and move forward with intense concentration and with a clear mind.

Nat pointed to the ship's present position on the navigation chart and discussed the next move.

Capt. Lawrence S. Wigley, USN (RET)

"Captain. As you already directed the conning officer, we should stay on course one-three-eight degrees true, speed twenty knots, and at depth of three hundred feet for one hour."

The navigator continued, "The conning officer should take a single ping sounding with the fathometer every thirty minutes and compare the depth of water received from the fathometer very carefully with the navigation track."

Bruce nodded in agreement.

"Then we will go to depth of two thousand feet at flank speed making a speed of advance or average speed through the ocean of thirty knots."

Stewart then added, "Also put into my night orders for the conning officer to clear baffles randomly about every two hours above and below the thermocline."

Clearing baffles was the process of changing the ship's course so that own ship's sonar can search and listen for submarine noises within twenty degrees either side of the propeller shaft, or in the baffles. This was done to observe if a hostile submarine was trailing or following behind you since the baffle area is a blind area for sonar detection of any contacts.

The process of clearing baffles was done randomly so that any adversary could not anticipate your movements.

Trailing another submarine was a very dangerous and exacting skill, especially a Soviet missile submarine. Trailing Soviet submarines was not new to Bruce. *Jackfish* had trailed the adversary's submarines in close on many occasions.

Establishing a trail of a hostile submarine was done to be able to maintain continuous contact with the submarine to keep an accurate and up-to-date torpedo shooting solution should this be necessary. This trailing of an adversary submarine also was done to record the generated noise profile of the enemy submarine. These recordings were put into the submarine force commander's file and distributed to all U.S. submarines.

These tape recordings provided for a rapid identification and classification of a particular submarine.

When clearing baffles, a Soviet submarine captain would sometimes drive his submarine at high speed back down the reciprocal of his present course. This ship's maneuver resulted essentially with a potential head-on collision with the United States submarine in trail.

This maneuver was called a "Crazy Ivan" and was guaranteed to turn the most stout-hearted U.S. commanding officer into putty when trailing close behind the Soviet submarine.

Mission Complete

Depth separation between the friendly and the Soviet was a must to minimize the potential of a collision when a close-in trail was in progress.

The thermocline was located at the depth where there was a significant change of water temperature and a salt water layer had developed.

There were many configurations of the thermocline so one had to find the profile by taking the submarine on a depth excursion and recording the gradient on the ship's internal bathograph.

The bathograph trace was a permanent record and allowed the operator to then evaluate what effect it would have on the sonar's ability to detect contacts.

A positive gradient in the ocean would have a completely different effect than a negative trace in capturing the generated noise of a contact and thus establishing range to detection of the contact and also the range of counter detection by the target.

The ability to evaluate how to use the existing gradient to best advantage was just another one of the arsenal of tactical knowledge and skill needed to be a successful submariner.

"Conn—captain. Take the ship to periscope depth at time zero nine hundred for housekeeping chores, including disposal of garbage and ship's refuge." The captain continued, "Also copy the communications broadcast. Hopefully, the submarine force commander will send some tactical information about our target."

The garbage and waste were discharged from the submarine into the ocean through the use of the garbage disposal unit.

The operation of this unit utilized the same principles as that of a submarine torpedo tube. There was an inner or breech door and an outer or muzzle door. With the muzzle door shut, the breech door was opened through the operation of valves and levers in the ship's garbage disposal room. Garbage then was loaded into weighted bags.

An operator then loaded the weighted bags into the disposal unit through the open breech door. After completing loading of the garbage, the breech door was shut. The unit then was equalized with sea water pressure using a series of valves making up the garbage disposal sea water pressure equalizing system. The muzzle door was opened and air pressure discharged the contents of the disposal system into the ocean. The weighted bags took the garbage to the ocean floor. The cycle was repeated as many times as necessary.

There were never any coupling of the identification of the weights used in the garbage disposal process to the United States.

Should a Soviet trawler dredging the ocean bottom for fish pick up a weighted bag, there could be no identification or confirmation that a United States submarine was operating in these Soviet controlled waters.

Bruce continued, "Since this will be Sunday and the crew is physically expended, we will have church lay services in the morning. We will need all the prayers and help from above that we can get in a very short time."

"Nat and Dave. Plan to start training in earnest after lunch today to have our battle station team well honed and up to speed both individually and as a team."

The battle station team consisted of the best, most knowledgeable officers and enlisted persons manning the crucial stations in the ship when preparing to shoot weapons or conduct other hazardous operations.

Examples of other hazardous operations included, but was not limited to, operating close in to a target to obtain photographs, underwater noise signatures, and photographs of the underwater hull configuration of the target.

The crucial stations manned included the conning officer, diving officer, engineering officer of the watch and key engineering watch standers, weapons room, damage control party, fire control party, and the supporting operators for these stations.

Bruce continued to review the navigation chart with *Jackfish*'s track plotted as if he had anticipated seeing the periscope of *Tigerfish* pop through at the submarine's present location. No such luck!

"Gentlemen. If all goes well, our track will cross the northeast tangent of the sixty-nautical-mile circle around Bermuda at twenty two hundred tonight."

Nat and Dave agreed.

"Then a course change to one-five-three degrees true for eight hours and thirty minutes will put us at the three-hundred-nautical-mile circle around Point Bravo."

Bruce delayed his discussion and took a sip of coffee. "We then will reduce speed at this point and put our sonar team on full alert." The captain continued, "Assuming all goes as planned, *Jackfish* will arrive at this point six-thirty on the twenty-third of December. This will give us forty-one hours and thirty minutes before Christmas to complete our mission."

Both officers were anxious and waited for an acknowledgment or some hints of what was next from their captain.

Bruce stated, "At the designated three-hundred-mile semicircle around

Mission Complete

Point Bravo, *Jackfish* enters harm's way. I want to flood the torpedo tubes at this time so that we will minimize making any additional noise when the torpedo shooting time arrives."

To completely ready the torpedo tube to launch a torpedo after the torpedo tube had been flooded only required equalizing the water pressure in the torpedo tube with sea water pressure and when equalized, opening the outer door or muzzle.

Equalizing the torpedo tubes with sea water pressure was a minimum noise generating evolution.

"Also, you and Dave will assume the command tactical officer responsibilities at this time. We then will cease using all ship's general announcing and alarm systems. A telephone talker will be stationed in each compartment to maintain silent communications."

This method of communicating with sound-powered telephones was used routinely by Bruce whenever his submarine was in close proximity of an adversary. This prevented the possibility of being detected through a sound short from a speaker or any other component not noise isolated from the submarine hull.

The captain had learned this lesson of noise generation and then becoming a target very early in his submarine career.

The nuclear submarine that he was initially assigned to was conducting a training exercise opposed by two United States diesel electric submarines. The submarines were traveling in leap frog process with final destination Bermuda.

The diesel submarines were very quiet, especially while making minimum speed. Whenever one of the diesel submarines detected Stewart's nuclear submarine, its crew would go to battle stations to obtain a torpedo firing solution.

Reverberating through the water, "MAN BATTLE STATIONS TORPEDO" would be heard clearly when the diesel submarine would use the submarine's installed general announcing system.

This noise in the water was caused by sound shorts with the announcing system to the diesel submarine hull.

This was a give away that the opposing diesel submarine had gained sonar contact on the nuclear submarine.

The grounded component provided Stewart's submarine a noise spoke in the water with a good bearing to the opposing submarine. This bearing provided the input allowing the nuclear submarine to generate a rapid target solution for a simulated "snap shot" firing evolution.

A lesson of the importance of sound isolation was vividly learned by the crews of the three submarines in this operation.

The increase of Nat and Dave's heartbeat could be heard throughout the control room. It was somewhat scary for both of them the way the captain emphasized, "When the shooting time arrives."

The captain's key supporting officers didn't understand the complete picture.

Bruce had told Nat and Dave that the target was a submarine of the *Jackfish* class. Now it was told to them that there actually would be torpedo shooting.

They both knew the only other submarine of the *Jackfish* class was the *Tigerfish*.

The captain continued. "Also, we will stream the floating wire at this point."

The floating wire or "tail" was a four-hundred-foot array towed behind the submarine on a four-thousand-foot cable. This array was used to pick up low frequency noises from submarines.

All submarines generate a system of sounds. The first spectrum of noises, in a very low frequency, generates from the propeller, then propeller cavitation, then machinery noise, both continuous and intermittent, and the flow noise over the hull and through piping.

The United States Submarine Force had spent years obtaining noise data from non U.S. submarines, and then analyzing and classifying the data of potential adversaries.

It was of the greatest importance to be able to classify each hull or class of ships by the spectrum of noises so that when a contact was located, it could be rapidly and correctly classified friend or foe.

The use of this detection, localization, classification, and tracking device would be instrumental in achieving a successful mission, especially since the *Tigerfish* was the second quietest submarine in operation by any country.

Bruce was somewhat concerned that his submarine was not deloused on departing port. This was a procedure where another U.S. submarine listened to your noise signature close in to ensure that you did not have any sound shorts or equipment generating a noise source into the water.

It was standard United States submarine policy to delouse a U.S. submarine when it was committed to a classified special operation; however, time was not available in this case.

Bruce then stared at Nat and Dave and stated very slowly and deliberately,

Mission Complete

"Gentlemen. Our success during these remaining forty-two hours will determine how future Christmases will be celebrated throughout the world!"

The captain knew he had said too much; however, he wanted to get it off his chest.

"Nat. Please prepare my night orders. I want to get a few hour's sleep. Give me a wake-up call at eight-thirty before we go to periscope depth at zero nine hundred."

"Also, please enter the satellite open-window time periods for tomorrow. Thank you."

Nat had already reviewed the open-window time periods and knew the *Jackfish* would be safe from satellite detection between zero eight thirty and zero ten hundred this morning.

After he reviewed and signed his night orders, Bruce collapsed on his bunk fully clothed.

This had been two days of stress, apprehension, and emptiness with the weight of his assignment getting heavier and heavier.

There was a light knock on the captain's door. This was followed by a voice saying, "Captain, your eight-thirty wake-up call as ordered, sir."

Bruce didn't need any reminder to awake.

He had gotten a minimal amount of sleep throughout the restless night. The pressures of the activities of the last two days were already starting to show. Increasing the stress was the fact that *Jackfish* was already more than six hours behind the original schedule.

He acknowledged the wake-up call and heard the messenger quietly depart.

In robotic habit, Bruce reached from his bunk and pushed the call button on his bunk transom to summon Bococo. He then looked at the ship's remote indicators located on the bulkhead at the foot of his bunk.

These three remote indicators, outlined by little red bulbs to make the data more visible in darkness, provided him the ship's current speed, depth, and course.

At a glance, Stewart saw that *Jackfish* was on course one-three-eight degrees true, at a speed of forty knots driving silently through the ocean at a depth of two thousand feet. All parameters were as Bruce ordered in his night order book before he hit the sack a very short time ago.

In less than thirty minutes, the conning officer would take the ship to periscope depth. Hopefully, the winds and wave action would have abated. Last night provided enough hostile weather to last for a long time.

All activities to be conducted at periscope depth had to be completed within one hour and thirty minutes. This was the time window when both the Soviet and United States photographic satellites would not be in an orbit to monitor *Jackfish*.

After completing housekeeping chores, including disposal of garbage and refuge and copying any priority communications, *Jackfish* then would return into its normal environment at depth two thousand feet and flank speed of forty knots.

The duty stewards mate gave a slight knock on the door, slowly opened it with a "Good morning, Captain," and placed a large mug of black coffee on the captain's desk.

As the ultimate responsibility for this ship and its crew sipped his coffee, the stark realization came before him that he had less than twenty-two hours remaining to arrive at the semicircle around Point Bravo and another forty-two hours before Christmas for him to accomplish the critical mission.

This meant traveling a total of almost seven-hundred nautical miles undetected by the enemy, then searching out more than thirty-five-thousand-square-nautical miles for a submarine of the same class and characteristics as *Jackfish*, but operating slower and more likely alerted.

Also, the anticipated location of the *Tigerfish* was based on the best judgment of one person without any assistance or input from other professionals.

One mistake could mean the end of *Jackfish* and resultant consequences for the United States and the countries of the free world.

Bruce recalled a quotation by Thucydides in four hundred and four B.C. and hoped that it did not refer to *Jackfish*. "Their want of practice will make them unskillful and their want of skill, timid. Maritime skills, like the skill of other kinds, are not to be substituted by the way or at chosen times."

Jackfish took a twenty degree up angle and started its climb to a depth of one-hundred-and-fifty feet. Speed decreased as the conning officer started the standard submarine ritual to bring his charge to periscope depth.

The standard practice on *Jackfish* when going to periscope depth from deep depth and fast speed was to start backing slowly without cavitating as the ship proceeded to a shallower depth. The trick was to get to periscope depth as rapidly as possible at the correct speed for periscope observations. The success of this evolution was obtained only with much practice.

Bruce observed the movement of the ship from the remote indicators in his stateroom. However, he sensed a problem as the ship started to slow

Mission Complete

rapidly and was still backing at three hundred feet with an up angle on the submarine. *Jackfish* continued to go deeper in the stern first position.

Bruce rushed into the control room to ascertain the problem. He knew that a casualty had occurred associated with the control of the main turbines.

"Conn—EOOW. Main turbine reverse throttle valves will not close from the propulsion control panel in the maneuvering room. Shifting to local control of the main turbines from the upper level engine room."

Jackfish was now at depth five hundred feet and still going deeper with an up angle on the submarine.

"Conn—EOOW. Throttle control of the main turbines has been shifted to local control. Opening throttles to answer ahead two-thirds bell."

"EOOW—conn. Very well. Answer all bells."

"Have you found the cause of the casualty?"

Seeing that the conning officer now had control of the depth control of the ship, Bruce went to the maneuvering room to see first hand what was the problem.

"Conn—EOOW. The cause of the casualty was the cotter pin holding the throttle linkages together broke. The main propulsion assistant is in the engine room and will inspect all cotter pins associated with the main turbine linkages."

"EOOW—conn. The captain is on his way to the engine room. Also give him the status report for the cause of the main turbine casualty."

"Conn—EOOW. Control of the main turbine throttle valves is now shifted to the propulsion control panel in the maneuvering room. All tests satisfactory."

A thorough investigation of all the linkage cotter pins associated with the main turbine showed no other deformities.

As the captain entered the control room, he told the conning officer, "Well done to you and your watch section on combating the depth control casualty."

The conning officer used the ship's 1MC general announcing system to inform the crew on the status of the turbine control problem and depth excursion.

At depth one hundred and fifty feet and speed of fifteen knots, the ship turned twenty degrees from base course. After five minutes, the ship turned to twenty degrees on the other side of base course. Sonar searched carefully in this baffle cone to ensure the detection of any ships, both on the surface and submerged.

"Captain—conn. At depth one hundred and fifty feet, speed fifteen knots on course one-three-eight degrees true. Have cleared the baffles. No contacts." The conning officer continued, "Request permission to take the ship to periscope depth. Will reduce speed to ten knots when en route to periscope depth."

"Conn-captain. Permission granted. Take the ship to periscope depth."

The periscope was raised as the ship approached periscope depth.

As the head of the periscope broke through the ocean surface, the conning officer pressed his forehead against the observation adaptor of the periscope and rapidly rotated the scope through three hundred sixty degrees, first in low magnification power, then in high magnification power.

The conning officer then made a much slower and more deliberate observation through three hundred and sixty degrees.

"Captain—conn. No contacts."

The conning officer directed the Electronic Countermeasures Mast (ECM) raised and the ECM electronic detection equipment manned by a trained operator.

This ECM operator searched through the complete spectrum of threat electronic frequencies searching for any signals from United States and USSR emitters.

The conning officer directed the auxiliary man of the watch to set up and start the garbage disposal operation. A junior officer was assigned to supervise and oversee this evolution.

Bruce required a thorough training for the operators who conducted this task. In addition, a qualified officer supervisor would be present to oversee the operation.

The rational for these requirements was that at different times during the garbage disposal evolution there was potential to have a single eighteen-inch muzzle or outer door opened between the sea water and inside the ship only contained by a single eighteen-inch breech, or inner door.

Also, there had been cases on other submarines when the disposal unit became fouled by improper operation and the disposal unit was not able to be used during the remaining mission.

The filled garbage bags then had to be put into the freezer and frozen. The frozen bags then would be shot out of a torpedo tube.

Bruce observed each evolution taking place in the control room and was satisfied that all were being accomplished smartly and safely.

The ECM Operator reported, "Conn—ECM. Searched all threat frequency bands. No contacts."

Mission Complete

"Conn—captain. I am going to tour the ship and then attend the protestant lay services in the crew's dinette."

These services started at ten-thirty and completed about eleven.

"When the garbage disposal is complete, take the ship to depth two thousand feet, speed flank. Take a depth sounding with the fathometer every two hours and clear baffles randomly every two hours. Put a new chart in the bathometer before we go deep to obtain a current trace of the ocean thermoclines. At ten-thirty, station the section tracking party and track some sonar generated submarine targets."

Bruce continued, "Let Dave know when you will commence the tracking exercise. I want him to observe and critique the team's performance. After lunch at fourteen hundred, we will exercise the battle stations party to remove any kinks and get us all up to speed."

The conning officer acknowledged the directives of his captain.

Bruce departed the control room and started his tour of the ship.

In every compartment that he entered, each watch stander had a questioning look on his face as his eyes met those of Bruce.

What was to happen at the end of this transit and how would it effect *Jackfish* and her crew?

Chief Keller was in the sonar room upgrading his sonar men by reviewing sonar tape recordings of Soviet submarine noises and of course a tape recording of the *Tigerfish*.

Bruce observed as the chief spoke. "As we get closer to Bermuda, there is the possibility that we will detect one of the Soviet's newest ballistic missile nuclear submarine (SSBN) of the *Rebel* class. The USSR has at least one ballistic missile submarine on patrol in this area at all times."

Keller waited for any questions and then continued. "If we detect a *Rebel* SSBN, be alerted for a Soviet nuclear attack submarine that would be riding shotgun for the SSBN."

Bruce nodded to Keller as a show of appreciation for the way the seasoned chief continued to upgrade his men. They both knew that the talent and knowledge of these sonar men would determine the outcome of this mission.

The captain then scanned the gathering and looked all the men in the eyes. He continued to talk in the same serious tone as their chief.

"Be alert for a third submarine with the two Soviet submarines. As a matter of routine, we should expect to detect a United States nuclear attack submarine trailing both the Soviet units. It is the United States' submarine's mission to shoot torpedoes and sink the Soviet ballistic missile submarine should there be any indication that the Soviet submarine is starting to go into the missile pre-launch procedure. It is mandatory that the SSBN gets sunk before any Soviet ballistic missiles are launched at the United States homeland."

Bruce continued, "*Jackfish* is responsible for not being detected by any of the three submarines and for not in any way alerting the Soviets to the fact that they are being trailed. We will track the three submarines and maneuver *Jackfish* out of their sonar detection sphere and give them a wide birth."

After waiting for any questions, Bruce stated, "There will be live torpedo shooting before Christmas. I expect every man to do what he has been trained to do, and do it well. Our future Christmas will depend on the outcome of *Jackfish*'s mission. Thank you, gentlemen."

Bruce departed the sonar room and continued his ship's tour.

It was obvious that the *Jackfish* crew was somewhat apprehensive and getting more uptight as this mission continued. This questioning attitude and the feeling of being left out was more pronounced with the officers, especially Dave and Nat.

This was the first time they had not been provided information about the mission being conducted. The complete crew didn't always get all the details of the mission; however, they usually received enough clues to make them comfortable.

Bruce entered the maneuvering room located in the engine room and talked with the engineering officer of the watch (EOOW).

This officer was responsible for the correct operation of the propulsion plant and ancillary equipment and for supporting the propulsion orders from the conning officer. He was well qualified to supervise the reactor operation and ancillary equipment, both in normal operation and to minimize the effect of any casualties.

"Well done to you and your watch section on rapidly finding the problem with the main turbine throttle linkage and expeditiously repairing the problem. Your actions adverted a potentially serious casualty from occurring to our submarine. Thank you."

In the maneuvering room, three additional watch standers performed specific responsibilities under the control of the engineering officer of the watch in supporting the conning officer.

One watch stander maintained the ordered speed of the ship by remotely adjusting the main turbine throttle valves to allow the correct amount of steam to enter through the throttles and rotate the main turbine rotors. The rotors were connected to the reduction gear that in turn drove the main propulsion shaft and propeller.

Another watch stander, the reactor operator, was responsible for maintaining the safety of the reactor and the correct stability of the reactor to maintain a specific pressure and temperature.

This operator controlled the movement of "control rods" into and out of the reactor to obtain the correct amount of nuclear fission to achieve a stable reactor configuration. The positioning of the control rods in the reactor core regulated the primary coolant temperature to provide steam at the proper temperature and pressure to operate the main turbines and provide ship propulsion.

The third operator was responsible for the proper electrical distribution to ensure safety and the maximum reliability of the ship's electrical system.

This operator controlled the electrical distribution through a mimic board that controlled the position of all the main electrical breakers. He was responsible for ensuring that the most reliable electrical configuration was available at all times during normal as well as during casualty control conditions.

The above watch standers were responsible not only for maintaining the reactor and propulsion plant in a safe and reliable condition during normal operation, but also had to be throughly knowledgeable in order to combat all abnormal and casualty conditions should they occur.

Engineering training with supervised initiated emergency drills for these watch standers was conducted frequently to ensure correct response was realized. These drills were performed under controlled conditions with safety observers.

"All is going well with the equipment and watch standers, Captain. We have many off watch men in the engineering spaces working on their submarine and watch stander qualifications." The engineering officer of the watch continued. "This keeps their minds occupied."

Bruce proceeded aft in the upper level engine room and stopped between the port and starboard main turbines.

He talked with the watch stander for a short time and thanked him for his timely action in casualty control to correct the depth control excursion.

Both the watch stander and Bruce reaffirmed the importance of thoroughly learning the ship and being able to operate equipment in the normal and also in the abnormal or casualty mode of operation as demonstrated by correct casualty control during the recent turbine throttle casualty.

When the watch stander departed, Bruce continued to observe in amazement the tremendous mass of metal, piping, valves, pumps, and switches that made up the main propulsion turbine systems.

The turbines were sound isolated and sound mounted with a free floating system allowing them to generate fifty thousand combined shaft horsepower with minimal noise output into the surrounding ocean.

Each main turbine had a separate support system. Both turbines had two main lubricating pumps that could be cross-connected to the other main turbine if necessary. Each had a low flow capacity independent emergency lube oil pump for use in casualty control situations.

The main turbines could be disconnected from the reduction gear drive by operation of a disconnecting clutch motor. This resulted in a single turbine operation driving the reduction gear and propulsion shaft. Maximum speed of *Jackfish* in this configuration with only one main turbine in operation was twenty-five knots. Both main turbines had to be stopped to allow this disconnection to occur.

Again there was the questioning look of his people as Bruce toured the lower level engine room.

Two men were in the space. Machinist mate second class Aaron Michael was the individual assigned the watch standing duties. He was observing gages and level indicators and recording the values on his hourly log sheet.

The petty officer was on his knees and bent over, slowly following the beam of his flashlight as he scanned the bilge area to ensure nothing unusual was present.

"Good morning, Michael. Is everything under control?"

"Yes sir, Captain. No problems." Michael continued. "Looks like we made our underway time as planned. Sorry about Petty Officer Jackson."

Sheepishly, with his head half hung, he looked up at Bruce and asked, "Captain, do you think we will be home for New Year's?"

"Not sure, son. Trust me—we will be home as soon as possible."

The other man in the lower level was machinist mate third class Dunn. He was working on his submarine qualification as he traced out the main circulating cooling water piping arrangement in his qualification notebook.

Submarine qualification required the individual to be knowledgeable about every system in the submarine including electrical components, power supplies, ratings, flow, normal operation, and casualty procedures for operating the systems as appropriate.

When underway on a submarine, an individual devoted six hours to carrying out the responsibilities of a watch station and twelve hours not manning a watch station.

Some of this off watch time was devoted to sleeping and eating. The majority of the remaining non watch standing time was devoted to qualification, training, and shipboard work, including conducting clean up and preventive maintenance on machinery equipment.

There was usually a movie shown twice each night for the benefit of the crew as the ship's schedule and mission permitted.

Qualification included both submarine and watch station, and also qualification for command for the more senior officers.

Training usually included at least one major shipboard drill each day, such as manning battle stations, fire, flooding in the ship, collision, reactor scramming, major engineering casualties, and weapons associated events. These drills were conducted more frequently as needed to satisfy the prerequisite for individual qualification requirements.

Section drills and evolutions included but were not limited to engineering drills and section tracking practice.

Emergency deep exercises were practiced routinely to prepare the section to take the ship deep under emergency condition such as potential collision with another ship.

Getting qualified in submarines was a time-consuming and demanding process. Officers usually took between twelve and fifteen months to qualify and get the gold dolphins pinned on their chest. This required qualification as an officer of the deck, diving officer, and engineering officer of the watch, both in port and underway.

A thorough knowledge was required of all systems and equipment in the ship, including starting, operating, and de-energizing of the equipment, power sources, and operation under normal and emergency conditions at a minimum.

After the officer had completed his qualification notebook, a review board of ship's officers assigned to the same ship as the candidate conducted a qualification board to assess the satisfactory knowledge of the qualifying officer.

Upon successful completion of the board and approval of the captain, the officer would be recommended to the squadron commander for qualification.

The next step was an examination by a commanding officer of another submarine on all in-port evolutions and events.

Successful completion of this step then resulted in the candidate going to sea on yet another submarine to be the "captain" for the underway to be evaluated on the underway aspects of being a submarine officer.

Satisfactory completion of all the steps resulted in the officer being "qualified in submarines" by the squadron commander.

Enlisted personnel took between six months and one year to earn qualification and the silver dolphins that came with it.

After satisfactory completion of all review boards of enlisted men, a qualification board of officers and chief petty officers examined the candidate to ascertain if he had a satisfactory knowledge to meet the standard required of all submariners.

The captain then would examine the candidate for the final certification of his qualification.

The same grueling process was required for qualification for watch station qualification. The standard established by the particular ship and adopted by all the men of the ship would be followed for qualification at all times.

It behooved individuals to be assigned to a submarine with high standards to improve the probability of return to port in a shooting war.

It was ten-thirty as Bruce took a seat in the crew's dinette to attend the last of the church lay services.

After the completion of the services, the captain spent a few minutes talking with the men at the services.

He then proceeded to the control room to observe the performance of the section tracking party.

All periscope depth evolutions were completed and the conning officer took the submarine down to a depth of two thousand feet, speed flank, en route to the next navigation position on the northeast semicircle sixty nautical miles off Bermuda.

At time eleven twenty-five, Bococo informed the captain that lunch was ready to be served in the wardroom.

Normal practice was to serve the first serving of food to the officers in the wardroom at eleven-thirty. All officers scheduled to eat at the first setting were present in the wardroom by eleven twenty-five, ready to take their seats when the captain arrived.

As a general policy of Stewart's, ship's business and politics were not acceptable conversation topics during meals in the wardroom.

The discussion at this meal was to be another exception to normal practice in *Jackfish*.

Mission Complete

The ship most likely would have sonar contact on the two Soviet submarines during the evening meal time tonight with battle stations and fire control stations manned.

Also, *Jackfish* would be in harm's way searching in the outer semicircle around Point Bravo during the next evening meal in the wardroom.

Stewart needed the present time available with his officers to discuss as much as he was allowed about the future milestones and significant events of the mission so that everyone was playing from the same sheet of music.

The captain opened up the discussion with a statement. He began, "I am limited by the highest authority not to discuss certain aspects and some of the details of this operation. Please bear with me and support our endeavors to the best of your ability." In a sincere tone, Bruce continued, "This mission is of the highest priority with the outcome dictating your future and that of the free world."

All present had questioning expressions, especially Dave and Nat.

"The key events remaining include exercising the crew at battle stations today at fourteen hundred until about sixteen hundred. Sonar will provide generated sonar contacts to allow the team to get geared up for the final performance in the next day and a half." Stewart continued, "The navigation track shows that we will pass the northeast point of the sixty-nautical-mile circle around Bermuda about twenty two hundred tonight. I expect that we will encounter a Soviet SSBN and a Soviet nuclear attack submarine riding shotgun transiting to the northeast during the time we are proceeding southeast. In addition, we should detect a U.S. nuclear attack submarine in trail of both the Soviet submarines."

With a more forceful tone in his voice, the captain stated, "It is mandatory that we avoid this trio and give them a wide berth. We will station the battle station fire control tracking party during this avoidance exercise."

This tracking party was composed of the same individuals who manned the key tracking stations during battle stations; however, the other stations, such as damage control party and weapons loading team, were not manned.

"After a course change to one-five-three degrees true, *Jackfish* will arrive at the three-hundred-nautical-mile circle around Point Bravo at zero six thirty tomorrow morning. At this time we will conduct the last of any noise-generating evolutions."

He looked at the weapons officer. "Five torpedo tubes will be flooded and made fully ready with the exception of opening the outer doors."

After scanning the remainder of the wardroom officers, Bruce continued,

"We will prepare two torpedo tubes with nuclear tipped Mk 56X torpedoes and three torpedo tubes with conventional non nuclear explosive warheads. Weapons officer, ensure that all preliminary tests and any preventive maintenance are performed on the torpedoes and torpedo tubes before this time."

Ray responded, "All work is in progress, Captain, and will be completed with the torpedoes ready in all respects by twenty one hundred this evening."

Bruce provided an approving smile. "Thank you, Ray."

The captain continued, "The floating wire will be streamed and the detection equipment manned continuously with a sonar operator. Sonar stations will be fully manned with the battle stations team during this relative short time period."

Bruce looked at the sonar officer and directed, "I want the sonar officer working with Chief Keller to ensure enough rest is provided the operators so that they remain alert. Nat and Dave will be on duty six on and six off as the command tactical officers stationed in the attack center."

Stewart sipped his coffee and then looked each officer in the face. He continued, "At this time, we will man the sound powered headsets in all compartments and establish silent communications. General announcing and alarms will not be used.

"Dave. I want you to develop the non-disclosure sheets for each member of the crew to sign pledging not to disclose or discuss any events that happen during this mission. Have each man sign the statement prior to noon tomorrow."

Dave replied, "I have the forms prepared and already distributed for signing. I will have them all signed and returned to me by noon tomorrow."

It was a standard practice to have signature sheets for non-disclosure of classified information for all classified and covert submarine missions.

The captain continued his briefing. "We will search out the northwest sector of the three-hundred-nautical-mile circle first. This area is the least probable for detecting our contact as determined by anticipated operations and tactical considerations of the target."

Bruce directed his comments to Dave, OPS, and the sonar officer. "We must decide the tactical plan, how much we sprint and drift during the search of this area to cover as much ocean as possible in the minimal time, and how much search time will be spent searching above and below the thermocline gradient. Also, bring Chief Keller into these preliminary discussions. He could have some good input. Bruce continued, "If our contact of interest is not detected, we then will search out the one-hundred-and-twenty-nautical-mile area. The final search area will be in the sixty-nautical-mile circle. We need to maintain the maximum time possible to search out this high probability area."

Stewart directed his statement to Dave. "After battle stations this afternoon, I want to meet with you, Nat, operations and sonar officers, and Chief Keller to discuss in detail our forthcoming tactical search plan. Think of all contingencies possible during your preliminary meeting and have "what-if" solutions ready to discuss with me."

"In closing," Stewart paused to ensure that he had the complete attention of all present, "the target will be a submerged submarine of the *Jackfish* class on station and ready to sink us if we are detected. This is a life-and-death situation and I ask for your continued support."

Dave thought that something was not right. *A crucial situation as described by the captain and I am not an integral player in the development of the success plan.*

The executive officer's scan back at Bruce let the captain know that one of his men was becoming more distraught at the way things were playing out. Bruce now knew that his officers were starting to cease their unfaltering allegiance to him. The cohesive organization was starting to come apart. Hopefully, the mission would be successfully completed before the total quasi mutiny occurred!

The captain scanned each officer in the wardroom with a stern but sincere look and then solemnly stated, "Please say a prayer for our success and for those men in the target submarine. Thank you."

Bruce did not open up the discussion for questions and general comments as he would normally have done. He knew the thrust of the follow-up discussion would be the classification of the target. That was a closed subject and Bruce didn't want to get involved in any further discussion on the issue.

Stewart knew that he possibly had said too much already about the mission and in too much detail. However, he also realized that he had a moral obligation to his men—men he could possibly be sentencing to death. He rationalized to himself that he had revealed only up to the limit of what he was authorized to say.

As Bruce excused himself from lunch and departed the wardroom, he could hear the many questions being directed to Dave with each officer making a statement or comment at the same time. The hornets were stirring and starting to buzz out of the hive.

Bruce took this opportunity to tour the submarine. His first stop, as usual, was the sonar room.

The captain got a sense of being close to the other inhabitants in the ocean deep when he scanned the multitude of sonar displays and multiplexed readouts in this room. Most submariners have the feeling that the sonar room is their security blanket. In most cases this is a reality.

Chief Keller, as usual, was in the space providing training sonar tape recordings to the off-watch sonar men.

"Good afternoon, Captain," the chief said with a happy smile on his face.

"How are your troops holding up, Chief?" questioned Bruce. The captain continued, "You know that you do need some rest once in awhile. You can't wear yourself out before the big game."

"Thank you for your concern, Captain. There is plenty of time to sleep on Christmas Day en route to Groton."

Both men had smiles of confidence on their faces as Bruce departed the sonar room.

Bruce ended his ship's tour in the attack center.

The conning officer reported to Bruce that everything was normal in the ship and in the ocean environment.

"It is now fourteen hundred, Captain. Request permission to man battle stations?"

"Permission granted, conning officer," answered the captain.

The conning officer announced over the 1MC general announcing system, "MAN BATTLE STATIONS."

Men moved rapidly throughout the ship to get to their assigned stations.

In the attack center, the executive officer was the officer in charge under the captain. He monitored all actions and supervised and coordinated the work of plotters, fire control panel operators, and others to achieve the best target solution for shooting weapons. He reported his solutions and other pertinent data to Bruce.

There was an officer who directed the activities of the operators manning the fire control panel who in turn reported his solutions to the executive officer.

Another officer coordinated the activities of the bearing plotters and attack center plotter. This officer monitored the source of target motion input to the plotting table to gain an output of best target speed, course, and range.

The exec received all these inputs and then established the best target data.

Mission Complete

Bruce, satisfied that the teams in the attack center were functioning well, proceeded to the torpedo room to evaluate the torpedo reload team.

The leader in the torpedo room had his team rehearsing a reload sequence for a non-nuclear conventional torpedo.

The captain was very impressed with this team's performance. "Well done. Looks like you all have been practicing during the off hours," said the captain to the torpedo men with a slight chuckle.

Everyone in the torpedo room appreciated this comment from their captain and provided wide smiles with their chuckles.

Morale is certainly good in this part of the ship with these troops, Bruce thought as he departed the torpedo room with a goodby wave of his hand.

The next stop for Bruce was to meet with the damage control team members. Their battle stations assignment location was in the crew's dinette.

The team leader had different pipe patches laid out on a table with a piece of pipe as a prop for his instruction. He gave a demonstration with each of the different pipe patches and then had team members repeat the application. All the team members looked proficient during their application of the patches.

Bruce spent some time with this team. He described to them the current strategy of the operation and then answered individual questions about the mission of *Jackfish*. Everyone in the group had some apprehension about the forthcoming events.

The captain was able to ease some of their fear of the unknown. All the team appreciated Bruce's concern and that he had taken the time to discuss issues with them.

Bruce visited the maneuvering room which was located in the engine room. He toured the engineering spaces with his engineer officer. Tom and Bruce both talked with the watch standers during the walk through.

Bruce agreed with Tom that all the engineers were in good spirits with a high morale.

The captain wandered back to the attack center, talking and greeting shipmates during his travel.

In the attack center Dave reported, "Captain. The battle stations team is honed to a sharp edge. I am satisfied that they are ready to perform. Request permission to secure from battle stations."

"Permission granted, Dave. Secure from battle stations. Bruce continued, "Dave. I want to meet with you, Nat, Chief Keller, and the operations/sonar officers in thirty minutes at sixteen thirty in the wardroom. I want to take this opportunity to develop a strategy for the sonar search plan."

"Yes sir. We'll be ready, Captain."

Bruce returned to his stateroom to relax and get ready for the sixteen thirty meeting to develop the ship's sonar search plan.

Bococo knocked on the captain's door, slowly opened the door, and placed a mug of black coffee on the captain's table.

"Thank you, Bococo."

The captain still had an outstanding commitment to write Petty Officer Jackson's wife a condolence letter. He knew he must do this; however, he needed to unscramble all the thoughts running through his mind and come to the table with a clear head.

The sound powered telephone in the captain's cabin buzzed twice.

"Captain speaking."

"Good afternoon, Captain. This is the conning officer. The ship is secured from battle stations." The conning officer continued, "Steering course one-three-eight degrees true, at a speed of thirty knots and depth of one thousand feet. Taking a fathometer sounding every one hour and clearing baffles randomly every two hours."

"Very well. Thank you."

"Sit down, gentlemen, and have a mug of coffee."

Dave, Nat, Chief Keller, and the operations and sonar officers all drew a mug of hot and freshly brewed coffee and then sat down at the wardroom table with the captain.

Bruce addressed the group. "You are going to get the best overall scenario as I assume it will play out. I want you all to put your heads together and develop the search plan for *Jackfish* to carry out the mission."

The captain opened up a chart and placed it on the table. The chart had Point Bravo shown with the three-hundred-nautical-mile semicircle and the sixty-nautical-mile semicircle plotted. An expanding cone with a one-five-zero degree true axis and with the point of the cone at Point Bravo also was plotted.

"My assumption is that the target will come from the northwest on course about one-five-zero degrees true towards Point Bravo." Bruce was able to deduct this information by drawing a course line from the position where the destroyer *USS Forbes* was torpedoed to Point Bravo.

"Assume the target will be in close proximity to Point Bravo and above the thermal layer about twenty two hundred to twenty four hundred on the twenty-fourth of December." Bruce asked, "Does everyone understand the scenario so far?"

Mission Complete

All the participants nodded to the affirmative.

Bruce continued. "We want to maximize the available time to search out the sixty-nautical-mile semicircle. Therefore, I recommend we search using sprint and drift techniques up to twenty knots in the three-hundred-nautical-mile semicircle."

All the officers sat straight up in their chairs with eyes wide open when Bruce stated, "Assume the target nuclear submarine will be generating self-noise sound shorts to aid us in detecting the submarine. Also, as I said before, the target will be a submarine of the *Jackfish* class."

Bruce sipped his coffee, glanced around the room, then continued. "This information is the best that is available. Most of the data are assumptions interwoven around some facts.

"Dave. When your team finishes the task, please have a template with courses, speeds, and depths shown that we can use as the road map for maneuvering the ship. Thank you."

After a slight pause, Bruce asked, "Are there any questions?"

Bruce was sure that there were many questions in the minds of the people present. He was sure the question most pressing was a verification of the classification of the target nuclear submarine. Dave didn't want to go there with the classification question. He had heard the answer too many times already.

Dave commented, "No questions, Captain. We have all the data needed to develop a worthwhile operating template."

Bruce excused himself from the table, thanked all the participants for their support, and proceeded back to his stateroom. He was pleased with the first sonar search plan meeting and was quite sure the team would deliver a professional and workable sonar search template.

Bococo brought the captain a large mug of black coffee. The stewards mate was getting worried about the captain's tired and run-down condition. "Can I get you anything to eat?"

"Thank you, Bococo. Please bring me a sandwich and a glass of milk."

"Yes sir. On the way."

Bruce could hear the sonar search team discussing many options to use in putting together the search plan. He was pleased that Dave was listening to the other members' input rather than taking over the project with his seniority.

The captain used this time to take a short nap. He climbed onto his bunk fully dressed.

He would be awakened either when *Jackfish* detected the Soviet submarines or when dinner was announced.

In a short time, the sound-powered telephone in the captain's stateroom buzzed twice.

"Captain speaking."

"Captain. This is the conning officer. Sonar has contact on a noise level bearing two-three-zero degrees true. Bearing is drawing right. The contact is classified as a Soviet *Rebel* class ballistic missile nuclear submarine."

"Very well, conn. Station the battle stations tracking team." Bruce continued, "Be alert for the Soviet nuclear attack submarine riding shotgun for the missile submarine." He paused. "There also should be an American nuclear attack submarine in trail of the two Soviet nuclear submarines."

The captain entered the attack center.

The members of the battle stations tracking team were rapidly assuming their assignments. Dave announced that he was in charge of this team and then started asking questions and giving directives.

Crew members were happy and talking loudly amongst themselves. They thought that the mission of *Jackfish* was to locate these two Soviet submarines.

Bruce directed Dave, "Slow to speed of ten knots. Stay on present course and ensure that the target bearing continues to draw right and that ranges to the Soviet submarines are open." He continued, "We need to search for the other Soviet nuclear attack submarine that is providing cover for the Soviet SSBN and the American nuclear attack submarine that should be trailing both Soviet submarines."

As the captain departed the attack center, he told his executive officer, "Dave. I will be in the sonar room."

Dave informed the sonar team, "Chief Keller, we are slowing to ten knots to reduce the probability of counter detection and also to try to gain contact on the other Soviet nuclear submarine and on the American attack submarine." Bruce directed Chief Keller, "Let the conning officer know as we slow down the best speed to hold solid contact on the Soviet SSBN. Also, the American attack nuclear submarine most likely is of the *Los Angeles* class."

"Thank you, Captain. The SSBN is quiet noisy and we held solid contact on the Soviet when we were slowing down through eighteen knots," Chief Keller reported to Bruce.

"Conn-sonar. Have contacts on two more nuclear submarines. Soviet

Mission Complete

nuclear attack designated "S2" bearing three-zero-zero degrees true. Sonar bearings are drawing right. American attack submarine of the *Los Angeles* class is designated "A1" bearing two-zero-zero degrees true. Sonar bearings are drawing right. Soviet SSBN designated "S1" now bearing two-three-zero degrees true. Bearings drawing right."

"Captain is in the sonar room and acknowledges these contact reports," sonar reported to the conning officer.

Bruce asked the sonar supervisor, "Can we hold solid contact on all three contacts at a ship's speed of eighteen knots?"

"Yes sir, at present environmental conditions. I will report to conn if any of the contacts should fade."

"Good work, Chief Keller. Your men are as sharp as ever."

Bruce departed the sonar room and entered the attack center.

"Dave. What are the target solutions at present?"

The executive officer responded to the captain, "We have a good target solution on the three nuclear submarines. The bearings of all targets are drawing aft of *Jackfish* with their ranges opening."

"Very well, Dave. Increase speed to thirty knots. Secure from battle stations."

Bruce returned to his stateroom and had a mug of coffee before dinner was served in the wardroom.

His mind was cluttered with demons laughing and telling bad stories about *Tigerfish* and her crew.

He visualized the torture being administered to the officers and sailors by the Soviet/Cuban terrorists. Also, his mind kept on bringing up images of the torture given to the key officers to get them to reveal nuclear safeguarded information.

Bruce got tears in his eyes as he put himself in Tom Morello's place, knowing that there was nothing he could do to save his ship and shipmates.

Bococo knocked on the captain's stateroom door, slowly opened it, and announced, "Captain, dinner is being served."

"Thank you, Bococo. I am on my way."

Although all seats were full for dinner in the wardroom, there was a distinct coolness being generated amongst the officers. Responses were short. No additional information was provided that was not requested. The normal happy comradeship was missing.

Bruce thought that this atmosphere could only get worst.

Five of the officers and Bruce stayed in the wardroom and watched a movie.

Bruce would have rather been doing something else than watching the movie; however, he decided that it was more important to spend as much time with his officers as practicable.

The sound-powered telephone in the wardroom buzzed two times.

"Captain speaking."

The conning officer reported, "It is time twenty two hundred and we are at the sixty-nautical-mile semicircle around Bermuda. Request permission to change course to one-five-three degrees true en route to harm's way?"

"Permission granted. Continue to take a fathometer sounding every one hour and randomly clear baffles every two hours."

"Yes sir, Captain."

Bruce toured the ship and was pleased to see that morale was as high as it had been, with the current hostile atmosphere slowly being generated.

The captain wrote his night order book and had it sent to Nat for his entries.

As Bruce turned out his bunk light, his thoughts were that there remained two hundred and sixty nautical miles to transit to Point Bravo undetected, arriving at zero six thirty on the twenty-third of December. Only forty-one and one-half hours remained to complete the mission before Christmas Day.

/7/ EN ROUTE TO HARM'S WAY

Over the normal noise of the propulsion plant generating fifty thousand shaft horsepower coupled with the peculiar noises caused by the ancillary components, a loud but calm yell dominated the spectrum of noise. "Fire in the lower level engine room. Starboard main turbine lubricating oil pump seal blew out. Lagging oil soaked. Fire and heavy smoke."

With a slight tremor in his voice, the engineering officer of the watch reported, "Conn-EOOW. Fire in lower level engine room. Starboard main lube oil pump seal let go. Heavy smoke." After a slight pause, the EOOW continued his report. "Stopping both main turbines to disconnect the starboard unit and put it on the jacking gear with emergency lubricating oil supply."

The 1 MC general announcing system reported to the crew, "Fire in the engine room," followed by the ship's fire alarm.

Sailors half dressed scrambled throughout the ship to take their assigned stations for combating a fire. Questioning looks were on many of the faces. Was this a real fire and if so, how much trouble do they have?

"Diving officer-conn. All stop. Make your depth one-hundred-fifty feet. Expeditiously establish a trim for ordered depth at minimum speed."

The diving officer responded to the orders verbatim with some anxiety in his voice.

The conning officer knew that he would have to reduce speed to de-clutch the main turbine from the reduction gear.

Water needed to be removed expeditiously from the ship's trim tanks and pumped to sea to achieve a satisfactory trim and maintain ordered depth for slow ship's speed. If the ship was trimmed heavy, speed would be needed to maintain ordered depth to keep the submarine from losing depth control and sinking.

The unknown casualty in the middle of the night was what the men in charge of operating the submarine always had nested in the back of their minds. To combat this type of casualty was the reason that the diving officer always trimmed the submarine a little bit light.

The diving officer directed the planes men to establish a fifteen degree up angle on the ship as the *Jackfish* moved towards a shallower and safer depth of one-hundred-fifty feet in this casualty situation.

Bruce rapidly entered the control room dressed in slippers and a robe and announced, "Captain is in the control room."

Dave followed closely behind the captain. "Captain. I am going to the reactor compartment tunnel. I will report the status of the casualty and damage control measures needed as soon as possible."

The captain gave an affirmative nod to Dave as his executive officer headed aft to evaluate the damage.

On a submarine, it is general operating procedure for the captain to go the control room and the executive officer to go to the scene of the casualty.

"Conn-diving officer. At ship's depth of one-hundred-fifty feet. Trimming the ship for minimum speed."

"Diving officer-conn. Very well."

"Steer course twenty degrees each side of base course to clear the baffles."

"Sonar-conn. Clearing baffles."

"Conn-sonar. Completed searching the baffles. No contacts detected."

The crew in the engine room donned emergency air breathing masks to prevent being overcome by smoke.

The crew members in the forward part of the ship each removed an emergency air breathing mask from the damage control lockers. They carried the mask with them ready to don it if necessary.

These emergency air breathing masks sealed around the whole face and had an air hose attached to the mask. The hose had a quick disconnect device on its end that allowed it to be plugged into the many air breathing manifolds located throughout the ship. This maneuverability and flexibility allowed the operators freedom to move throughout the smoke-filled spaces while disconnecting and connecting the hose to different emergency air breathing manifolds.

This emergency air breathing system for providing breathing air to operators in an emergency was developed and installed in nuclear

Mission Complete

submarines after the need was identified when the U.S. nuclear submarine *Nautilus* had a fire on board while traveling under the pack ice at the North Pole in the late 1950s.

"Conn-EOOW. Two badly burned men are still in the smoke-filled engine room. Both men are conscious with normal breathing in emergency air breathing masks."

Bruce acknowledged the sequencing of reports by nodding to the conning officer. He then directed the conning officer, "Have the hospital corpsman don a self-contained oxygen breathing apparatus and take station in the reactor compartment tunnel with the damage control team."

The engineering officer of the watch ordered the propulsion throttle man in the maneuvering room to reverse the main engines until both turbines were stopped.

The throttle man rapidly spun the throttle operator wheel hand over hand to the shut position. He then slowly opened the reverse throttle valve to allow steam to operate the turbine in the reverse direction. Steam was slowly admitted into the main turbines to stop the forward rotation of the main shaft.

When the throttle man observed the speed of the main shaft to be zero, he reported "EOOW- Throttleman. Turbines indicate all stop."

"Upper level engine room-EOOW. Stopping the main turbines from the maneuvering room. When you have local indication that the turbines are stopped, locally trip shut the steam throttle valve to the starboard main turbine." The engineering officer of the watch continued, "Disconnect the starboard main turbine shaft coupling. Engage the starboard emergency lubricating oil pump and then put the starboard turbine on the turning gear."

The upper level engine room operator reported back verbatim these orders as he expeditiously carried out the directives.

The turning gear rotated the main turbine shaft very slowly to prevent bowing the rotor shaft. Bowing of the turbine rotor took place when the rotor was stopped without a cooling medium available to equalize the heat applied to the metal rotor.

It was mandatory to accomplish this evolution of stopping and de-clutching the main turbine as fast as possible. This de-clutching operation was required to permit regaining ship's speed with the port main turbine.

Also, it was necessary to get lubricating oil applied to the turbine bearing housing to prevent wiping the starboard main turbine bearings. Wiping the babbitt metal from the main turbine bearings would put the turbine out of commission until the submarine returned to port to effect the repairs.

This procedure of rapidly stopping main turbines was practiced often by the ship's crew under controlled and supervised conditions by the ship's drill team to ensure proficiency in combating this casualty.

The damage control party with the engineer officer and damage control assistant assembled in the reactor compartment tunnel awaiting directions from the engineering officer of the watch for them to enter the engine room. The executive officer also was wearing a breathing device and was assembled with the damage control party.

The hospital corpsman was waiting in the reactor compartment tunnel to administer medical assistance to the two burned shipmates. He would not enter the engine room but would be waiting the transfer of the casualties to the reactor compartment tunnel.

Each member of the damage control party was wearing an oxygen breathing apparatus that was a self-contained system that provided oxygen to the wearer.

A fine oil vapor mist filled the engine room, resulting in minimum visibility.

"Captain-conn. Request permission for the damage control team to enter the engine room and for the transfer of the burned men into the reactor compartment tunnel."

"Permission granted."

"EOOW-conn. Transfer the burned men from the lower level engine room to the reactor compartment tunnel watertight door. The support team in the reactor compartment tunnel will enter into the engine room when the two casualties are made ready to be transferred into the reactor compartment tunnel."

Opening the reactor compartment tunnel watertight door would then contaminate the reactor compartment tunnel with heavy black smoke from the engine room. However, the hospital corpsman would be standing by in the reactor compartment tunnel to provide medical attention.

The valves for control of the turbines were positioned by the upper level engine room watch stander. His proficiency and thorough knowledge of the piping systems made it possible for him to complete this evolution with minimum visibility available.

"EOOW- Engine Room. Starboard main turbine is disconnected and on the turning gear with the emergency lubricating oil system in operation."

The engineering officer of the watch repeated back the report verbatim.

Propulsion now was restored to the submarine with single turbine

Mission Complete

operation. The speed of *Jackfish* was limited to twenty-five knots with only the port main turbine in operation.

The captain directed the conning officer. "Ensure that the high pressure air compressors are not started to charge up the air banks until the ship's atmosphere is cleared of the oil mist." Bruce continued, "We don't want to contaminate the high pressure air system and the air supply for the emergency air breathing system."

A suction with the air compressors from the presently contaminated environment would make these valuable systems not useable for emergency air breathing purposes.

"Conn-EOOW. Port main turbine is available for propulsion up to maximum speed of twenty-five knots. Answering all stop."

"EOOW-conn. Very well. Answer all ordered propulsion bells."

Bruce acknowledged the report to the conning officer.

The damage control team rapidly entered the engine room, proceeded to the lower level, and started to combat the fire caused by the spraying of the hot lube oil.

The damage control team leader reported to the EOOW, "Heavy black smoke still is being generated from the oil soaked lagging."

A damage control team member connected the salt water fire hose to the ship's fire main in the lower level engine room.

Dave observed and assured himself that all correct damage control practices were being followed.

The nozzle of the hose was positioned to the minimum flow position and was pointed into the bilge area away from any mechanical or electrical equipment. Two operators manned the hose nozzle. The hose nozzle control valve was slowly opened by the hose attendants.

This discipline in the control of the hose nozzle and of the water flow minimized the possibility that the hose would get loose and spray electrical distribution panels and other components causing more damage.

"EOOW- damage control. Have energized the fire hose and commenced minimum spray on the lagging and general area. Fire is out. Black smoke still is being generated by the oil soaked lagging."

"Damage control-EOOW. Very well."

The combating of this exact type of casualty was practiced often by the crews on nuclear submarines. This casualty was usually the one simulated drill that was imposed on every nuclear ship during the annual operational reactor safeguards examinations by the fleet commander's inspection team.

Stewart was very familiar with combating this type of casualty and had the utmost confidence in the damage control team leaders. He remained in the attack center and monitored each event and provided moral support and backup to the conning officer.

During an event such as this, the ship normally would proceed smartly to periscope depth. At periscope depth, the diesel engine or low pressure blower would be used to emergency ventilate the effected compartments overboard. This emergency ventilation mode would rapidly rid the effected spaces of smoke.

However, both the diesel and low pressure blower were significant noise generators in the water and could possible cause the *Jackfish* to be detected.

Also, the ship must be at periscope depth to use this emergency ventilating equipment. This configuration would make the *Jackfish* susceptible to detection by the Soviet orbiting satellite.

Nat reported to Stewart, "The clear window when the *USSR* satellite will not be able to detect *Jackfish* will be available in one more hour at zero one forty-five."

This meant all the crew in the reactor compartment tunnel and the engine room had to remain in air breathing masks or oxygen breathing apparatus for at least another hour.

"Conn-captain. At zero two hundred, take *Jackfish* to periscope depth and ventilate the ship overboard with the emergency ventilation fans."

These fans were sound mounted well and noise isolated from the hull, thus reducing the possibility of any heavy noise generation into the surrounding water.

"Tunnel-conn. Report the status of our two burned casualties."

The hospital corpsman reported, "Both men are stable; however, I would prefer if they were in the forward part of the ship where more medical support can be provided in a cleaner environment."

Dave was now in the reactor compartment tunnel and concurred with the hospital corpsman's recommendation.

Bruce made the decision to open the reactor compartment tunnel watertight door and move the two burn casualties forward out of the reactor compartment tunnel. He knew this would cause some smoke to enter the forward part of the ship; however, he considered this the best decision for the stricken shipmates.

"Conn-captain. Place the ventilation fans in fast speed recirculating."

This mode of operation would rid the ship's atmosphere of some of the

Mission Complete

smoke concentration using the HEPA filters installed in the ventilation system.

"Captain-conn. Ventilation fans are in fast speed recirculating."

"Conn-captain. Make your depth four hundred feet and increase speed to twenty-five knots." Bruce continued, "When the satellite window is out of detection orbit at zero two hundred, take the ship to periscope depth and emergency ventilate the engine room and the rest of the ship overboard with the emergency ventilation fans."

This evolution of eliminating smoke from the ship and cleaning the ship's environment of contaminants should be completed in thirty minutes.

"Dump trash and garbage at periscope depth also."

The captain talked with his executive officer. "Dave, I want to rig your stateroom as a clean area for the medical treatment of the two burn casualties. This will allow better treatment to be administered by the hospital corpsman." Bruce continued, "Have the stewards mate rig both bunks in your stateroom with clean linen and thoroughly clean the stateroom."

"Yes sir, Captain. Will have the directives accomplished expeditiously."

Dave continued, "I will sleep in the empty bunk in the operations officer stateroom."

In this single main turbine arrangement using just the port main turbine, *Jackfish* was limited to twenty-five knots. Normal speed would be available after the starboard main lubrication oil pump was repaired.

Tom provided an engineering status of the repair. "I will have my mechanical experts start repair work on the mechanical seal for the main lubrication oil pump as soon as the engine room has been cleared of black smoke."

In the interim, Chief Machinist Mate Douglas reviewed the main lubrication oil pump technical manual to ensure all needed repair parts were available and on hand. He ensured that the repair team was familiar with the repair and the post repair test process.

The red tag protection system was completed, listing all the valves and electrical switches that needed to be isolated and tagged out of service. This tag-out system provided mechanical and electrical protection for the lubrication oil system and safety protection for the maintenance personnel.

"Captain-engineer. We have all the repair parts assembled for repair of the starboard main turbine lubrication oil pump." Tom continued, "The repair team headed by Chief Douglas has reviewed the repair procedure. Estimate that the complete work package will take four hours to tag out the system, rig out the main lubrication oil motor, replace the pump mechanical seal, reassemble the motor, and then test the system."

"Very well, Tom," Bruce responded. "Engineer. It is mandatory to get this work completed expeditiously to allow us the availability of flank speed to do battle on an even footing against the enemy. Have your team with repair procedure, parts, tag-out log completed, and ready to tag out the starboard main turbine lubrication oil system and commence work as soon as sufficient visibility is available in the lower level engine room."

The captain met with his navigator. "Nat, looks as if we will lose another four hours in the transit to Point Bravo. Revise the navigation chart to show our new track after including the lost time and reduced speed due to our main turbine casualty. We should arrive at Point Bravo about zero eight- thirty with both main turbines capable for full operation."

After a slight pause, the captain continued, "I want Dave, ops/sonar, you, and Chief Keller to meet with me in the wardroom at zero six hundred this morning. We will have to reevaluate our tactical search plan to make up for the additional lost time. I want each of you to think out all options available and 'what ifs' and also be ready to discuss a solution for all the contingencies."

Dave reported to Bruce, "The burned men are resting in my stateroom and the hospital corpsman is administering medical support for them."

"Captain-conn. Request permission to take the ship to periscope depth and emergency ventilate overboard with the ventilation fans."

"Permission granted, conn."

Bruce continued, "After the ship is clear of all contaminates, have the emergency air breathing masks centrally located in both the forward and after parts of the ship. Have the hospital corpsman supervise the swabbing out of the masks with alcohol and then have the masks properly stored."

Bruce visited with the burned shipmates in the exec's stateroom. They both were resting comfortably after receiving morphine shots to ease the pain.

"Conn-captain. Request permission to have the engineer commence work on the starboard main lube oil pump after emergency ventilating the ship. Tom estimates the complete job will take four hours."

"Permission granted." The captain continued. "Let me know when the system has been tested satisfactorily. Also, inform me if any problems are encountered during the repair process. Have the hospital corpsman report to you and the executive officer hourly the status of the burned casualties."

Mission Complete

"Yes sir, Captain."

At zero two hundred, the head of the *Jackfish* periscope broke the surface of the ocean.

The conning officer swept three hundred sixty degrees and announced to the watch standers in the control room, "Periscope sweep completed. No visual contacts."

"Ballast control panel operator, raise the ECM mast."

The ballast control panel operator raised the ECM mast.

"ECM Operator, search for any threat frequencies."

The ECM operator searched all bands for threat frequencies. He reported, "No threat frequencies detected."

"Captain-conn. No visual contacts. No threat frequencies detected with ECM."

"Request permission to commence emergency ventilating overboard."

"Conn-captain. Very well. Permission granted to emergency ventilate the ship overboard."

"Also, copy the force commander's broadcast to see if any tactical messages are addressed to *Jackfish*."

"Conn-captain. I am going to hit the rack for awhile. Ensure that I am awakened at zero six hundred."

"Captain-conn. Yes, sir."

Bruce laid down on his bunk fully clothed. He was exhausted already with no clear opening available in the near future for a good rest.

"Ballast control panel-conn. "Raise the snorkel mast and commence ventilating the ship. It should take about thirty minutes to clear the contaminants out of the environment. Have the air monitored frequently. I want to minimize the ventilating time."

After a report from the auxiliary man of the watch that the atmosphere environment readings were normal, the conning officer ordered, "Secure emergency ventilating. Lower the snorkel mast." The conning officer continued, "Secure the ECM equipment. Lower the ECM Mast."

"EOOW-conn. Notify the engineer officer that permission is granted to commence repair work on the starboard main turbine lube oil pump."

Following normal ship's procedure, the conning officer slowed the ship and cleared baffles every two hours to search the baffle cone for contacts.

Dave reported to the conning officer, "The two burned men are sleeping well. The hospital corpsman will keep them on intravenous fluid throughout the night and provide them antibiotics to prevent infection."

Dave went to the wardroom for a cup of coffee before getting a few hour's sleep.

Nat had the same idea.

The two officers sat in the wardroom, both waiting for the other to open the dialog about the current conditions in *Jackfish*.

Finally Dave opened the conversation. "Do you know any more about this mission than what has been provided to us by the captain?"

Nat stared at Dave and continued the conversation. "No, I don't. These are completely unsatisfactory conditions to work under." He continued, "The best that I can surmise is that the target is the *Tigerfish*."

"But why and how could this be?"

Dave added, "This is one dangerous mission, to say the least."

"We loaded advanced nuclear torpedoes in Groton. There should be at least a two-man rule to determine if and when the nuclear torpedoes should be fired."

"At a minimum, we should be operating under a classified Top Secret operations order."

Nat continued the conversation with Dave. "How could the *Tigerfish* be alive and why is our mission to sink a U.S. nuclear submarine?"

Both officers become more angry and distressed as the conversation continued.

It was obvious now that the wedge had been inserted between Stewart and his top two trusted officers.

This coolness was to continue as the mission proceeded, with dissension rapidly forming between the captain and the rest of the officers.

"Conn, this is the engineer. The repair work on the starboard main turbine lube oil pump is proceeding well. The motor has been disconnected from the pump and cleared out of the way to allow installation of a replacement mechanical seal into the pump. We are on schedule and should complete installation and pump testing by zero six-thirty. I will provide you progress reports and let you know if any problems surface."

The conning officer responded, "Thank you, Tom, for the update."

There was a light knock on the captain's door. This was followed by a voice. "Captain, your zero six hundred wake up call as ordered, sir."

Bruce didn't need any reminder to awake. He had had a minimal amount of sleep throughout the restless night. The pressures of the activities of the last four days were already starting to show. Increasing the stress was the fact that *Jackfish* was already more than eight hours behind schedule.

Mission Complete

He acknowledged the wake up call and heard the messenger quietly depart.

In robotic habit, Bruce reached from his bunk and pushed the call button that summoned the duty stewards mate.

He then looked at the ship's remote indicators located on the bulkhead at the foot of his bunk. These three remote indicators, outlined by little red bulbs to make the data more visible in darkness, provided him the ship's current speed, depth, and course.

At a glance, Stewart saw that *Jackfish* was on course one-five-three degrees true, at a speed of twenty-five knots driving silently through the ocean at a depth of one thousand feet. All parameters were as Bruce ordered in his night order book before he hit the sack a very short time ago.

In less than two hours, the conning officer would take the ship to periscope depth. Hopefully, the winds and wave action would abate.

All activities to be conducted at periscope depth would have to be completed within thirty minutes. This was the time window when both the Soviet and United States Photographic Satellites would not be in the orbit to monitor *Jackfish*.

After completing housekeeping chores, including disposal of garbage and ship's refuse and copying any priority communications from the force commander, *Jackfish* then would return into its normal environment at depth one thousand feet and ship's speed of twenty-five knots.

In about two more hours at zero eight-thirty, *Jackfish* would enter the three-hundred-nautical-mile circle around Point Bravo.

The duty stewards mate gave a slight knock on the door, slowly opened it with a "Good morning, Captain," and placed a large mug of black coffee on the captain's desk.

As the ultimate responsibility for this ship and its crew sipped his coffee, the stark realization came before him that he had less than forty hours remaining to accomplish the critical mission.

This meant traveling almost fifty nautical miles more undetected by the enemy nuclear submarine and then entering harm's way.

Subsequently, *Jackfish* would have to search out more than thirty-five thousand square nautical miles for a submarine of the same class and characteristics as *Jackfish*, but operating slower and with the target ship's sonar operators most likely alerted.

Also, the anticipated location of the *Tigerfish* was based on the best judgment of Stewart without any assistance or input from other professionals. One mistake could mean the end of *Jackfish* with the resultant disastrous consequences for the United States and the other countries of the free world.

Bruce again recalled the quotation by Thucydides in four hundred and four B.C. and hoped that it did not refer to *Jackfish*. "Their want of practice will make them unskillful and their want of skill, timid. Maritime skills, like the skill of other kinds, are not to be substituted by the way or at chosen times."

The sound-powered telephone sounded in the captain's cabin.

"Captain-conn. The engineering officer of the watch reports the starboard main turbine lubrication oil pump has been repaired and tested satisfactorily. Ready to answer all bells."

"Conn-captain. Very well. Thank you."

"Increase speed to flank."

Bruce entered the control room and discussed the current tactical status with the conning officer and Nat.

Bruce directed his conning officer, "At zero eight hundred, take a single ping sounding. Make speed fifteen knots and go to depth one thousand feet for a bathograph trace. Then return to an operating depth of two hundred feet." The captain continued. "I will provide more tactical directives before zero eight-thirty."

The conning officer and Nat both acknowledged the captain's directives.

Bruce then visited the sonar room and talked with the sonar operators on watch.

It was reaffirmed to these young sailors by their captain that the crew of *Jackfish*, their families, and their country were depending on their performance during the next two days.

The captain entered the wardroom for the tactical meeting with his key officers. Chief Keller also was present. The sonar chief's vast knowledge of the performance and operation of the sonar installation in *Jackfish* would be beneficial in developing the tactical plan for the future encounter.

All the participants got a large mug of coffee and a few hot sticky buns. Everyone was quiet. All eyes and ears of the group were focused on Bruce, waiting for him to provide enough information to bring them on the team.

Bruce opened up the discussion with a synopsis of the current information.

"As I discussed earlier, our contact of interest is a submarine of the *Jackfish* class. I am not at liberty to discuss anything more about the target

Mission Complete

classification except to reaffirm that the target will sink *Jackfish* if we do not sink the target submarine first."

Bruce delayed this conversation as he sipped his coffee. "*Jackfish* represents the free world in this international game of who is standing last."

These comments only irritated Dave and Nat more than they already were.

Dave looked Bruce in the eyes and questioned, "Captain. What is our objective and why can't you trust us with more details of the mission?"

Although the other officers present and Chief Keller had the same questions, they were surprised by this outburst by the executive officer against the captain.

Bruce momentarily flushed with anger, then regained his composure.

"Gentlemen. The success of this mission is so important to national and to world freedom that *Jackfish* is authorized by the president of the United States to use the nuclear tipped MK 56X torpedo against the target submarine should it be necessary as a last resort."

The chief and the officers present in the wardroom all dropped the lower lips of their mouths and looked at each other with questioning thoughts.

Dave was the only officer questioning his captain. He continued with the question, "Captain. Do we have an operational order from higher authority and if so, does the order authorize the use of nuclear weapons?"

Bruce wished that these questions had not been asked.

The captain responded to these questions in a firm voice giving the indication that there would be no more discussions associated with this question. "*Jackfish* has not been provided an operational order for this mission nor has the ship been authorized in writing by higher authority to shoot nuclear weapons."

Everyone present at the meeting realized that they could be held accountable for terrorist activity for shooting weapons without authority.

It was obvious that the wedge had been driven further between the captain and his wardroom. It was not going to take much time for the rumors to start to spread throughout the ship.

Bruce provided his best judgment to the meeting participants as to the current tactical situation. He laid out a chart showing his best expected weapons launch location for *Tigerfish*.

"Using the best intelligence available, I evaluate that the target nuclear submarine will be located around Point Bravo at launch time. Expect the nuclear submarine to be at periscope depth from about twenty two hundred until twenty-three fifty the twenty-fourth of December."

Bruce intentionally handed out a tidbit of information to his officers with the statement "at launch time."

Every member of the group immediately picked up on this statement and started to look at each other as if to say "Did you hear the statement also?"

Bruce took another sip of coffee as the participants absorbed the information provided.

He continued, "I have drawn a circle with a three-hundred-nautical-mile diameter line on the axis of two-two-five degrees true and zero-four-five degrees true. We only are interested in the northwest half semicircle.

"Put an expanding cone in the circle with the point of the cone at Point Bravo. The center line of the cone is course one-two-five degrees true and the length of the arc of the cone at the circumference of the circle is to be twenty nautical miles."

Bruce already had the cone and circle drawn on the chart around Point Bravo. Also on the chart was drawn the sixty-nautical-mile semicircle.

All the officers and Keller looked at the chart and waited for the next bit of information or directives. They all continued to be aroused with the latest tidbit about "target launch time" and anticipated that more information would be forthcoming to them.

After enough time for those present to absorb the information on the chart, Bruce continued. "I anticipate that the target will be on course about one-two-five degrees true proceeding toward Point Bravo. Expect the target to be below the gradient until about twenty two hundred."

Without allowing any time for questions, the captain commented, "After about twenty-two hundred the nuclear submarine then should be at periscope depth. If all goes as planned, anticipate the target to be transiting towards Point Bravo making five knots. The submarine then will linger around Point Bravo, alerted and making five knots."

The captain slowly scanned the eyes of his audience and stated, "There is a very good possibility that *Jackfish* will pick up noise spokes on our sonar equipment from the target submarine. The noise would be generated by the target self initiated sound shorts. This data is the best that I can develop from the minimum information provided for this mission."

Again, the questioning looks on the faces of the audience became more pronounced.

Bruce continued, "Dave, I want you to head this team and expeditiously develop the best tactical plan for making our searches. We want to search above and below the gradients. Use sprint and drift search plans when searching the farthest areas from Point Bravo.

Mission Complete

"Also," Bruce continued, "allow sufficient time in the plan to thoroughly search the sixty-nautical-mile area in the proximity of Point Bravo and in the cone drawn on the chart."

"Gentlemen. I want to meet with this team again at zero eight hundred to review the results of your tactical think tank. Thank you for your continued support."

Bruce again sipped his coffee and then stated, "For information, the conning officer has been directed to slow to fifteen knots, get a bathograph trace down to one thousand feet, and then make ship's operating depth two hundred feet."

The amazed audience continued to look at Bruce with questioning eyes. They all were in sheer shock at the information just provided to them.

Bruce excused himself from the wardroom table.

As he departed the wardroom he looked at his executive officer. "Dave. Please notify the conning officer that I am going to make a tour of the ship. I will be back in the wardroom at zero eight hundred."

"Yes sir, Captain."

Dave's response was not given in his normal cheery style but was a little more crisp.

During his absence, the group in the wardroom started questioning the information received from their captain concerning the mission.

Nat questioned Dave, "Are we violating any laws, either military and civilian, if we shoot weapons and sink the target submarine?"

The operations officer added, "I have never read anything, including operations during World War II, where an operations order is not provided to conduct critical submarine operations."

The executive officer ended the conversation before the captain returned. "I don't have an answer yet. I'll try to resolve the issue soonest."

The captain completed touring the ship and entered the control room.

The conning officer reported to Bruce, "I completed taking bathograph trace to one thousand feet. We are now operating at two hundred feet. The trace shows a strong layer at one hundred and fifty feet. Below this depth the trace goes strong negative. A good place to hide and not be detected."

"Very well. Make speed ten knots."

Bruce gripped the 1MC general announcing system hand microphone in his hand. He delayed talking momentarily while he thought out his announcement.

"Let me have your attention please. This is the captain speaking." He continued. "In thirty minutes *Jackfish* will enter harm's way and commence the localize, hunt, and attack phase of our mission. Our target is a nuclear submarine. The objectives of this nuclear submarine target is to change our way of life in the United States and how others live in the free world. Within the next two days, there will be torpedo shooting."

After a slight pause, Bruce continued. "You men of *Jackfish* are trained professionals and I am confident that your knowledge, expertise, and overall skill in your individual tasks will prevail and we will be successful in carrying out our mission. Thank you, shipmates, and God speed.

"As of zero eight-thirty this morning, all alarms and announcing systems will be secured throughout the ship. A telephone talker will be stationed in each compartment and at key watch stations."

Using hand set communications would eliminate any possibility of generating a noise source into the water through a sound short.

The conning officer was directed by Bruce to set the communications watch at zero eight-thirty. He also was directed to stream the sonar floating wire.

Bruce entered the wardroom. He felt certain that his first-rate team would have a search plan developed.

Dave opened up the discussions. "Captain. We have developed what we consider to be a realistic and thorough search plan."

"Excuse me for a moment, please." Bruce picked up the hand telephone in the wardroom, dialed the telephone, and then commented, "Weps. This is the captain. Make five torpedo tubes ready in all respects except for opening the outer doors. I want two torpedo tubes containing the Mk57X torpedo and three tubes with the non nuclear conventional torpedoes readied. The tubes are to be flooded and equalized with sea water pressure."

Ray repeated back the orders to the captain, and then gave a "Cheery aya aye, sir."

"Also notify the conning officer of my directives, please."

The non-nuclear conventional torpedoes operate at a speed of sixty knots to a range of twenty thousand yards. This type of torpedo has multiple sensing devices and is detonated by either acoustical or contact features.

"Dave. At zero eight-thirty, please set the battle stations sonar team."

Keller responded. "I will station the team as soon as we finish here with the search plan. My guys are ready to go to work."

Dave and Bruce both thanked the sonar chief for his dedication.

Mission Complete

The executive officer led the discussion of the tactical sonar search plan with the other members of the team adding information as appropriate.

Bruce looked at the chart as Dave discussed the search plan. Templates were marked on the chart to indicate courses and speeds required.

There were essentially three areas of interest: the outer area with a three-hundred-nautical-mile diameter, the inner area with a sixty-nautical-mile diameter, and the expanding cone area. The outer area encompassed thirty-five thousand square nautical miles. The inner area of interest had fourteen hundred square nautical miles.

Dave pointed to the chart as he provided the tactical information to his shipmates. "In the outer area, we will sprint and drift at our best search speed except when crossing the cone. We will slow to ten knots during this period. The section tracking party will plot own ship's course along the tracks we have projected on the chart."

Bruce commented, "The plan looks good. Now to implement it successfully!"

The captain continued. "Dave and Nat. We will station the section tracking party and the command tactical watch in ten minutes at zero eight-thirty. At this time we will have entered harm's way."

Nat told Dave and the captain, "I will take the first six hour watch."

Dave asked Bruce if he had time to discuss some issues.

"Yes, Dave, let's go into my stateroom."

The executive officer took this opportunity to place all his cards on the table. "Captain. I am concerned that I do not have all the answers to this complicated and apparent dangerous mission. Without all the information, it is hard for me or the wardroom to support you properly. Also, the rest of the wardroom feels left out as they enter into a dangerous mission."

Bruce responded, "Dave, I completely understand your concern plus the concern of the other officers." Bruce took a sip of his coffee. "I have been directed by the president of the United States not to tell anyone the details of this mission. I disagree with the directive; however, I am required to comply."

Dave acknowledged Bruce and then departed from the wardroom.

It was obvious by the executive officer's facial and body expressions as he departed the wardroom that he was not completely satisfied with the captain's rationale.

/8/ HELL TRIP TO CUBA

As Bruce continued to sip his coffee, he became remorseful as he relived the words that described the barbaric conditions on *Tigerfish* after the takeover by the Soviet/Cuban pirates. These barbaric actions had been described to Vice Admiral Hasting, the Chairman of the National Security Council in Washington, D.C., by Lieutenant Michael Hodges of *Tigerfish*.

These conditions then were related to Bruce by Vice Admiral Hasting in Bill Walter's office four days ago.

Hodges also reported that these conditions continued during the undetected submerged transit of the U.S. nuclear submarine out of the Mediterranean Sea into the North Atlantic Ocean and then to Cuba.

Hodges was taken off *Tigerfish* prior to the submarine getting underway from Cuba on the morning of the fifteenth of December. He was to remain in Cuba until the nineteenth of December. The pirates then would put him on a plane from Key West, Florida, with his destination Washington, D.C. At this time he would deliver the ultimatum to the president of the United States.

While he was confined in a small dungeon on the pier in Baracoa Harbor, Cuba, he heard and saw the horrible sight concerning his *Tigerfish* shipmates.

About thirty *Tigerfish* sailors had been taken off the submarine before the ship got underway. These sailors were considered unnecessary for the accomplishment of the pirates' mission. They then were cramped into a barbwired compound with the access to the compound locked.

Four guards fired automatic weapons into the barbwired complex until all the sailors were assassinated. The guards then fastened weighted objects to the bodies and loaded them into a boat at the pier. Three trips to the outer harbor were necessary to dispose all the bodies into the ocean.

Mission Complete

Hodges had been unable to hold his composure and wept profusely as he told the details of this incident to his superiors in Washington.

The young *Tigerfish* officer was now confined at a military complex outside of Washington. The medical experts believed that Hodges was very close to the edge and was capable of going over and revealing all he knew about the *Tigerfish* incident.

Admiral Hasting assured Bruce during their conversation that the following events that took place on the *Tigerfish* were as accurate as possible.

"Also, Bruce, the brutality and assassination of the thirty *Tigerfish* sailors after *Tigerfish* got underway were captured on photographs by both a United States photographic flyover mission and a United States photographic satellite."

The admiral looked the young commanding officer in the eyes and sternly stated, "Payback is being planned at the present time by United States military forces."

After the successful takeover plot by the Soviet/Cuban team Tracy Smith, the senior Soviet submarine officer aboard *Tigerfish*, assumed the role as commanding officer of *Tigerfish*.

Tracy Smith, the new commanding officer of *Tigerfish*, pressed the actuator for the ship's 1MC general announcing system and announced, "Let me have your attention please. I have now assumed the position of commanding officer of *Tigerfish*. Congratulations to the takeover team. Each of you performed superbly. We are now in control of the American submarine and en route to our intermediate stopover in Cuba."

Roars and cheers were heard throughout the ship from the Soviet/Cuban team.

Tracy's initial major responsibility included adding credibility to the Unites States Navy's belief that *Tigerfish* had sunk with all hands aboard.

As was rehearsed during the Soviet/Cuban team takeover training sessions, Tracy would direct the Soviet/Cuban crew organization to be able to oversee the American crew as they successfully transited the pirated submarine from the Mediterranean Sea through the Strait of Gibraltar and across the Atlantic Ocean to Cuba undetected.

By the time the ship reached the concealed destination port in Cuba, all of the ship's safes would be opened and their contents examined. Contents of significant importance would be copied by the pirates for shipment to Russia.

The combinations to the two safes containing the fire control panel security keys would be in the crew's possession. Classified equipment and documents, including one of each type torpedo carried by *Tigerfish* and an Axehandle nuclear missile, would be ready to be removed from the U.S. submarine for further transporting to the Soviet Union.

As part of the plan, the captors built a model of a large container ship in the Cuban harbor that would house the *Tigerfish* and its crew. This container ship would keep the submarine from being detected by outside activities, including United States satellite and reconnaissance aircraft fly overs.

This concealment would house the *Tigerfish* during the last phase of the transit into the port and during the ship's stay in port.

The model ship was well-equipped to permit all necessary work to be accomplished on the captured American submarine. Inside the concealment houses were cranes big enough to remove torpedoes and the Axehandle missile from the *Tigerfish*, and there was also space available for these weapon's stowage.

The two Russian psychologists assigned to this project were proven experts in brain manipulation. They would board the *Tigerfish* off Africa and complete their task—obtaining from Tom Morello, the captain of *Tigerfish*, and key responsible individuals the combinations for the secret communications codes and the necessary information to be able to arm and launch the nuclear torpedoes and nuclear tipped Axehandle missiles.

The Soviets would use mind altering drugs, truth drugs, and whatever else was required to obtain the information needed. They didn't initially plan on using physical torture unless it was needed as a last resort.

While completing each assignment in the Cuban port, Tracy would also have to ready the *Tigerfish* to leave Cuba on schedule and transit submerged and undetected to the predetermined Axehandle missile launching station off Bermuda.

Food would have to be loaded aboard *Tigerfish*. Repairs would have to be made on failed equipment. Thorough cleaning and purification would need to be accomplished in all United States crew berthing areas.

Some of the unnecessary *Tigerfish* crew members would be taken off the submarine to be disposed of later.

The Soviet submarine crew had to complete all preparations to launch the dreaded Axehandle missiles by Christmas Eve if the demands of the pirates were not accepted by the president of the United States.

Most of the U.S. crew were still unconscious and all were bound in hand and leg irons.

Since some of the American sailors were needed to operate the ship

Mission Complete

safely, the pirates would wait until they had all awakened and then would keep the *Tigerfish* crew under close supervision as they initially submerged and subsequently operated the ship.

Tracy met with his Soviet/Cuban team in the wardroom and reviewed the details of the remaining milestones of the takeover plan.

When the *Tigerfish* crew awakened, key American operators would take their stations for submerging and then operating the ship undetected en route to Cuba. They would be closely supervised by trained submariners.

They would then maneuver *Tigerfish* in close proximity to a United States warship. Explosive charges then would be discharged from the submarine's torpedo tubes to simulate a distressed submarine.

Then Tracy would announce a casualty using the *Tigerfish*'s underwater communications system. The ship then would transit on the navigation track established by the *Tigerfish* navigator to exit the Mediterranean Sea.

All the American crew members in each watch section would sleep in the same berthing location. Each would be padlocked in their bunk after a head call subsequent to coming off watch. The sailors would not be unchained until it was time to eat and then the invaders would set the watch.

Officers, chief petty officers, and the other crew members—except the captain, executive officer, engineer officer, and operations and weapons communications officers—would berth in the same berthing area.

These latter six officers would berth in the same location and be dressed in anti-suicide garments. These garments were orange-colored one-piece coveralls. The suits had fibre buttons that would dissolve if swallowed. The suit cloth was too strong to be torn to form a noose to hang the individual. Each suit had an opening in the front and back for body disposal functions. The prisoner's feet would be covered with lightweight slippers with no shoelaces.

This select group of officers would be under constant visual guard by one of the terrorist takeover team members.

It would be necessary to be sure that these six officers could not commit suicide and deprive the Soviet/Cuban team of information necessary to carry out their future mission.

In employing nuclear weapons, the two-man rule was always instituted in U.S. nuclear submarines. For entry into a classified safe, one officer would have the combination to the outer safe door and a second officer the combination to enter the inner safe containing the security keys and/or combinations and codes.

Therefore, these six officers now had the combined information needed by the Soviet/Cuban team to succeed in their dramatic plan.

Tracy planned to start administering tranquilizers and truth drugs to this initial group of officers on the first of November. This would be two days before *Tigerfish* departed from the Mediterranean Sea and picked up the Soviet mind manipulation experts from the Soviet trawler off the west coast of Africa.

Two officers would be separated from the rest of the group on the first of November and put into separate staterooms, with the mind games to begin.

With information gained from his Soviet intelligence organizations, Tracy knew well the security procedures established in U.S. nuclear submarines to protect nuclear weapons.

The commanding officer is the only person who has the combinations to the belly bands for each of the nuclear torpedoes. When installed in place around the torpedo, this belly band prevents the torpedo from being moved from the torpedo room and loaded into the torpedo tube.

There are two keys that need to be installed into the attack center fire-control panel to launch either a nuclear-tipped Axehandle missile or a nuclear torpedo. Each key was located in a separate high explosive combination safe. Each safe had an inner door and outer door combination. The executive officer had the combination to the outer door and the operations officer had the combination to the inner door. Both doors must be opened to get one of the keys.

The combination to the safe holding the other set of keys was controlled by the weapons officer and the engineer officer. Both officers had to be present to allow the combination safe to be opened to obtain the key.

The commanding officer was the overall monitor who ensured that the security procedure was carried out correctly.

All the crew members' heads would be shaven, except for the captain's, executive officer's, and engineer officer's, to further humiliate the sailors.

One submarine shower would be allowed weekly for each *Tigerfish* crew member.

This type of shower was first used in American diesel electric submarines where pure water was at a premium. These non-nuclear submarines had a small capacity for making pure water with the priority for the distilled water being used to refill the batteries that provided ship's propulsion and ancillary support functions.

When taking a submarine shower, first you would wet your body, turn off

Mission Complete

the water, soap and scrub the body, and then rapidly use the shower water to rinse.

To conserve the availability and supply of food since the number of people onboard the *Tigerfish* had increased, only two meals per day would be provided the captives.

All meals for members of the *Tigerfish* crew would be served in the crew's dinette.

The wardroom would be reserved for the Soviet/Cuban team.

All jewelry, rings, medals, wallets, and all personal identification would be confiscated.

Tracy Smith continued by directing his number two officer to "Set up a schedule for opening the stateroom safes and any other safes throughout the submarine. Use low detonation shape charges to open the safes if needed." Tracy continued,"Have the contents of each safe examined carefully for information to support our cause. We will wait until the safe expert comes aboard in a couple of days to open the larger safes."

Tracy ended the meeting without asking for any questions.

He then directed his team to take pre-assigned stations for operating the *Tigerfish*.

Key watch stations in the forward part of the ship and the engineering spaces were manned by the American crew.

The Soviet monitors, armed with 9 millimeter side arm pistols and billy clubs, closely observed every action taken by the *Tigerfish* U.S. operators.

The Soviet/Cuban monitors and operators all were graduates of the Soviet *Tigerfish* Take-Over Course and fully understood the basics of operating the U.S. nuclear submarine.

It was made very clear to the American captives that no deviation of the proper operation of the ship would be tolerated.

Tracy ordered the *Tigerfish* conning officer under the close scrutiny of the Russian monitor to submerge the ship and make the ship's depth two hundred feet.

Two blasts of the diving alarm klaxon echoed throughout the ship in unison with the order "DIVE. DIVE" heard over the ship's 1MC general announcing system.

The gushing of water was heard as sea water replaced the air in the main ballast tanks when the main ballast tank vent valves were opened.

The conning officer reported, "Ship is at two hundred feet, trim is satisfactory."

Tracy directed the conning officer to make ship's course two-two-five degrees true and make ship's speed ten knots.

After receiving a verbatim repeat back of his orders given to the conning officer, Tracy ordered, "Make a depth excursion to one thousand feet to obtain a bathograph trace of the thermal conditions."

Tracy directed Tom Morello and the *Tigerfish*'s navigator to review with him and his Soviet navigator the intended track out of the Mediterranean Sea into the North Atlantic Ocean.

The four officers closely observed the ship's outbound track on the navigation chart in the attack center.

This track had been previously prepared by the *Tigerfish* navigation team.

The ship's navigator pointed his finger along the ship's track as he explained in detail each movement of the *Tigerfish*, including course, speed, and depth.

The transit speed laid out on the chart was for *Tigerfish* heading home to Groton, Connecticut. The ship's speed now would have to be reduced and the track recalculated to meet Tracy's requirements for non-detection of *Tigerfish* during the transit.

Initial course was two-two-five degrees true out of the Gulf of Naples through the Tyrrhenian Sea for a distance of one-hundred-eighty nautical miles.

The ship then would maneuver to course two-five-five degrees true for one hundred twenty nautical miles south of Sardenia. For the next five hundred forty nautical miles, *Tigerfish* would be on course two-seven-zero degrees true. Course then would be changed to two six four degrees true. They would remain on this course for eighty nautical miles. The ship then would go to periscope depth to obtain a final navigation fix on the light located on the Isle of Alboran.

Tigerfish would continue to transit the remaining one hundred eighty nautical miles on the same course to the Strait of Gibraltar. The total transit distance from takeover of *Tigerfish* to the Strait of Gibraltar would be eleven hundred nautical miles.

Tracy interrupted the conversation and directed, "I want the speed of advance or average speed for *Tigerfish* to be ten knots for the total trip into the North Atlantic Ocean and then to Cuba. Using this reduced speed and judicious use of depth and sound layer protection should ensure that no detection of *Tigerfish* will be made by United States or Soviet warships."

Tracy also would use his knowledge of the thermal flow through the Strait of Gibraltar to make an undetected exit from the Mediterranean Sea.

Mission Complete

At the Naval Academy in Moscow, Smith had studied the tactics and strategy used by the German submarine force during World War II. He was particularly impressed with the tactics used by the German submariners to transit the Strait of Gibraltar. The German U-boat commanders had used the knowledge of ocean flows to pass through the strait undetected and with minimum propulsion by keeping on either side of the thermal gradient when going into or exiting the strait. They could maneuver their submarines in this fashion because they knew that the Atlantic water entered at Gibraltar as a surface flow. It then followed the north coast of Africa to Cyprus.

In this path of the Mediterranean, high evaporation rate increased the salinity of the surface water. This high salinity water then sunk to become the Mediterranean Intermediate Water and flowed westward through the Strait of Gibraltar into the Atlantic Ocean.

The conning officer reported, "The ship has completed depth excursion to one thousand feet and now is maintaining depth at two hundred feet at a ship's speed of ten knots." He continued, "There is a sharp positive thermocline located at one hundred and forty feet."

Noise rays captured in this positive water area above one hundred and forty feet would bend upwards and travel to extreme ranges, allowing possible long-distance detection of *Tigerfish* by surface ship or submarine sonar equipment.

At a deeper depth below the thermocline, the water temperature goes negative very sharply, bending the noise rays downward significantly and reducing the possibility of *Tigerfish* being detected at long distances by sonar equipment.

This was the same sound profile that Tracy had expected from his study of the water temperature conditions in this part of the Mediterranean Sea in preparation for the takeover and outbound transit of *Tigerfish*.

Tracy directed the Soviet monitor, "Have twenty pound TNT explosive charges placed into two of the torpedo tubes."

These charges were brought aboard *Tigerfish* with the transfer of the Soviet/Cuban team at Naples.

Tracy continued, "Also, load into the same two torpedo tubes some ship's debris that is identified with the ship's name—*Tigerfish*."

The orders were given to the torpedo room watch stander and the Soviet monitor stationed in the room to load the two torpedo tubes.

The explosive charges were loaded into two torpedo tubes as well as the debris. Breech doors were shut and dogged down. The torpedo tubes were now flooded and would be ready to shoot after being equalized with sea water pressure and the outer doors opened.

This status report was provided to Tracy in the control room and acknowledged by the Soviet commanding officer.

The TNT explosive charges had a ten minute time delay set on them before they would detonate. This time delay would allow *Tigerfish* to launch the charges and then move to a safe distance away from the detonation.

The detonation of the charges at a deep depth, coupled with the bogus distress signals from the *Tigerfish* underwater communications telephone, would develop a realistic condition that a United States nuclear submarine was in distress and probably sunk.

The next phase was to use ship's sonar detection equipment, periscope visual observations, and Electronic Coutermeasures (ECM) Detection Equipment to locate a United States warship.

The *Tigerfish* then would close the warship and simulate a distressed United States nuclear submarine.

Tracy directed his Soviet conning officer monitor, "Take the ship to periscope depth."

The conning officer repeated the order back verbatim to Tracy. "Ship is at periscope depth at a speed of five knots," reported the conning officer. He continued, "ECM mast is raised, searching for United States Navy electronic signals."

Conn reported, "Have a visual contact at a distance of about twenty thousand yards. Estimate the speed of the contact to be fifteen knots and closing our track. Target evaluated to be a United States destroyer."

The tracking party was directed by the Soviet captain, "Track the contact using the attack console. Establish a ship's course for *Tigerfish* to close the destroyer to a range of eight thousand yards."

The conning officer directed, "Diving Officer. Make the ship's depth one hundred fifty feet. Make ship's speed ten knots."

At this depth, the ship would be just below the thermal layer, thus minimizing the possiblility of detection by the destroyer's sonar equipment.

At eight thousand yards from the closing destroyer, the speed of *Tigerfish* was reduced and the ship's depth made shallower to just above the thermal gradient.

The two filled torpedo tubes were equalized with sea water pressure and the outer doors opened.

Tracy picked up the hand microphone for the ship's underwater

Mission Complete

telephone. He pressed the actuator button and made the announcement, "NUCLEAR SUBMARINE *USS TIGERFISH*, FLOODING CASUALTY, LOSING DEPTH CONTROL."

The message was repeated twice.

Tracy directed the firing of the two torpedo tubes.

The explosive charges and debris were launched from the two torpedo tubes. The outer doors then were closed.

Tigerfish slowly changed depth to below the thermal gradient to three hundred feet and steered course two-two-five degrees true at ten knots to clear the area.

The many questions from the U.S. destroyer's underwater telephone about "the submarine name, status, repeat transmission" reverberated through the ocean.

The noise of the explosive charges drowned out any more conversation from the destroyer.

Tigerfish proceeded out of the area on course two-two-five degrees true. The plan was to remain on this course for eighteen hours. The time was now twenty hundred on the twenty-eight of October.

At time fourteen hundred on the twenty-ninth of October, the pirated submarine changed course to two-five-five degrees true.

All the crew of *Tigerfish* had now awakened.

Most of the American sailors were in an unbelieving state of mind. Unfortunately, some of the crew doubted that the pirates really had control over their ship. Some also doubted any possible brutality would occur from the captors.

All doubts of any possible brutality were quickly erased.

During the watch change on the morning of the thirtieth of October, petty officer second class Henry, the off-going reactor operator, attempted to scram or shut down the engineering reactor plant from the secondary reactor control station outside of the maneuvering room.

If his attempt had been successful, all the control rods would have entered the reactor core and poisoned the core, thus stopping criticality and the generation of neutrons and ship's power.

The *Tigerfish* would have to go to periscope depth to take in air through the snorkel mast to operate the installed diesel engine. The diesel engine noise would make *Tigerfish* a predominate noise source into the ocean. Also, the ship at periscope depth allowed the possibility of being detected by a United States photographic satellite or surveillance aircraft.

Taking air into the ship through the snorkel mast was required to operate the diesel engine. The diesel engine in turn rotated the diesel generator. The operation of the diesel generator was necessary to provide a source of electrical power to operate the ship and allow a recovery of the reactor plant.

Henry was captured by the Soviet monitor before he was able to complete his objective.

The pirates dragged the petty officer into the crew's dinette beating him continuously with their billy clubs. One of the Russian officers narrated step by step over the 1 MC general announcing system the punishment of the American petty officer as it was administered by the Soviet guards.

The *Tigerfish* crew members throughout the ship listened in awe and disbelief at the narration of the punishment.

Each finger on both hands was broken and his hands were smashed with a sledge hammer. After Henry soberly confessed over the ship's 1 MC general announcing system that what he had attempted to do was a foolish act, the guards hung him by his neck until he was dead.

The limp body of Henry was hung in the crew's dinette for all to observe as a message that noncompliance with the pirate's orders would not be tolerated. After four days, the stench of the U.S. sailor's body became unbearable in the confines of the submarine.

Henry's body was put into a body bag, weighted down, and put into a torpedo tube.

With a few of Henry's shackled shipmates present in the torpedo room, the commanding officer of *Tigerfish* said a prayer for Petty Officer Henry as the Soviets closed the breech door of the torpedo tube.

The tube was flooded, equalized with sea water pressure, and the outer door of the torpedo tube opened.

With a slight push on the firing key by the Soviet's number two officer, the submarine shuddered slightly as the torpedo tube was discharged.

A good American submariner entered the ocean deep.

The rule of no talking by any of the U.S. crew while eating meals also was enforced religiously by the pirates.

After another week of captivity, a crew member of *Tigerfish* attempted to push the guards to the limit. As the American sailor was eating lunch, he started to ridicule one of the guards.

Three guards administered a severe punishment. Two guards held the sailor down and the other guard cut half of his tongue out of his mouth.

The guards laughed as they watched the terror in the eyes of the tortured

Mission Complete

sailor while the blood splattered out of his mouth as the tongue muscle fell to the deck.

Most of the watch section that was having lunch in the crew's dinette regurgitated what they had already eaten after seeing the awful sight of what befell their shipmate. The complete watch section having their lunch in the crew's dinette was marched out of the space and back to the berthing area and chained into their bunks.

Their remaining food was dumped into the garbage cans.

Again, another lesson in strict compliance with directives from the barbaric pirates.

Each member of the watch section slept in the same berthing compartment and would be padlocked after coming off watch. They would not be unchained until time to eat before watch time.

After about one week, the urination stench was overwhelming throughout the American sleeping compartment.

Two Cuban guards took a liking to one fair seaman. Each night the seaman was awakened. His shackles were removed and then he was dragged off screaming to the shower area by the two guards. Shortly afterwards they would drag the sobbing prisoner back to his bunk.

As the repetition of this routine continued, his crying in bed all night didn't keep his shipmates awake. After receiving this abuse for over a week, the young sailor committed suicide by suffocating himself with his pillow case.

Again, the U.S. commanding officer of *Tigerfish* led the prayer in the torpedo room for another one of his crew as the torpedo tube launched the dead seaman to his underwater burial site.

For the remainder of the transit, all the American sailors were solemn, depressed, and in a state of shock and fear.

On the first of November, the engineer officer and weapons officer were put into separate staterooms. The start of the deadly mind games commenced. Only red lights were energized in the two staterooms. Intravenous input of truth drugs into the two officers commenced. Their heads were covered to eliminate the sensations of night and day. The normal patterns of waking and sleeping and normal time to eat were deliberately disrupted.

A Soviet guard was placed in each stateroom to oversee the captives and to ensure they remained awake during the complete ordeal. Tracy assured the two officers that they would be ready to provide the information desired by the interrogators upon their arrival onboard *Tigerfish* in two days.

On the second of November, *Tigerfish* changed course to two-six-four degrees true in preparation for going to periscope depth.

At mid-afternoon, a navigation fix would be taken through the periscope on the navigation beacon light on Point Alboran. This navigation fix of the ship was necessary prior to going through the Strait of Gibralter submerged.

At periscope depth, a visual observation was taken through the periscope on three different landmarks on the island. Each line of bearing from the observation was plotted on the navigation chart.

These landmarks were accurately located and well established on the navigation chart of the area. The position where the three lines of bearing crossed on the chart was the location of the *Tigerfish* at that time.

Tracy directed the conning officer, "Steer course two-six-four degrees true at speed ten knots. Maintain depth of two hundred feet." He continued, "Take a single-ping fathometer reading every fifteen minutes."

The conning officer and the Soviet monitor acknowledged the directives.

Tracy ordered his Soviet monitor, "Ensure that the soundings received agree with the depths shown on our navigation track."

The transit from the present position through the strait and into the North Atlantic Ocean would be one hundred eighty nautical miles.

Tracy gathered with the U.S captain of *Tigerfish* and the U.S. and Soviet navigators and reviewed the track laid down for the *Tigerfish* transit to Cuba. "At twenty-four hundred tonight, our course will be changed to two-zero-zero degrees true and we will proceed southwesterly parallel to the coast of West Africa."

Tracy waited for a short time to ensure that he had the attention of the three officers.

"This will provide some coverage from the United States maritime air patrol airplanes flying surveillance patrols out of the Azores. At time zero-five-zero on the third of November, *Tigerfish* will rendevous with a Soviet trawler and we will receive onboard *Tigerfish* three people from the trawler." Tracy continued, "One of our comrades being transferred to *Tigerfish* is an expert locksmith. The other two comrades are renown psychologists."

Tracy spoke proudly, "Both of these psychologists are truly experts in their field of brain manipulation. Each has had much experience and practice developing their techniques in North Vietnam working against American prisoners. These two experts have never failed to break down captives and get all the information desired from their prisoners."

The Soviet navigator interrupted the conversation and stated, "I have

Mission Complete

verified that our scheduled time of personnel transfer from the trawler will take place when the United States satellite will be out of orbit to detect us and the trawler."

Tracy discussed the timing with the conning officer and the Soviet monitor. "Sonar must be alert to pick up a chirping noise source from the trawler beginning at time zero four-thirty. Also, we will be at periscope depth at zero four-thirty. The trawler will transmit a radio signal one minute on and four minutes off every five minutes starting at zero four-thirty."

Tom Morello sat on a bench in the corner of the control room listening to the conversations and directives. The captain of the *Tigerfish* was helpless to do anything to help his crew or ship. He thought that maybe the United States would send a nuclear attack submarine to resolve the issue. Tom's real prayer was that the skipper of the dispatched American submarine would be Bruce Stewart. Then he would know the mission of destroying the *Tigerfish* would be accomplished.

He then put his mind to the task of thinking what could they do aboard *Tigerfish* to aid a U.S. nuclear submarine attack on themselves. From listening to the discussions between the Soviets submariners on board, Tom understood that the major event was to take place sometime before midnight Christmas Eve. Also, that a message would be received by *Tigerfish*. Therefore, the *Tigerfish* would have to be at periscope depth, probably at twenty-two or twenty-three hundred, to be able to communicate.

Tom's first thought was to cause a sound short in the submarine that would put out a distinctive sound spoke into the water. An opposing submarine would definitely be able to pick up the sound short noise spoke with its sonar at a long distance.

This bearing from the sound short would be enough information for the searching submarine to develop a torpedo shooting solution to the target submarine.

Tom knew that the best way to cause a sound short was to place a wrench between machinery piping in the *Tigerfish* engine room bilge area and the submarine hull. Tom needed to make sure that his selected crew members in *Tigerfish* understood what was to happen.

The *Tigerfish* sonar operators would have to de-energize the ship's self noise monitors prior to execution of the plan. This would prevent the self noise monitors in the sonar room from lighting up, alarming and alerting the Soviet submarine officer stationed in the sonar room as a monitor that the ship was putting out a noise source.

The sonar operators on watch needed to be especially alert during this crucial time frame before Christmas to pick up the U.S. nuclear submarine in the attack phase. Then they had to reduce the volume level of the sonar equipment audible pick-up signals in the sonar room.

The Soviet officer monitors were not that proficient with the advanced *Tigerfish* sonar equipment to be able to distinguish a sonar signal put out by a quiet submarine like *Jackfish* from the many traces displayed on the computer-like sonar equipment.

All this planning was again based on Tom's logic that a U.S. nuclear submarine would be searching out the ocean to sink the *Tigerfish*.

Tom would have his team alerted before the *Tigerfish* departed Cuba en route to the Axehandle missile launching station.

Tracy then discussed the future tactical plan of the *Tigerfish* with the assembled officers in the control room.

"The trawler will be at the rendezvous location sending out signals in the water and transmitting radio signals. The Soviet ship will patrol on a circle five hundred yards from the rendezvous point."

Tracy directed his number two officer, "Have the snatch blocks and pulley arrangements assembled in the control room."

This equipment had been brought aboard *Tigerfish* when the pirates boarded the ship off Naples.

At zero four-thirty, sonar reported, "Conn-sonar, have a high pitch noise on bearing two-zero-zero degrees true."

"Sonar-conn, that noise is probably from the Soviet trawler we are to rendevous with for the personnel transfer."

Tracy Smith directed the conning officer, "Take the ship to periscope depth."

The conning officer responded with a verbatim repeat back of Tracy's directive.

Conn reported, "At periscope depth, have visual contact on a surface ship. Initial classification of the contact was a Soviet trawler."

Tracy directed the conning officer, "Surface the ship and proceed towards the trawler."

"SURFACE.SURFACE.SURFACE" was announced over the ship's 1MC general announcing system.

The conning officer sounded three blasts of the ship's diving klaxon in unison with the verbal announcement.

Air was released into the main ballast tanks, an up angle was put on the

Mission Complete

ship, and the sleek American submarine squirmed out of the deep onto the ocean surface.

The conning officer scrambled up the stainless steel vertical ladder to the bridge cockpit area followed closely behind by Tracy.

The sky was clear with many stars visible. The submarine experienced a slight swell and soothing roll. A good night for a personnel transfer.

"Control room-officer of the deck. Send a flashing light to the bridge and the quartermaster qualified to send and receive Morse code with the flashing light."

"Yes sir, both are on the way to the bridge."

The quartermaster followed Tracy's directives and was able to establish Morse code communications with the trawler using the flashing light.

The trawler was directed to make speed five knots on course two-six-zero degrees true and to prepare to send the lightweight heaving line to *Tigerfish*.

Tracy directed the quartermaster to send the following message to the trawler, "When *Tigerfish* and the trawler are on parallel course at minimum distance apart, shoot the heaving line across the bridge area of the submarine."

The directive from *Tigerfish* was acknowledged by the trawler.

Minor course changes were made by Tracy to put both ships on the optimum course with minimum rolling in the sea way.

The pulley arrangement had been rigged on the top of *Tigerfish*'s sail area and the submarine was ready to receive the heaving line from the trawler.

The seaman on the trawler deck took good aim with the heaving line rifle and the heaving line passed directly over the cockpit area of the submarine sail area.

The *Tigerfish* lookout grabbed the line out of the sky as he would the football for the winning touchdown in the Super Bowl Football Classic.

The lightweight heaving line was pulled through the pulley arrangement above the sail area of the submarine until the one inch personnel transfer line was hauled onboard *Tigerfish*. This line was passed through the pulley and retrieved back onto the deck of the trawler.

The seaman on the trawler reported, "Ready to transfer."

This was responded to by Tracy in the *Tigerfish* bridge cockpit, "Ready to receive."

Three people were seen on the deck of the trawler dressed in orange-colored inflatable cocoon- type suits. The complete suit was inflatable and had enough padding throughout to prevent injury should the person being transferred get hurled against the side of the submarine. The transferees were fully encapsulated in the protective suits. They also wore reinforced helmets.

All three people were transferred without incident.

The three comrades were directed down the access ladder into the control room. The new arrivals were met by the number two Soviet submariner and taken to the wardroom. Hot coffee and breakfast were waiting for the new arrivals in the wardroom.

Tracy then had the message sent for the captain of the trawler, "Please transfer three cases of your best vodka. Thank you."

Again, the transfer was carried out without any problems.

The complete transfer was accomplished within thirty minutes and within the time frame when the vessels were invisible to the United States surveillance satellite.

The pulley and shackle arrangements were removed from the *Tigerfish* cockpit area and lowered into the submarine.

The officer of the deck directed over the announcing system, "Clear the bridge. DIVE.DIVE."

In unison with this verbal order, two blasts of the diving alarm klaxon were heard throughout the ship.

Tracy directed the *Tigerfish* conning officer and the Soviet monitor, "Make ship's depth two hundred feet and speed ten knots. Steer ship's course two-six-zero degrees true."

Both officers acknowledged the orders verbatim as given.

Tracy, Tom Morello, the *Tigerfish* navigator, and Tracy's navigator then further examined the navigation track laid out for *Tigerfish* en route to Cuba.

Tracy moved his finger across the navigation chart as he explained his plans.

The Soviet continued, "We will continue on our present course to the Bahamas Islands. On course two-three-five degrees true the ship will pass through the Crooked Island Passage on thirteen November, then course one-seven-two degrees true to the port of Baracoa, Cuba."

Tracy stoped talking so as to get the attention of all participants.

He then continued, "We will take station five miles off the entrance to the port and rendezvous with a large container ship scheduled for zero five hundred on the fourteenth of November. This ship is just the silhouette of a large container ship and will be the concealed home for *Tigerfish* and her crew during our stay in Cuba. We will enter the ship facade after dark on the fourteenth of November. Four sea-going tug boats, two on either side of the facade, then will lead us into the port."

Mission Complete

Tracy again stated, "The average speed or speed of advance of *Tigerfish* for the complete trip will be ten knots. Also, the depth will be limited to two hundred feet unless we need to evade threat ships. This depth limitation is necessary to avoid being detected by the United States SOSUS installations."

The SOSUS installations were based on a system of sound spectrum analysis called LOFAR.

Every ship had an orchestration of sounds. It started first of all from the propellers and had a very low frequency. Then there was propeller cavitation, then machinery noise, then flow noise over the hull and through the piping.

SOSUS was originally developed against the non-nuclear diesel electric submarine snorkeling.

When the discussion was completed, Tracy moved closer to Tom and whispered to him, "Captain, please have your men provide all the information that my comrades will desire. As I said earlier, these men are experts in their field and will do whatever is necessary to complete their assignment."

Tracy stated with a grin on his face, "Thank you, Captain, for your cooperation."

The shackled Tom Morello, under Soviet guard, was escorted back to his holding stateroom with the other orange coverall wearers.

Tracy went to the wardroom to have breakfast and meet the three new arrivals.

A brief status report of the current situation with *Tigerfish* was provided to the three new Soviets by Tracy. Tracy gave the Soviet safe cracker a layout of the *Tigerfish* that showed all the safes aboard the ship.

Tracy told him, "I want your first priority to be getting the contents out of the classified safes in the torpedo room."

The Soviet weapons officer added, "Particularly the classified operation and maintenance technical manuals for both the nuclear torpedoes and the Axehandle missiles. The weapons officer continued, "These manuals are needed on a high priority basis. We need to become extremely proficient on all facets of the weapons including torpedo tube pre-load prerequisites, loading the missiles into the torpedo tubes, and the fire control panel alignment for launching the weapons. Also, we need to get all the details to prepare us to safely offload a missile and nuclear torpedo when we get to Cuba."

These two weapons would be transferred to a Soviet cruiser while in the Cuban port for further transfer to the Soviet Union.

The weapons officer added, "After breakfast, I will be your escort to the classified safe locations."

The safe cracker and Soviet weapons officer departed the wardroom en route to the torpedo room.

Tracy continued his briefing on the status of the key *Tigerfish* officers to be interrogated and his initial plan for obtaining the required information.

After some exchanges about the plan for extracting information, all the participants agreed to the course of action.

The interrogators estimated that it would take about two days to retrieve all the information needed after the American officer was "prepared" for interrogation. The preparation, or mind manipulation period, would last about two days.

Both Soviet interrogators would interrogate each captive officer. Sometimes the interrogation would be one-on-one and sometimes two-on-one depending on the mental and physical condition of the officer and also the credibility of the responses received from the interrogated officer.

As Tracy led the two interrogators to the staterooms of the first two "prepared" officers he commented, "Gentlemen. I would rather have you carry out your mission without applying any torture or punishment. However, the mission must be a success at any cost."

Tracy introduced the first interrogator to the operations officer and then the second interrogator to the weapons officer.

"Please keep me informed of the status of obtaining the required information. We will test the data received from the first two questioned officers to ensure that the information is correct and the double door safes are opened before going to the next set of officers for interrogation."

Tracy directed his number two officer, "Put the executive officer into a separate stateroom and prepare him for the interrogators."

As before with the engineer officer and weapons officer, the deadly mind games commenced.

Only the red lights were energized in his stateroom. Intravenous input of truth drugs into the officer commenced. His head was covered to eliminate his perceptions of night and day. The normal pattern of waking and sleeping and normal eating time would be deliberately disrupted.

A Soviet guard was placed in his stateroom to oversee the captive and to ensure that the executive officer remained awake during the complete ordeal.

Tracy was quite pleased with his team's progress to date in completing the mission. He now had visions of becoming a Soviet hero. Also, he had sorrow that his father was not alive to nurture the honor for the family.

At dinner, Tracy again served a glass of vodka to each attendee.

Mission Complete

"Gentlemen. Please give me the status of your progress after your evaluation of the subjects."

"Yes sir, Captain," responded the safe cracker. "Making good progress at this time. Anticipate that I will be able to enter the high-armor explosive-proof classified safes in the torpedo room by early tomorrow."

"Well done. Please keep to your schedule," replied Tracy. Tracy continued, "And the status of the interrogation schedule?"

The older of the two interrogators answered the captain's question. "Anticipate that we will be able to maintain the schedule that we discussed earlier. Essentially, we are working with a two day 'mind preparation' time for each officer. This will be followed by two complete days of intense interrogation."

The older interrogator looked across the table at the second interrogator and questioned, "Do you agree with the estimate?"

He nodded to the affirmative and added, "If all goes as planned, we will have the inner and outer door combinations to the first safe from the engineer officer and weapons officer by close of business on the fifth of November."

Tracy responded with the grin of a pussy cat. "Thank you very much. Please keep me informed of your status."

The tension was growing between the Soviet/Cuban sailors and the crew of *Tigerfish*.

On the morning of the fifth of November, one of the ship's cooks was carrying an armful of food to prepare for lunch as he passed a Cuban guard in the ship's galley.

The ship's cook accidentally bumped into the guard.

The Cuban guard immediately started to beat the cook unmercifully in the back and head with his billy club. The cook continued to be beaten by the guard as he fell to the galley deck.

In a desperate act to protect himself, the cook was able to gain control of a very heavy skillet. He caught the guard off balance and knocked him down as he started to smash at the guard's head, face, and shoulders.

By the time the two other Cuban guards were able to separate the two combatants, the guard was dead. The two guards were able to wrestle the skillet out of the cook's grip.

Again, the punishment as administered by the guards was narrated by the lead Soviet guard to the complete crew over the 1 MC general announcing system.

The two Cuban guards held the cook on his hands and knees. A third guard slit his throat from ear to ear. The cook immediately died.

To make a more pointed expression for the requirement for strict compliance, the guards also assassinated the young *Tigerfish* supply officer.

The *Tigerfish* supply officer was the dead cook's immediate supervisor.

The captors indicated that the American officers would be held responsible for the actions of their subordinates.

The shackled U.S. commanding officer of *Tigerfish* again was called to say a prayer at the torpedo tubes holding his two shipmates. Tubes were flooded, equalized with sea water pressure, and discharged. Two more U.S. sailors took their final resting place at the bottom of the sea.

Tom's head was bent over, tears flowed from his eyes and he was dumbfounded at knowing he could do nothing to change the current climate in *Tigerfish*.

The few shipmates of the cook allowed to attend the burial, in leg and arm irons, observed and said a prayer. They were solemn, in total disbelief, and also had tears flowing down their checks.

The body of the dead Cuban guard was discharged to sea from the torpedo tube without any ceremony or respect by his shipmates.

/9/ TECHNOLOGY TRANSFER

Mid-morning the fifth of November, the safe cracker and the Soviet weapons officer reported to Tracy. "We have the classified safes in the torpedo room open. Currently we are examining the contents of the safes."

Tracy acknowledged the report. "Weps. Let me know if we have all the documents and manuals in the safes for us to do our mission."

"Yes sir, Captain," replied the young Soviet weapons officer.

The safe cracker continued throughout the ship opening safes holding classified and sensitive information.

Tracy entered the reddened stateroom where the interrogator was questioning the American engineer officer. He nodded at the interrogator as an acknowledgment.

The engineer officer still had his head covered. His speech was groggy and he appeared incoherent at times.

The "thumbs up" signal by the interrogator was interpreted by Tracy to mean that all was proceeding well and on schedule. Tracy got the same response from the interrogator working on the *Tigerfish* weapons officer.

The Soviet weapons officer proceeded to the torpedo room.

He directed his two assistants, "Examine all the manuals and documents in the classified safes to ensure we get all the pertinent classified information. After your examination is complete, start a thorough study of the Operation and Technical Manuals for the Axehandle missile and nuclear torpedoes. Ensure we become proficient first with the prerequisites for tube loading the missiles and then the post loading tests and surveillance requirements."

The Soviet weapons officer continued, "I want to get the Axehandle missiles loaded into the torpedo tubes as soon as practicable." He continued,

"The current *Tigerfish* torpedo tube loading plan has two Axehandle missiles, one nuclear torpedo, and five conventional non-nuclear warhead torpedoes loaded in the eight torpedo tubes available in this *Jackfish* class of nuclear submarine. This appears to be a standard tube loading arrangement for this class nuclear submarine en route to its home port from an extended deployment."

After a slight pause to ensure that his assistants fully comprehended his directives, the Soviet weapons officer provided more direction. "Continue reading the manuals to prepare for our tube loading the weapons. I will put together a tube loading plan for the captain's approval."

At evening meal in the wardroom, Tracy continued to be joyful. Vodka was again served with a toast given to the success of the mission. Tracy asked his new comrades, "Please provide me the latest status of your endeavors."

The Soviet weapons officer started the briefing. "As you already know, we have the classified safes opened in the torpedo room. All the contents are being examined to locate anything valuable to our cause. My two assistants are becoming proficient with all facets of the Axehandle missile and the nuclear torpedoes. I will provide you a recommended weapons tube loading plan tonight. I recommend that we start tube loading the missiles as soon as possible."

"Concur with your recommendations, weps. Well done," replied Tracy with a large smile.

The safe cracker followed. "I am following the schedule of classified safes to be opened as laid out by your number two officer. See no difficulties yet."

"Thank you. Keep me informed of any problems in your endeavors," responded the newly self- appointed *Tigerfish* captain.

The lead interrogator reported, "We are proceeding on schedule. Expect to have all the information needed from the weapons officer later this evening." He continued, "The engineer officer is showing more grit than we have seen in our past interrogations. However, we will complete his interrogating before breakfast tomorrow morning. As soon as we finish with the first officer and confirm that the information is correct, we will start interrogating the executive officer. His two-day 'mind preparation' period will be completed early afternoon the sixth of November. As per schedule, we will start the 'mind preparation' phase with the operations officer starting early tomorrow afternoon on the sixth of November."

Tracy again showed outwardly his pleasure with the progress being

Mission Complete

shown by his new team members. "Again, thank you, comrades, for your proficient work ethic and results." The Soviet commanding officer was so elated with his progress to date that he poured himself another glass of vodka.

"Good evening, Captain."

"'Good evening, Russell. Have a glass of vodka and relax somewhat." Tracy continued, "Haven't seen much of you since the ownership of the *Tigerfish* changed hands over to the good guys."

Both officers chuckled somewhat like new proud parents with bragging rights.

Russell sat erect in his chair as he sipped his vodka and commented, "Have been spending most of my time with Lynn in the engineering spaces. Want to ensure no problems are encountered. The *Tigerfish* engineers are quite proficient and take good care of their engineering plant."

The Soviet weapons officer and his two assistant weapons officers spent much of the night studying the operational and technical manuals for the Axehandle nuclear missile and the nuclear torpedo. They now had a recommended loading plan to present to Tracy for his approval.

The Soviet weapons officer discussed the plan with his assistants along with the rationale for the weapons selection. "Want to have tube loaded five Axehandle missiles. We will need to launch four missiles if launching missiles is necessary to carry out our mission. However, I want one spare missile ready to launch to account for any contingencies. The other three tubes will contain conventional non-nuclear torpedoes. This will give us the fire power to complete our mission and be able to fight against another vessel, should that be necessary."

His assistants concurred with the plan. Now to present the plan to the captain, get his approval, and then start to load the nuclear missiles.

"Loading the missiles will be a very time consuming and exacting process." The Soviet weapons officer continued, "The torpedo room has to be rearranged to allow the unloading and reloading process to take place."

Tracy's number two officer reported, "Captain, the interrogators have gotten the safe combinations from the engineer officer and the weapons officer. The combinations to both the inner and outer doors of the safe have been tested satisfactorily. We now have in our possession the first fire control panel security key. The interrogators worked so expertly that neither of the two officers remember anything about their interrogations and what was revealed." He continued, "The two officers have been returned to the stateroom with the other orange-suited officers.

"The interrogators have started the 'mind preparation' process with the operations officer. Also, we have started interrogating the executive officer for the combination to the outer door of the second safe."

Tracy almost laughed with contentment on hearing the report. "Well done. We are on or ahead of schedule."

Tracy took control of the first fire control panel security key. He changed the safe combination for the safe in the *Tigerfish* commanding officer's stateroom and then stored the precious key in this safe.

The Soviet weapons officer and his team examined the torpedo handling, loading, and storage schemes in the torpedo room. They would need this knowledge to prepare for the movement of weapons to meet the desired weapons loading plan.

The room had eight torpedo tubes in two vertical columns of four tubes each. There were two horizontal banks of weapons skids. Each bank had four horizontal levels of holding skids and had storage for three weapons on each level. Overall, there was a total storage capacity for twelve weapons for each bank.

Each bank had a hydraulic operator that allowed the complete bank to move up one level and down one level. This gave added flexibility for the movement of weapons throughout the torpedo room.

The total storage capacity for this class of submarine was eight weapons tube loaded and space for twenty-four weapons in the torpedo room. Four of the holding skids were kept empty to allow for relocating weapons in the room and tube loading purposes.

Hydraulic hoists and locking mechanisms were used to move the weapons. Locking devices attached to the weapons prevented them from rolling out of the weapons skid when the weapon was being moved for loading into the torpedo tubes.

The Soviet weapons officer knew that to end with the tube loading scheme he needed would take many weapons movements in the torpedo room and would be time consuming. In addition, he had to rely on the cooperation and work performance of the *Tigerfish* sailor weapons handlers. Hopefully, all would go well without the need for another "compliance" lesson.

The senior interrogator and Tracy's number two officer reported to Tracy. "We have gotten the combination to the outer door for safe number two. The results are correct and the outer door has been opened."

As before, Tracy was elated with the report. "Right on schedule. Well done."

Mission Complete

"We are going to start the commanding officer with 'mind preparation' this afternoon. We want to complete the interrogation of the operations officer first."

Tracy acknowledged to the affirmative this report from his number two officer.

The Soviet weapons officer sat down with Tracy in the wardroom. They both started to drink black coffee from large mugs with the *Tigerfish* ship's emblem on them.

After a thorough brief on the weapons loading plan, Tracy answered, "Permission granted to implement your loading plan. It is well thought out as usual."

Tracy and his weapons officer departed the wardroom en route to the torpedo room. Tracy wanted a first-hand look at the storage configuration and to appreciate the work necessary to obtain their desired weapons loading scheme.

"You are going to have a tough task achieving the final loading configuration." Tracy continued as he departed the torpedo room, "Let me know if you have any problems."

The next step before starting to work with the weapons this afternoon was to talk with the *Tigerfish* lead torpedo man. He wanted to ensure that he had the support of this petty officer before starting the weapons operation. If this were not the case, additional measures would be necessary.

In the afternoon of the ninth of November, the number two Soviet officer smiled from ear to ear and reported to Tracy, "We have the combination to the inner door to safe number two. Both doors now are open and we have access to the contents of the safe. Here is the second security key for the fire control panel."

Tracy took the security key and gave his number two officer a big hug. "Well done, comrade!"

The second security key was placed into the same safe in the commanding officer's stateroom as was the first security key.

Tracy spoke to his number two officer, "The prerequisites of the mission are close to being achieved by our well trained team."

Tracy's number two officer reported to Tracy, "We only need to complete interrogation of the *Tigerfish* commanding officer and the communications officer. Both of these officers will complete their 'mind preparation' tomorrow afternoon, the tenth of November. We should have results by the close of business on the twelfth of November."

The Soviet weapons officer completed his motivation speech to the *Tigerfish* lead weapons handler.

The American sailor knew without a doubt that his team's cooperation was a must. Success in achieving the requirements of the approved loading plan must be accomplished. The *Tigerfish* sailor also understood the serious consequences of non compliance.

The weapons handling team would assemble in the torpedo room after lunch today. The *Tigerfish* weapons officer also would participate in a supervisory role.

The Soviet weapons officer and his two assistants met with the *Tigerfish* weapons officer and his lead weapons handler in the torpedo room to discuss the game plan for moving weapons It was emphasized by the Soviet officer that they would work together to have a smooth operation.

The two *Tigerfish* crew members agreed to cooperate with the Soviets to achieve a safe and satisfactory operation.

The basic scenario was to move three conventional non-nuclear torpedoes from the torpedo tubes and replace them with Axehandle missiles.

The *Tigerfish* weapons officer commented, "This seems like an easy evolution; however, it will be extremely difficult and time consuming. We will have many individual weapons to move to get into the proper weapon configuration according to our plan. We must ensure the correct weapon is lined up with the designated torpedo tube to accept the weapon. This will be like a complicated game of chess to line up the empty skids to receive and then have an opening to transfer the weapon."

The American officer continued, "Recommend that we lay out all the moves on the drawing board. When satisfied we have a satisfactory solution, then start the operation."

The Soviet weapons officer agreed with the recommendation. "Let's start now with the drawing board. I want to commence the weapons movements as soon as possible."

The officers put their heads together and fully cooperated with the task of developing the game plan for moving the weapons.

The *Tigerfish* weapons handlers were assembled in the torpedo room. The weapons officer talked with them about the task at hand. "We must move the weapons and relocate them to the desired positions as soon as possible; however, the work must be done safely. The *Tigerfish* lead weapons handler is in charge of the movements."

By mid-afternoon, the weapons started to be moved.

Mission Complete

Two Axehandle missiles were moved into the torpedo tubes and the third missile was relocated in position to be tube loaded first thing the next morning. The weapons leaders agreed that the positioning work in the torpedo room would be finished for the evening. The task would be completed tomorrow morning the twelfth of November.

After breakfast on the twelfth of November, the number two Soviet officer reported to Tracy, "Good progress is being accomplished with the interrogation of the *Tigerfish* captain and communications officer. Anticipate that all interrogations will be completed by mid-afternoon."

The number two continued, "I have directed the conning officer to clear baffles every two hours as you directed. Also, a fathometer sounding is being taken every hour. The soundings compare favorable with our navigation track."

The weapons team assembled in the torpedo room after breakfast ready to complete the task of loading the third Axehandle missile into the torpedo tube.

Before lunch, the weapons loading task was completed.

The *Tigerfish* weapons movement lead petty officer opened the *Axehandle Missile Operations Manual* to the section titled "tube checkout."

He discussed the manual with his weapons officer and the Soviet weapons leaders. "We don't need the reload team anymore." He paused, then continued, "The pre-firing checks with each missile need to be completed at this time. This encompasses the requirement to complete the electrical checkout of each missile, the hydraulic check of the control features of the missiles, and the firing continuity check from the missile through the fire control panel."

The Soviet weapons officer questioned the time duration to complete the pre-firing tests remaining for each missile.

The *Tigerfish* sailor responded, "Estimate that it will take about two hours to complete the remaining checkouts for each missile. We should be finished by late this evening."

Most of the weapons handling party were dismissed from the torpedo room. Four of the *Tigerfish* torpedo men remained. The remaining four were responsible for the required final readiness inspections of the missiles.

With detailed checkoff sheets in their hands and wearing telephone headsets, the men started the tedious and exacting process of completing the post-load missile checks.

In the late afternoon, the lead interrogator and the Soviet number two officer reported to Tracy, "Captain, the interrogation process is complete. We have the belly band combinations for the nuclear torpedoes from the captain. The communications officer provided us the combinations and information needed to encrypt and decrypt all classified messages."

The Soviet number two officer continued his report. "Both of these officers have been returned to the berthing area with the other officers wearing orange coveralls. Our interrogators did such a good job that none of these officers remember anything about the interrogation, what was discussed, and what was disclosed to the interrogators."

Tracy smiled and gave his number two officer a positive nod of appreciation.

Dick Varley, under escort, met with the lead electronics technician. He verified that the SINS equipment was functioning correctly and that the navigation track of *Tigerfish* was accurate.

Tomorrow morning the submarine would pass through the shallow waters of Crooked Island Passage. Varley wanted to ensure the submarine was located as shown on the navigation chart.

After evening meal, Tracy met with his number two officer in the wardroom.

Tracy questioned his assistant, "How many of the *Tigerfish* crew should be off loaded from the ship when we depart Cuba on the fifteenth of December?"

"We don't need the complete crew to operate the ship or to help us complete our mission. Think about the number of *Tigerfish* sailors we will leave behind when we get underway."

"I want you to discuss the subject with Tom and his executive officer and get their recommendation as to how many enlisted and the specific ratings of the sailors needed to remain on board to operate the submarine." The captain continued, "Ensure that they both are aware that one Axehandle missile technician and one sailor expert with the nuclear torpedoes will be transferred to the Soviet cruiser prior to our geting underway. Let Tom and Varley think that we will return to Cuba after our mission to pick up the sailors off loaded from *Tigerfish* prior to getting underway. We will discuss the topic again in two days. Thank you."

At twenty-two hundred on the twelfth of November, the Soviet weapons officer reported to Tracy, "We have completed all weapons movements. All post-load and pre-launch checks on the Axehandle missiles have been completed. All tests are satisfactory."

Mission Complete

"Well done, weps. Thank you for your effort," Tracy responded with a pleasing smile.

At zero eight hundred on the thirteenth of November, Tracy and the shackled Tom Morello entered the control room.

"Take three soundings with the fathometer. Compare the depths received from the soundings with the depth shown at our current position on the navigation chart," ordered Tracy.

The conning officer responded, "All soundings agree with the depths shown on our navigation track."

The Soviet captain ordered, "Steer new course two-three-five degrees true to pass through the Crooked Island Passage. Take the ship to periscope depth for a visual observation." Tracy continued, "I just want a comfort observation to ensure the track is clear and out future navigation track is not fouled."

The conning officer reported, "At periscope depth. No visual contacts."

"Very well. Make your depth one hundred and fifty feet," answered Tracy. "Start taking sounding every thirty minutes. Verify the depths received with the fathometer agree with our laid out navigation track." Tracy continued, "Stay on this course until midnight."

"At twenty-four hundred, change course to one-seven-two degrees true to head towards the entrance of Baracoa Harbor."

The *Tigerfish* conning officer and the Soviet monitor both responded, "Yes sir, Captain."

Tracy then stated smugly, "We will rendezvous with a mock container ship five miles from the entrance to the harbor."

At dinner, the conversation was very light and casual. Tracy was beaming more than usual since all his milestones had been met. *Tigerfish* was ready to carry out the mission.

Tracy again served glasses of vodka to the members of the wardroom. A toast for continued success was made by the captain and joined in by all his subordinates at the table.

The Soviet weapons officer started the discussions about business. "Captain, request permission to rig the torpedo room in preparation for off loading the Axehandle missile, a nuclear torpedo and a convential non nuclear torpedo."

"Permission granted. Be sure to work with caution, weps," replied the Soviet captain. "We can not afford any accidents this late in the game since we have come this far on top."

Tracy was sitting in the captain's stateroom when his sound-powered telephone rang.

"Captain-conning officer. It is now midnight. Request permission to change course to one-seven- two degrees true and proceed towards Baracoa Harbor."

"Permission granted. We should rendezvous with the container ship five miles off the harbor at zero six hundred. The container ship will contact you by radio." The captain continued, "Please wake me up at zero five-thirty. Set the maneuvering watch also at zero five-thirty. Good night."

"Yes sir, Captain."

The Soviet and the U.S. weapon officers supervised the preparations for off loading the weapons from the *Tigerfish*. These weapons would be off loaded to a Soviet cruiser that would moor outboard the container ship in the harbor.

This preparation process to ready the weapons for off loading was slow and deliberate. Developing a fault in the movement equipment or a mistake in the task could be costly to the mission.

With the Axehandle nuclear missile in the hoist and raised to the ready to off load position, the team stopped the operation. They would continue with the other two weapons after off loading the missile.

"Captain-conn. It is now zero five-thirty and time for your wakeup call as ordered. The water is starting to shoal up. Depth is now three hundred feet."

"Very well. Take the ship to periscope depth," responded Tracy. He continued, "Station the maneuvering watch."

"STATION THE MANEUVERING WATCH" echoed throughout the ship over the 1MC general announcing system.

The conning officer maneuvered the *Tigerfish* up to periscope depth.

After careful scanning through three hundred and sixty degrees with the ship's periscope, the conning officer reported no visual contacts.

"Ballast control panel-conn. Raise the ECM mast and have the operator search for any electronic signals. Pay particular attention for signals from a Soviet commercial shipboard radar."

"Sonar-conn. Be alert for a Soviet commercial surface ship on approximate bearing of one-seven- two degrees true estimated range fifteen thousand yards."

"Radio-conn. Be alert for a radio transmission to us from the Soviet commercial ship."

The Soviet captain entered the control room, raised number two periscope, and stared into the periscope eye piece as he made a three hundred and sixty degree sweep.

Mission Complete

"Captain-conn. The maneuvering watch is stationed throughout the ship, sir."

"Very well, conn."

Sonar, radio room, and the ECM Operator reported almost in unison that they had received a signal from the container ship on a bearing dead ahead of the submarine.

"Captain-conn. Have a visual contact of a large container ship on a bearing of one-seven-two at a range about five thousand yards."

"Very well. Slow ship's speed to five knots." Tracy continued, "The container ship is propelled by four sea-going tug boats, one on each quarter of the ship. They will make three knots speed. When we direct, the container ship will float open its stern door allowing access for *Tigerfish* to enter the shell of the ship. We will make speed five knots and maneuver into the bowels of the container ship. Once inside, we will match the container ship's speed and surface *Tigerfish*. Our topside sailors then will moor us firmly to the container ship."

After a pause, Tracy continued, "We will remain inside the container ship for our duration in Cuba. A Soviet cruiser will enter the harbor at zero ten hundred this morning and moor outboard of the container ship. *Tigerfish* will receive potable water, top off food, shore power electrical support, and any other repair support needed from the cruiser. We will transfer an Axehandle missile, one nuclear torpedo, one conventional non-nuclear torpedo and any other equipment, documents, technical and operation manuals, and information of our interest to the cruiser for transporting back to the Soviet Union. The admiral in charge of the Murmansk Cruiser Squadron is embarked onboard our support cruiser."

Tigerfish moved into the container ship slowly taking the correct position for surfacing.

"SURFACE.SURFACE.SURFACE" echoed throughout the ship. The upward movement of the submarine was felt as the multi-ton *Tigerfish* scratched its way out of the deep.

All deck hatches opened allowing many sailors to exit the submarine. Deck cleats were rotated out of the currently faired position within the hull. Mooring lines were received from the container ship.

"Maneuvering-conn. All stop. Spin engines as needed. We are now under the control of the container ship."

The container ship moved into the Cuban harbor uneventfully by skillful use of the four sea-going tug boats and moored starboard side to the pier. All mooring lines from the pier were attached to the container ship and without much difficulty the vessel was moored snugly against the pier. A personnel brow was put over to the pier from the moored container ship.

Immediately many guards armed with automatic weapons crossed over the brow from the container ship to the pier and set up an armed personnel perimeter fence on the pier.

About two hours after the *Tigerfish* moored, a large, sleek, and well-preserved Soviet cruiser made up mooring lines to the port side of the container ship. Access brows for personnel movement between the two ships were installed. Brows were installed for movement of material between the ships. All the personnel brows and access walkways between the ships of the nest were covered. The coverings prevented American satellite and airplane reconnaissance overflight photographs from detailing the activity taking place in the complex.

Shore power cables were hooked up to the *Tigerfish* from the cruiser. These cables provided the electrical power to support the needs of the submarine while in a reactor shutdown condition. The electrical system for the Soviet cruiser operated with a frequency of fifty hertz. This was the same frequency used throughout Russia and in most other countries other than the United States.

The *Tigerfish* electrical system was based on a system with sixty hertz frequency. To make both systems compatible, the Soviets had installed a frequency transformer in the shore power system that changed the shore power frequency provided to the *Tigerfish* to sixty hertz.

Tigerfish shut down both the reactor plants and used the shore power from the Soviet cruiser for electrical requirements.

"ADMIRAL ARRIVING" was heard over the 1MC general announcing system as the Soviet admiral crossed the brow from the cruiser and landed on the deck of *Tigerfish*.

Much congratulations and praises were handed out to Tracy and his officers by the admiral and his chief of staff. Vodka was provided to all with a toast by the admiral on the success of the mission.

Tracy and the admiral went into Tracy's stateroom and the admiral was provided all the details of the success. The Soviet captain provided the scenario of the movement of *Tigerfish* after departure from Cuba.

"Excuse me, admiral and captain. Request permission to start transferring the Axehandle nuclear missile and the other weapons to the cruiser," the Soviet weapons officer said.

Mission Complete

Tracy introduced his weapons officer to the admiral and provided much praise for the young officer's professionalism and overall skills.

"Permission granted, weps. Again, ensure we follow the approved weapons movement check-off list for the transfers. Please inform number two before you commence the operations."

The Soviet cruiser put a liberty launch into the water. There were four men armed with automatic weapons in the launch. The launch established a patrolling pattern around the nest of ships. A search light was mounted in the launch for night surveillance.

Many Soviet civilian engineers came aboard *Tigerfish* from the cruiser armed with cameras, diagrams, and measuring devices. Their task was to gain as much information as possible to give the Soviet ship designers, builders, and engineers in the Soviet Union a good start on developing a "Soviet *Tigerfish*."

Large duplicating machines were installed temporarily in the cruiser just for this support mission.

The engineers would use these machines for the purpose of mass duplicating all technical and operation manuals, documents, prints, and anything else of importance.

The weapons handling team completed the transfer of the Axehandle missile shortly after dinner. Being on schedule, they secured the transfer for the night. The other weapons would be transferred tomorrow morning.

Before getting underway, one sailor from the *Tigerfish* expert with the Axehandle missile and one thoroughly knowledgeable with the nuclear torpedo would be transferred to the Soviet cruiser to accompany the weapons back to Russia.

After three days into the weapons, equipment, and information transfer, the Soviet captain evaluated that his team was ahead of schedule.

To relieve the routine and resultant boredom from becoming a morale problem, Tracy had set up a covered space on the pier to house a temporary bar facility. Beer, bar games, and snacks were provided. The bar opened in the late afternoon and remained open until midnight to provide relaxation for the Soviet sailors.

After the first week in port, Tracy established a covered area off the bow of the container ship for relaxation for his officers. Bar facilities and space for lounging and dancing were provided. Local area ladies were brought into the facility each night.

Tracy and the admiral would go into the local town for dinner and drinks each night.

Tracy was not his jovial self at breakfast this morning. It was obvious that he and the admiral had many vodka toasts last night while telling each other sea stories and war adventures.

The Soviet weapons officer reported to Tracy, "All weapons have been transferred to the Soviet cruiser. The *Tigerfish* torpedo room is being cleaned and stowed for sea." He continued, "Routine preventative checks will have to be conducted on all the *Tigerfish* weapons before the submarine goes out to sea. The checks are being scheduled so that plenty of time is available for any corrective maintenance if required."

Tracy responded, "Very well, weps. Keep up the good work. Thank you."

The number two Soviet officer gathered Tom and Dick Varley for a conference in the *Tigerfish* wardroom.

"Gentlemen. It is obvious that we can not take the complete *Tigerfish* crew with us when we go the sea." The number two continued, "When discussing the crew overload with Tracy, he recommended that about thirty unnecessary sailors be left ashore when we put out to sea to complete our mission."

Number two waited to let Tom and Dick regain their composure. He then continued, "For information and planning, one of your Axehandle missile experts and an expert with the nuclear torpedoes would embark in the Soviet cruiser for the return trip to the Soviet Union."

Both Tom and Dick were shocked at the request for the transfer of the *Tigerfish* sailors and that two of the *Tigerfish* crew were being transferred to Russia.

Number two delayed his statements, awaiting the attention of the two American senior officers and then spoke. "We plan to return *Tigerfish* back to Cuba and pick up your sailors after we complete our mission."

Both Tom and his executive officer knew immediately that the Soviet submariner was telling a lie. They both knew that these sailors would become shark bait as soon as *Tigerfish* departed the port.

Again, another situation where the U.S. commanding officer of *Tigerfish* had no options available to him to protect his sailors.

"Please give me your recommendations tomorrow morning with the list of the crew members and their ratings who will make the voyage with us. We are scheduled to depart for sea in four days on the fifteenth of December. Thank you."

When Tom was permitted to go topside of the container ship, still in shackles and under guard, he was able to observe a barbed wire stockade being constructed on the pier just forward of the container ship. By mentally

Mission Complete

calculating the size of the stockade, it was obvious to Tom that his sailors would be herded into the space. He shuttered when he imagined the next step in the lives of the captives.

"Excuse me, Captain. Do you have time for me to review with you the navigation track from here to our launching station on the twenty-fourth of December?"

"Yes, navigator. Let's review the track now."

Tracy's number two was summoned to the wardroom to also participate in the review.

Number two entered the wardroom and the three officers drew a large cup of coffee.

The Soviet navigator started with an overall summary of the trip. "We will get underway at zero nine hundred on the fifteenth of December and arrive at our missile firing station at sixteen hundred on the twenty-fourth of December."

After assuming an agreement by the attendees to his summary, the navigator continued, "We will remain inside the container ship for the first five miles outside of the harbor. At this time, we will submerge the submarine, disengage from the container ship, and steer course three-zero-zero degrees true. Recommend depth two hundred feet at a speed of eight knots. At this location, change course to three-five-zero degrees true."

The Soviet navigator pointed to the desired location on the navigation chart and stated, "After passing through the Straits of Florida, continue on course until we arrive at this location." The navigator again pointed to the desired location on the navigation chart. "*Tigerfish* will change course to one-four-zero degrees true and decrease speed to five knots. We are now six hundred and twenty nautical miles from our calculated missile launching point."

He continued with his briefing and prior to completing, he repeated for effect the *Tigerfish* time- on station. "Estimate time to arrive on station is sixteen hundred on the twenty-fourth of December."

Number two then provided Tracy a status report of the current conditions aboard *Tigerfish*. "Anticipate getting from Dick Varley after lunch the final list of sailors who are to remain embarked in *Tigerfish*. I will have all the others sailors load their belongings the evening of fourteen December. We will move them ashore and into the barbed wired compound early the fifteenth before we get the submarine underway. All berthing areas will be cleaned and purified on the thirteenth of December. The complete *Tigerfish* crew will be showered also on the thirteenth."

He reviewed his notes and then continued, "Clean mattresses in *Tigerfish* will replace the present ones the evening of the thirteenth."

Number two remained quiet awaiting any questions or comments from his captain.

He then continued. "Request your permission to rig the ship for dive starting the morning of the thirteenth of December."

Tracy responded to his number two, "Permission granted to rig the ship for dive with the exception of the bridge access hatch and the main ballast tank vent valves." Tracy continued, "Ensure that the people designated to do the rigging review the check-off sheets earlier so that they are knowledgeable with all the equipment, valves, and switches."

As number two started to depart the wardroom, he informed his captain, "Russell will be ready to brief you on the reactor and engineering plant before dinner. He anticipates no problems meeting our commitments."

"Very well. Thank you."

Tom had made valuable use of the small intervals of time available when not under constant supervision by the Soviet guards to brief select members of the *Tigerfish* crew on future events. The principal individuals involved in the plot were the lead sonar technicians and the engineer officer. Anticipating an attack from an American nuclear submarine against the *Tigerfish* late the evening of the twenty-fourth of December was the linchpin of the ploy.

It was very crucial that Tom only bring into the circle of confidence those crew members who would support aiding the U.S. nuclear submarine against *Tigerfish* and knowing that if the attack was successful, all in *Tigerfish* would be killed.

Tom's plan was to take effect about twenty-one hundred on Christmas Eve. The *Tigerfish* U.S. commanding officer believed the submarine would stay below the layer until about twenty-one hundred and then go to periscope depth to await the receipt of an extremely important message.

No crew member in *Tigerfish* knew how sensitive and important to world peace the results of this message would be.

From twenty-one hundred until midnight, it was important that no *Tigerfish* sailor report an opposing submarine to the Soviet monitors. Tom had directed that the self-radiated noise monitors in the maneuvering room, sonar room, and the control room be turned to the lowest volume. Also, the *Tigerfish* sonar operators must be especially alert to detect a submarine making an attack on *Tigerfish*.

At twenty-two hundred and every ten minutes thereafter, the watch stander in the lower level engine room would place a wrench between the pipe of a system with liquid flowing and the hull to develop a sound short. This noise producing device was to be initiated continuously commencing at twenty-three hundred on the twenty-fourth of December.

Russell entered the Soviet captain's stateroom before dinner and provided Tracy with a status report of the engineering plant. "Captain, request permission to commence heating up the reactor plants starting at zero nine hundred tomorrow morning. The Soviet cruiser does not have a primary coolant retention facility on board to accept our excess primary coolant from coolant expansion as we heat up the pressurizer. Therefore, I plan to discharge our excess primary coolant overboard into the harbor." The Soviet engineer officer continued, "This will give us all day tomorrow the thirteenth and also the fourteenth to go critical, heat up the plant, and become self sustaining. Plan to remove shore power cables by late afternoon the fourteenth."

"The reactor startup pre-critical check-off has been completed with no problems and all of our corrective and preventive maintenance have been completed," Russell reported with a smile. "Plan to top off our pure water from the cruiser early on the fourteenth and potable water late the fourteenth."

"Well done, Engineer," Tracy acknowledged with a smile. "Keep me and number two informed of any problems completing your plan."

There was much laughter during dinner. Again, Tracy had vodka served to the wardroom and a well-wished toast for continued success of the mission. Tension was just about erased from the Russian officers.

The Soviet weapons officer started the business discussions as dessert was being served. "Captain, I have about four hours remaining to complete required preventive maintenance and surveillance checks on all the weapons. Should have everything complete by noon tomorrow."

Tracy responded, "Thank you, weps. Let your troops know they have done a good job overseeing the American sailors in accomplishing their required tasks."

Russell added, "For the information of everyone, we will heat up the plant and go critical starting tomorrow morning at zero nine hundred. Plan on having the engineering plant self sustaining with the shore power cables removed by noon the following day on the fourteenth."

"Thank you, Engineer. Let me know if you have any complications," answered Tracy.

Number two reported, "The start of rigging the ship for dive will commence tomorrow morning, the thirteenth. On the fourteenth, want to have the personal belongings for the thirty *Tigerfish* sailors not going with us loaded into thirty-gallon plastic containers and moved to the stockade at the head of the pier." He continued, "We will transfer the selected sailors off the submarine early the fifteenth before we go to sea. Also, we will transfer the two weapons technicians with their baggage to the cruiser the evening of the fourteenth."

Tracy completed the discussions with words of caution. "We must keep a constant vigilance and run a taut ship during these last few days in port. We have performed flawlessly to date and it is no time to fall on our face. Well done."

Later in the evening, number two met with Tom and Dick in the *Tigerfish* wardroom.

"Please let me have the list of thirty enlisted to be transferred before the *Tigerfish* goes to sea. Also, I want to review the names and rates of those men to operate the submarine when we leave port."

Tom put the two lists on the table and the three officers reviewed the names and associated ratings of the enlisted on the lists. Some questions were asked about some specific names and rates.

"I agree with the names on both the lists," responded the Soviet officer. He continued, "The men leaving the ship will pack all their personal belongings into a thirty-gallon bag prior to twenty-one hundred on the fourteenth. Their bags will be put into the stockade at the head of the pier later in the evening. The men will depart the ship at zero five hundred the morning of the fourteenth and be put into the stockade."

Number two then looked at Tom and Dick and half heartedly told them, "We plan on coming back to Cuba after our mission to pick up your men."

Both the senior U.S. officers knew that the above statement was an absolute lie.

The Soviet officer let Tom and Varley know, "The two weapons technicians will be transferred bag and baggage to the cruiser the evening of the fourteenth and be transferred to Russia. The two men are needed to support our advanced weapons program in the Soviet Union."

In closing, number two told Tom and Dick that "Lieutenant Michael Hodges will be transferred off the ship on the fifteenth. He is to remain in Cuba until sent to the United States on the nineteenth to deliver a message from Tracy to your president."

Mission Complete

This was a tremendous surprise and shock to both Tom and Dick. Neither had any idea what the plot was to be; however, they both agreed it was to be big!

By observing the number of Axehandle missiles loaded and the significance of having an admiral on site observing the preparations for the *Tigerfish* to get underway, both officers pretty well pieced together what was in store for the free world. Tom and Dick both agreed that their plan for Christmas Eve to alert a possible U.S. nuclear submarine attack on *Tigerfish* must be successful.

On the afternoon of the thirteenth, Tom and Dick, still under Soviet guard and wearing shackles, met with the assembled *Tigerfish* sailors who were to be transferred off the submarine before underway. They discussed what to expect and that they would be off the ship when the submarine got underway. Each had to pack all his personal belongings tomorrow night for transfer to the stockade early the next morning.

Although Tom knew it to be a lie, he repeated what the Soviet number two had said about *Tigerfish* returning to Cuba after its mission to pick up the sailors.

Tom had all the men gather with hands together for a prayer. Many of the men were weeping. Some were on their hands and knees crying profusely.

The *Tigerfish* captain met with Michael Hodges and let him know what the future intentions were for his travel to the United States.

"RIG SHIP FOR DIVE" was sounded over the ship's 1 MC general announcing system.

The sound-powered telephone in the commanding officer's stateroom rang. Tracy answered and heard Russell's voice.

"Captain. We have finished heating up the reactor plants. Request permission to take the reactors critical."

"Permission granted, Russell. Take the reactors critical. Keep me informed."

The *Tigerfish* sailors completed loading out the ship with food provisions from the cruiser.

The Soviet number two took a walk through the submarine to ensure that progress was being made to properly store the ship for going to sea. Areas in need of increased attention were rapidly directed to the person responsible for the task.

Prior to noon on the fourteenth, the ship's 1MC general announcing system reported that the reactor was critical and that shore power cables were being removed.

Russell reported to Tracy, "Shore power cables are removed from the ship. We are now self sustaining on our own generated electrical power." The engineer officer continued, "Topping off the pure water tanks now. Will top off all potable water after dinner tonight. My assistant engineering officers are supervising the securing and battening down of the engineering spaces for going to sea."

"Very well, Russell," responded Tracy.

After dinner on the fourteenth, all personal belongings of the selected *Tigerfish* sailors were taken ashore and loaded outside the stockade. All of Mike Hodges personal belongings were packed.

The young *Tigerfish* submarine officer was ready to disembark the submarine tomorrow morning, the fifteenth, before the submarine went to sea.

Tracy had provided Mike the sealed envelope. Mike had been cautioned by Tracy of the consequences to the *Tigerfish* crew members on board should he not deliver the letter and should he disclose the status of *Tigerfish* to anyone.

Shortly after lunch, number two reported to Tracy, "Rig for dive is complete. There are some minimal exceptions to the completed rig that can be controlled."

"Thank you. Maintain the completed rig for dive check lists up to date so that we can make our commitment for underway and submerging," Tracy replied.

At zero five hundred on the fifteenth, the designated thirty enlistees from the *Tigerfish* were marched off the container ship under armed guard to the stockade at the head of the pier. The Cuban guards cursed at the prisoners, yelled and verbally harassed them as they solemnly walked to the barbed wire stockade.

Lieutenant Mike Hodges was marched off the container ship shortly afterwards. A single armed guard escorted him to his wooden holding area. The spaces between the boards of the wooden walls in his holding area allowed the young officer to observe the *Tigerfish* sailors cramped into their barbed wire compound.

The admiral came aboard *Tigerfish* to say goodby to Tracy and to wish him and his crew good luck.

At zero eight-thirty, "STATION THE MANEUVERING WATCH" was heard throughout *Tigerfish*.

The Soviet cruiser sounded three short blasts with its signaling horn and

Mission Complete

slowly backed down away from the cargo ship and maneuvered to a course to steer out of the harbor.

"Officer of the deck-control. The maneuvering watch is stationed throughout the ship."

The engineering officer of the watch got permission from the bridge to test the main engines.

Tigerfish surged slowly forward and then aft as the main engines were being tested in both ship directions.

"Officer of the deck-engineering officer of the watch. Main engines tested . Test satisfactory."

All mooring lines to the container ship were singled up.

Tracy moved to the bridge area at zero eight-fifty. "Radio the container ship that we are ready to get underway."

The officer in charge of the container ship started giving signals to the four sea-going tug boats. The mooring lines to the pier were cast loose. Three short blasts of the ship's horn were sounded.

The container ship was maneuvered by the four sea-going tugs one hundred and eighty degrees and headed seaward from the harbor.

Once clear of the harbor, Tracy directed that the mooring lines from the *Tigerfish* to the container ship be slipped loose.

The deck cleats were repositioned into the hull with the cover plates making a flush configuration with the hull.

All personnel topside were directed to lay below decks.

The submarine topside hatches were dogged down and rigged for dive.

The container ship and *Tigerfish* both made three knots through the water with the submarine maneuvering to remain positioned evenly inside the bowels of the container ship.

Number two reported to the bridge, "The ship is rigged for dive with the exception of the bridge access hatch and the main vent valves."

"Very well," replied the officer of the deck.

Tracy directd his number two officer to rig the main vent valves for dive.

When clear of the harbor, both ships increased speed to five knots.

At the five-mile point from the harbor, the stern plate was opened from the container ship and the *Tigerfish* slipped into the deep en route to carry out its assigned mission.

Mike Hodges lost sight of the container ship from his holding area. He desperately wondered what his fate would be and the fate of his shipmates in the compound.

It didn't take long to discover the fate of his thirty selected shipmates.

Four Cuban guards armed with automatic weapons took station outside the barbed wire compound. All four started spraying bullets into the bodies of the *Tigerfish* sailors. This continued until there was no movement from any of the sailors.

The assassinated bodies were loaded into a harbor launch at the pier. The launch had to make three trips to the outer limits of the harbor to drop all the bodies into the ocean.

Unknown to the Soviet/Cuban team or to Mike Hodges, the complete assassination of the *Tigerfish* sailors and the dumping of their bodies into the ocean were captured on photographs from both an American over-flight mission and from a United States photographic satellite.

Hodges was distraught as he watched the massacre of his shipmates. For the next four days he sat in the corner of his compound and wept.

On the nineteenth of December, Lieutenant Michael Hodges was smuggled into Key West, Florida, with follow-on transportation to Washington, D.C.

/10/ TARGET LOCALIZATION

Bruce glanced at the highly polished brass clock on the wardroom back bulkhead. The time was zero eight-thirty on the twenty-third of December.

Jackfish was now operating in harm's way with a maximum of thirty-nine hours remaining to complete this critical assigned mission.

Bococo entered the wardroom very quietly with a pot of hot steaming coffee. Without asking, he filled the captain's half-full mug to the top.

"Good morning, Captain. Can I get you some breakfast?"

"No thank you. Not too hungry at this time," responded the captain with a forced smile.

He really was hungry; however, his stomach was rapidly churning, a condition caused by a mixture of uneasiness, uncertainty, and apprehension.

The wardroom telephone buzzed. "Captain-conn. I am steering the courses and making the speeds laid out on the navigation chart by Nat and Dave. Five torpedo tubes are flooded and equalized with sea water pressure. The outer doors are shut." The conning officer continued, "Chief Keller reports that the battle stations sonar team is on station. The chief will rotate the sonar operators over the next two days to provide for sleep and food. The communications watch is stationed throughout the ship as you directed. Also, the section fire control tracking party is stationed."

Bruce felt comfortable that he had everything in place at the present time in the "approach and attack phase" of this mission. "Thank you, conn. Keep me informed."

The captain completed his ritual tour of the submarine.

He spent more time than normal this morning in the sonar room as if his presence would help the sonar men detect the target nuclear submarine sooner.

"Good morning, Chief." Bruce delayed his conversation as he scanned the many sonar consoles and displays. "Please ensure that your troops are well fed and rested." He continued, "This is going to be a long day and a half."

"Yes sir, Captain. We are all ready to do our job," responded the proud chief petty officer.

Bruce departed the sonar room with a nod of approval to Chief Keller. The captain knew that he had the best sonar team with the best leader in the fleet.

The torpedo room was Bruce's next destination. His rationale was that the sonar gang finds the nuclear submarine target and then the torpedo gang sinks the enemy.

Usually with this battle condition set, there were two torpedo men on watch in the torpedo room. Bruce was surprised to see five torpedo men in the room just talking and doing those thing that make men life long comrades. These men were ready for combat.

"Good morning, men." Bruce said with a smile on his face."Are you all talking to the torpedoes to ensure they remain our friends?"

All the men smiled and the pressure of getting ready to go into combat was relieved.

The leader of the group responded, "Good morning, Captain. We are staying close to ensure that our torpedo buddies don't get lonely."

As the captain started to depart the torpedo room, the torpedo man leader smiled and replied, "Rest assured, Captain, we won't let you down."

Bruce then moved into the attack center. He wanted to take this opportunity to observe the performance of his men on the fire control section tracking team.

Some of the team were quiet and solemn. Others had their heads bent over looking at the chart or plotter as if they were looking for a correct answer. Essentially, the men were all scared.

The conning officer asked different men questions about tactical problems and the correct development of the solutions. This kept their minds on their current assignment with not much time to think about the "what ifs."

Bruce took this opportunity to create small talk with his troops in the attack center to take some of the edge off the high level of stress that was developing.

The captain directed the conning officer, "Be at periscope depth to copy the twelve hundred communications broadcast. Hopefully, the force commander will send us some tactical information about our target. Ensure that you clear baffles slowly so that we don't cut or foul the trailing sonar wire in the propeller."

Mission Complete

"Yes sir, Captain," responded the conning officer.

Nat departed from the sonar room and entered into the attack center. He made it part of his watch to spend some time with Chief Keller in the sonar room to get a better appreciation of the sonar conditions.

Bruce queried his command tactical officer, "Good morning, Nat. Is everything under control?" The captain continued, "I have directed the conning officer to be at periscope depth for the noon communications broadcast. Also, take good care of our sonar tail when clearing baffles on our way to periscope depth. We don't want to cut the wire or get it tangled in the propeller or propeller shaft."

"Yes sir, Captain. Will ensure that we have a sonar tail with good conductivity when we return to our operating depth."

Nat delayed his conversation as he moved closer to the captain and then stated in a quiet voice, "Everything is under control, Captain. The troops are a little jittery at present but they will settle down soon."

Bruce followed up with a caution before leaving the attack center. "Make sure the conning officer realizes we only have until twelve-thirty at periscope depth. After that time, we are in the vulnerability window of the Soviet photographic satellite. Thank you, Nat. I will be in the wardroom for lunch."

"Yes sir, Captain."

As Bruce proceeded to the wardroom, he got a warm sense that Nat was a solid member of the team and would support Bruce's every wish.

Bococo notified the captain, "Lunch is being served in the wardroom."

Bruce entered the wardroom and took his seat at the head of the table. The executive officer and two other officers were not present.

Bococo explained to the captain that the executive officer would not be eating lunch during the first seating. "He said that he has some work to get completed before going on watch. The other two officers did not provide an excuse."

It was obvious to Bruce that the deep freeze was starting between his officers and himself. The wedge was driving his team further apart.

Bruce began to question himself whether his crew would support him through the shooting phase of this mission.

After knocking on the wardroom door, the messenger of the watch entered and stood at attention. "Excuse me, Captain. The conning officer reports the hour of twelve hundred, sir."

Bruce responded with a smile. "Thank you, Petty Officer Jones."

The telephone at the captain's seat in the wardroom buzzed twice. "Captain speaking."

"This is the conning officer. At periscope depth. Have copied the communications broadcast. No priority messages for *Jackfish*. Sky is clear with minimum wave action. Permission to return to search depth of two hundred feet?"

"Conn-captain. Permission granted to return to search depth of two hundred feet. Continue to clear baffles every two hours above and below the gradient."

Bruce spent some time during lunch again reviewing with his officers the tactical plan for *Jackfish* and what each officer was to expect during the next day and a half. He also emphasized what was expected from each officer and crew member during this forthcoming stressful period.

After this lunch time discussion period, Bruce was content that everyone in the wardroom had received the same message from him.

That message was that full allegiance and dedication to country and ship were a must to ensure the successful completion of this mission and to ensure the safety of all hands onboard *Jackfish*. No less would be unacceptable.

At fourteen hundred Nat knocked on the door to the captain's stateroom. He was accompanied with the off-going conning officer.

"Captain. I have been relieved as the command tactical watch by the executive officer. The ship is searching at two hundred feet at ten to twenty knots in accordance with the speed laid out in the developed tactical search plan. Toured the ship and all is well." After a slight pause, Nat continued. "Visited our two burned shipmates resting in the executive officer's cabin. The hospital corpsman is feeding them well. They are making a marked improvement in their health."

"Thank you, Nat, and also your assistant. Stay loose and keep up the good work."

Bruce considered this to be a good time to write the condolence letter to Petty Officer Jackson's wife and family.

He also needed to prepare a message to Commodore Walter giving the details of Petty Officer Jackson's loss of life and also the details of the burn casualties associated with the main turbine lubricating oil fire.

Both of these items were listed on Bruce's "to do action calendar."

In the interim, Bruce was establishing an informal investigation of both accidents in accordance with the Uniform Code of Military Justice. This way, all the details of the two casualties were preserved and documented by the investigation.

Should higher authority desire another investigation, the results from

Mission Complete

these initial informal investigations could be an addendum to the second investigation.

Bruce called for the ship's yeoman.

"Prepare for me the convening documents for informal investigations for the death of Petty Officer Jackson and the main turbine lubrication oil casualty. Assign the weapons officer and the operations officer as the two investigating officers. Let the executive officer review the documentation before they are signed by me."

The ship's Yeoman acknowledged the captain's directives and departed smartly to accomplish his tasking.

Bruce departed his stateroom en route to the engineering spaces. He stopped in the attack center to discuss the current status of the ship with Dave.

"Good afternoon, Dave," Bruce said with a cheery tone. "What is the ship's status at present?"

The command tactical watch officer smiled at Bruce and responded, "All is well at present. We are sprinting at fifteen knots now for another thirty minutes. Will then slow to ten knots and search below and above the layer. It is like being in a sound isolated cave when we are below the layer." Dave was a little more spirited now and out of his pouting mode as before.

Bruce observed the watch standers and members of the section tracking team.

He took this opportunity to talk with the troops in the attack center on the light side. Again, it was obvious that the tension was high with the crew. The unknown always provided an apprehensive feeling.

Dave provided the captain a brief of *Jackfish*'s track, courses, and speeds using the navigation display laid out on the plotting table in the attack center. He used his finger as a pointer to show the submarine's projected track over the next four hours.

"It looks like your team developed a splendid search plan for *Jackfish*. Well done," Bruce said to Dave with a smile. "However, the bag of gold is still at the end of the rainbow. Dave. I am going to the engine room and talk with Tom for awhile. By the way, I want to have the informal investigation concerning the death of Petty Officer Jackson and the investigation germane to the main turbine lube oil fire completed before we get into port. Both the weps and ops officers will have a lot of time to complete the investigations after we finalize our mission and head for the barn."

Hearing this statement from the captain about the mission made the muscles in the executive officer's face tighten.

The captain thought to himself and regretted that the commander in chief did not allow Bruce to conduct this mission as a team effort, the proper way and the way he had done so many times before.

"Yes sir, Captain. Will make sure that they both understand their commitment," responded the executive officer.

Bruce stopped in the executive officer's stateroom made over to be a hospital ward and chatted with the two burn casualties. Both were in good spirits and very talkative.

"Captain. We are ready to go back to the engine room and stand our watch," they both spoke almost in unison.

Bruce acknowledged with a smile, "Enjoy the rest while you can. We will put you back to work soon enough." The captain looked them both in the eyes and said sincerely, "Thank you for your good work. Now rest some more."

Bruce put his head into the communications center. "Good afternoon, gentlemen. Everything under control?"

"Yes sir, Captain. We are waiting to send out the big messages," the chief radio man said with a grin on his face.

The two other radio men in the communications center smiled with the comments of the chief.

The chief had been in the Submarine Force and on submarine special missions enough to know that a highly classified patrol summary "high lights" message was dispatched on conclusion of every mission. He had hit it on the head about "the big message" but the three radio men didn't know what the contents of this message would be or what the contents would mean.

Bruce waved to the three jovial crew members as he departed the communications center.

As the captain passed through the crew's dinette, some sailors were playing bridge. Two were playing acey duecy and the chairs of two eight-man tables were filled with chow hounds feeding their faces.

The captain answered some questions, made himself a sandwich, and sat at one of the tables. He continued to talk with his shipmates as he ate his sandwich.

The questions asked by the sailors covered all spectrums, including return time to their home port of Groton, status of the burned shipmates, when the next operation at sea would be for *Jackfish*, and most importantly, if the nuclear submarine target would shoot weapons at *Jackfish*? The most important question asked by all the troops was whether their submarine was the better of the two that were getting ready to engage in mortal combat. All ears listened for the answer to the question and all eyes stared at the captain as he provided the answer.

Bruce responded slowly and deliberately as he scanned his shipmates who were waiting for some reassurance of their survivability. "As I have repeatedly told you over many years, you are the best crew operating the best ship in the world. We have not failed as a team in the past and don't plan on the team failing now." Bruce saw a smile of confidence come across all faces in the crew's dinette. A proud band of sailors were ready to take on the unknown. Bruce was the proud leader of a group of professionals who only needed a little encouragement from their boss to perform.

The captain continued aft through the submarine to the maneuvering room in the engine room. Tom was standing watch as the engineering officer of the watch. As the ship's engineer officer saw his captain looking into the maneuvering room, he greeted him with a "Good afternoon, Captain. Everything is going well. No problems with the plant." Tom continued, "Many of the crew are up and about. They don't want to miss anything when and if it happens. Others are working on their submarine qualification."

Bruce directed Tom to have the engineering watch supervisor relieve him of the duties as engineering officer of the watch so the two of them could chat.

The engineering watch supervisor was the second in charge of the engineering watch section. He was an enlisted man, usually a chief petty officer, and his qualification requirements were almost as stringent as those of the engineering officer of the watch.

The engineer officer reported to the captain that he had been relieved by the engineering watch supervisor. The captain used this chat time to ensure that Tom fully understood the tactical situation that *Jackfish* was committed to complete.

Tom was a little taken back when Bruce sternly told him, "As of this Christmas morning, there will only be one nuclear submarine that survives. It is to be either *Jackfish* or the enemy nuclear submarine." Bruce delayed to allow Tom to recover his senses. "Should the other guy survive, the world will be made up of two dictator powers governing the world."

Tom replied, "What can I do to help ensure that the good guys win?"

Bruce explained that there appeared to be a wedge being driven between himself and many of the officers in the wardroom. "The major question or dispute point is that the enemy target is a nuclear submarine of the *Jackfish* class. We all know that the only nuclear submarine of this class besides *Jackfish* is the *Tigerfish*. Unfortunately, I have been directed by the president of the United States not to disclose to anyone more than I have already done." Bruce paused. "Carrying out your responsibilities with only half of the mission information must be done by trust and loyalty. I need your support when the shooting time comes. It is crucial to world freedom that we sink the enemy nuclear submarine before midnight Christmas Eve."

"I have always supported your directives and followed you into many challenging and dangerous situations." Tom paused, looked Bruce in the eyes, and stated, "This time is no different."

Bruce got a lump in his throat. "Thank you, Tom."

He nodded as he turned and started out of the engine room.

The captain hit the call button in his stateroom. Within two minutes the duty stewarts mate knocked lightly on Bruce's stateroom door. He entered quietly with a large mug of black coffee for the captain.

"Thank you very much" was Bruce's acknowledgment for his expeditious service.

"You're welcome, Captain" was the response.

Bruce took out a blank radio communications message form. He wrote out a FLASH unclassified message "MISSION COMPLETE" on the form. The message was addressed to the commander of submarine force, Atlantic fleet (Norfolk, Virginia), the commander, submarine squadron two (Groton, Connecticut), and the chief of naval operations in Washington, D.C.

He would hold the rough message form in his stateroom until hopefully the deed was done and the message was ready to be released.

The captain's stateroom telephone buzzed twice. "Captain speaking."

"Captain, this is the conning officer. Sonar has picked up a contact, evaluated as a tanker, range about twelve thousand yards on course parallel to *Jackfish*'s course."

"Very well. I will be in the attack center shortly," responded the captain as he departed his stateroom and proceeded to the attack center.

Bruce entered into the attack center. He reviewed the plots and examined the solution developed by the fire control attack console.

"Dave. It would be good to go to periscope depth and validate your solution. However, we can't take a chance of being detected." Bruce directed Dave, "Continue to refine your solution using bearing overlaps. We can devote some time now to freshen up the fire control tracking team to solve bearings only target solutions."

Dave and Bruce reviewed the search plan template laid out on the plotter in the attack center.

Mission Complete

Dave pointed his finger to the position of *Jackfish*. "This is our current position and projected track for our search plan."

The executive officer waited while the captain examined the track.

Dave then stated, "Anticipate that we will be ready to start the sonar search of the sixty-mile circle starting at ten hundred tomorrow morning the twenty-fourth of December."

The captain responded, "Agree with your projection, Dave." He continued, "I will write in my night order book and you publish in the plan of the day that the ship would man battle stations tomorrow at zero nine-thirty. Also, Dave, let the crew know that we expect to remain at battle stations throughout the day and night. We will rotate the watch stations through meal time so that everyone can eat a hot meal." Bruce continued, "Also, have the cooks prepare many sandwiches and have them available for the crew around the clock while we are at battle stations."

Dave gave an affirmative nod to the captain.

As Bruce reviewed the projected track for *Jackfish* to conduct the search plan, he smiled and told Dave, "Your team did a wonderful job of developing the projected search plan."

Looking at the chart on the plotter table it was easy to document where *Jackfish* had traveled and forecast the projected track of the submarine. The plotted track also provided a historical review of the ship's travels.

"Dave, when you are satisfied with the skills of your section tracking team, you can secure tracking the surface tanker. Take some time before the end of the watch to critique your watch section. I will be in my stateroom until evening meal is served."

Dave responded, "Yes sir, Captain. I am quite pleased also with the team's performance tracking the tanker. A couple of false starts initially, but the bugs have been worked out now."

Bruce departed the attack center and went to his stateroom.

Bococo knocked on the captain's door, opened it slowly and placed a mug of coffee on the captain's table. "Do you want anything to eat before evening meal is served?"

"No thank you, Bococo."

At eighteen fifty-five, Bococo knocked on the captain's door again. The stewards mate partially opened the door and announced, "Captain, evening meal is being served in the wardroom."

"Thank you, Bococo. I am on my way."

At nineteen hundred all the officers present took their seats at the wardroom table following the lead of the captain.

During the meal, Bruce discussed with the officers the good work done by the team headed up by Dave in developing the search plan. Also, Bruce acknowledged the performance of the section tracking team now on watch for the way they rapidly solved the fire control solution for the tanker that randomly passed *Jackfish*.

Bruce announced, "*Jackfish* will enter the sixty-nautical-mile circle tomorrow morning at ten hundred. We will man battle stations at zero nine-thirty and plan to remain at battle stations throughout the day and into the evening. We will rotate watch standers during meal times so that everyone gets a warm meal. The cooks will prepare sandwiches and the sandwiches will be available in the crew's dinette around the clock."

Bruce continued his stay in the wardroom after the first seating of the evening meal was completed. He wanted to spend some time with Dave and the off-going officer watch standers while they ate their evening meal.

"Good evening, Captain," Dave started his report. "I have been relieved as the command tactical watch by Nat. Everything is routine. No sonar contacts."

The captain received relief reports from the conning officer and the engineering officer of the watch. Everything was normal. Bruce wondered if this was this the calm before the storm.

During the meal, Dave discussed the success of the search plan template that his team had prepared. It appeared to be a very useful tool for preparing and then implementing the search routine for *Jackfish*.

Dave commented, "Captain, it looks as if we will complete the search of the sixty-nautical-mile circle about twenty-one hundred tomorrow evening. This will give us some overlap search time at the highest priority target locations. Our current search plan calls for a fifty percent probability of detection in the outer area. Traveling at the planned slower speed in the inner area will greatly increase our probability of detection," Dave stated as if answering a question in submarine school.

"It appears that everything is proceeding as planned," Bruce commented with a smile. The captain sipped his coffee and continued, "Our non-nuclear torpedoes have a speed of sixty knots and a range of twenty thousand yards. At this speed, the torpedo will travel six thousand yards in three minutes."

The after dinner session with Dave and Bruce was now turning into a tactical development plan for the shooting scenario that was to take place tomorrow evening.

Bruce continued his discussion. "Dave, the target probably will be above the layer at periscope depth. I guess that between twenty-two hundred and midnight the enemy nuclear submarine will be standing by to copy a broadcast message."

Dave's face flushed and became tight as he heard all this intelligence information coming from his commanding officer. He realized that Bruce was not guessing or making up all this information without a solid base.

The captain stared at Dave and stated, "Recommend that we continue to search as planned. Once contact is generated, we will take *Jackfish* under the layer, speed five knots and close target range to four thousand yards. We want to approach from the stern of the target to prevent counter detection. We can validate our target solution by short trips above the layer. At four thousand yards or less, *Jackfish* will launch two conventional torpedoes to run at depth two hundred feet. At three thousand yards, program the torpedoes to run at depth sixty feet." Bruce continued, "Set contact mode of detonation with a program shift to acoustic detonation when the torpedo travels to the target generated range as shown on the fire control attack panel." After a pause, Bruce stated, "We will have two Mark 57X nuclear tipped torpedoes in standby as a backup contingency. There is the possibility we may need the extra speed of these eighty-knot torpedoes."

Dave almost fell out of his chair after hearing the captain discuss nuclear tipped torpedo shooting.

"Dave. I want to discuss the tactical approach and the weapons firing plan more with you, Nat, and Ray in the morning. Please set up a meeting in the wardroom for zero eight hundred with all participants. Thank you."

Bruce continued his discussion with Dave. "Prepare a recommendation for a meritorious service medal for Petty Officer Jackson. I want to send the recommendation to the squadron commander by message after we complete our mission. This way, hopefully, the award will be approved by higher authority and processed in time to be presented to Mrs. Jackson at the military funeral for the petty officer."

Dave responded, "I will arrange the tactical meeting for tomorrow morning as requested. Also, I will start work expeditiously on the award recommendation for Petty Officer Jackson."

"Thank you, Dave, for your continued support."

"Captain. The movie is set up and ready to be seen," the duty movie operator reported.

Five officers, including Dave, took their seats in the wardroom waiting for the showing of the movie. They had already started eating popcorn.

Dave directed the movie operator, "Start the movie."

Bruce called the conning officer on the ship's telephone. "Conn-captain. Be at periscope depth to copy the twenty-two hundred broadcast. The open satellite window is from twenty-one fifty until twenty-two forty-five." Bruce continued, "While at periscope depth, dump trash and garbage. This will be the last time we dispose of garbage until the completion of this mission."

"Captain-conn. Very well, sir."

The movie was not very good; however, it provided a distraction from the ever increasing tension growing amongst the officers.

At twenty-three hundred, the captain toured the ship. The watch standers throughout the ship enjoyed Bruce being in their space with them and also providing the opportunity for them to discuss issues with the captain. Just seeing the boss close to them at this time provided somewhat of a security blanket for these dedicated sailors.

Bruce returned to his stateroom and prepared his night order book. In addition to the standard directions listed in the book on how to operate the ship while the captain was sleeping, he added that battle stations were to be manned at zero nine-thirty, the ship would enter the sixty-nautical-mile search area at zero nine-thirty, ensuring that all hands were careful not to make any unnecessary noise, and the trailing sonar wire would be reeled in as soon as *Jackfish* detected the target nuclear submarine.

The night order book was signed by the captain and given to Nat to add his requirements. The book then was distributed to the cognizant people to read and sign. Bruce added the requirement for a wake up call at zero seven-thirty.

The tired and stressed out captain thought to himself, *Only a maximum of twenty-four hours remain to complete this mission!*

Bruce got out of bed, opened his combination safe, and checked his thirty-eight caliber Smith and Wesson revolver. He cleaned the revolver with a towel and loaded the gun with six bullets.

I hope that there will be no need for the revolver, Bruce thought to himself. *Just to be sure, I will carry the gun with me after lunch this afternoon.*

Bruce rapidly fell into a deep sleep.

Shortly afterwards, the captain bolted to a sitting position and was wide awake. He was perspiring and his body was wet all over. The thought came to him how vulnerable he was shooting and sinking a United States nuclear submarine without a written operation order signed by higher authority. Only seven very senior people including the president of the United States and

Mission Complete

Bruce knew of this plan. Michael Hodges also was aware of what had happened during the takeover of *Tigerfish*; however, he was confined and could easily be eliminated from the picture if needed.

Bruce slipped halfway back into sleep.

His thoughts were of Tom Morello and himself in their days at the United States Naval Academy. During their first class, or senior year, Bruce had been engaged to Ann. She had an apartment in Annapolis, Maryland, and was a teacher in the local grade school. One weekend, Bruce had his sister Carole visit the Academy for a football game. Bruce was the quarterback and Tom the tight end of this great Academy football team.

Tom was Carole's date, or drag, for the weekend. They both hit it off well and soon were engaged. Carole moved into the apartment with Ann and also was hired as a teacher in the local school. After graduation, Bruce and Tom had a double wedding in the Naval Academy Chapel.

Both officers went to submarine school together and then to nuclear power training and subsequent nuclear power prototype training at Boston Spa, New York. Bruce now was godfather to both of the Morello's two children. Tom was godfather to Bruce's three children.

After this mission of sinking the *Tigerfish* was completed before midnight tonight, Bruce wondered if he could ever look Carole and the two Morello children in the eyes again.

The messenger of the watch made a slight knock on the captain's stateroom door, slowly opened the door, and announced, "Captain, your zero seven-thirty wake up call as ordered, sir."

Bruce pulled his tired body to the side of his bunk. He then religiously followed his ritual of pushing the call button for coffee and then examining the remote dials on his bulkhead that provided him the *Jackfish* current course, speed, and depth. Course, speed, and depth were just as ordered.

Stewarts mate Bococo knocked on the door, slowly opened it, and placed a mug of coffee on Bruce's desk. "Good morning, Captain. Breakfast is being served."

"Thank you, Bococo. I will have some breakfast."

Bruce rapidly finished his breakfast and had another mug of coffee.

He tried to put his mind in gear to get ready for the forthcoming tactical meeting on selecting the final torpedo firing approach solution.

At zero eight hundred, the executive officer, operations/navigation officer, and weapons officer entered the wardroom, each poured a large mug of black freshly brewed coffee, and took their seats at the wardroom table with the captain.

Bruce started the discussion with how he envisioned the tactical problem would play out. "Nat, Ray, and Dave, my best projection is that the target submarine will be at periscope depth between twenty-two and twenty-four hundred." Bruce delayed, then continued, "The submarine is waiting for a message. In the interim, the target is most likely preparing to launch missiles."

Both Dave, Ray, and Nat, wide-eyed, looked at each other in total disbelief!

Bruce knew that he was revealing too much detail of the mission; however, the survival of the free world depended on the action of these three men during the next sixteen hours.

"Also," stated the captain, "there is a high probability that the target submarine will initiate sound shorts for us to be able to detect and localize the target."

Bruce got up from the table and poured another mug of coffee. He also topped off the coffee mugs for his three officer shipmates.

"Thank you, Captain," uttered Dave as he looked Bruce in the face, still bewildered.

Nat, slowly and in a timid voice, asked Bruce, "Your best estimate is that *Jackfish* will be at the shooting position after twenty-two hundred tonight?"

"That is correct. We need to develop the shooting tactics based on the following scenario," Bruce continued. "Assume the target is at periscope depth generating sound shorts giving us a good bearing solution. *Jackfish* approaches the target submarine below the temperature gradient to a range of four to six thousand yards. With a good firing solution, we launch two conventional non-nuclear torpedoes to run at one hundred fifty feet depth. At one thousand yards from the target, the running depth of the torpedoes is programmed to go above the layer and attack the target at a running depth of sixty feet." Bruce sipped his coffee, then continued. "Detonation of the torpedoes is set for the contact mode in both torpedoes. If the torpedoes have not exploded after running the fire control panel generated range, the mode to detonate is reprogrammed to the acoustic mode."

Ray, the weapons officer and expert with the weapons characteristics stated, "The speed of the conventional non-nuclear torpedo is sixty knots. The torpedo will travel six thousand yards in three minutes. So, in less than three minutes we should have success."

Bruce, with a stern and sincere look on his face, stated, "As a backup at the firing point, I want two of the nuclear tipped Mark 37X torpedoes in standby

Mission Complete

ready to launch as the contingency plan. This provides us the opportunity to shoot an eighty knot torpedo."

Again, Ray, Nat, and Dave went white-faced and both looked at Bruce with a questioning look.

These three officers had been high-voltage shocked by their captain's comments more times in the last four days than during their complete tour of duty aboard *Jackfish*. Neither Dave, Nat, nor Ray realized the real surprise in this scheme was that Bruce had already programmed the Mark57X torpedoes to be able to detonate in the nuclear mode by just initiating the nuclear lever on the front of the weapons fire control panel in the attack center.

In closing, Bruce cautioned his three professional officers. "Remember and plan accordingly that the nuclear submarine target that we are searching for also can launch weapons at *Jackfish*."

At zero nine-thirty, the telephone talker in each compartment announced that "MAN BATTLE STATIONS" was directed throughout the ship.

All hands rapidly moved throughout the ship to the designated stations that they had been assigned.

Bruce departed the wardroom to tour the ship. The other three officers remained in the wardroom. For a short period the officers just seemed to stare into the ceiling, Then Dave started the discussion.

"We are in a deep mystery that might have a bad ending," Dave stated in a timid voice. "I believe that the captain is providing us all the information that he is allowed to provide; however, that puts us into a precarious position. Sinking a submarine without written authorization from higher authority is not usually attempted." Dave delayed while the other two officers digested what he was saying.

Both Ray and Nat agreed with Dave; however, they both stated that they had allegiance to the captain and would follow his directives.

The three officers departed the wardroom and manned their battle station assignments.

Bruce first visited the executive officer's stateroom to talk with the two burn casualties. The hospital corpsman was present and was happy with the get well progress of the men.

"Thank you, Doc, for your professionalism in taking care of our shipmates. You did a good job," Bruce said with a happy smile on his face.

"Thank you, Captain. I really appreciate your comments."

The two burned victims chimed in. "He certainly did a good job, but he kept sticking us with the blunt needles, those with the square ends."

All present had a laugh.

Bruce entered the sonar room. Chief Keller, as usual, was in the space caring for his brood.

"Good morning, chief. I assume that you have been ensuring that your followers get enough food and rest? Today is going to be a big one. This is Super Bowl Sunday!"

The chief smiled and the sonar men also chuckled a bit.

"Yes sir, Captain. The troops are ready for kick-off time." Chief Keller commented, "We have a continuous tape recording of *Tigerfish* running on the spare tape recorder. The off sonar watch stander refreshes himself by listening to the sonar tape."

Bruce responded, "Chief, I have the utmost confidence in you ability and your well trained sonar men."

During this visit, the captain also discussed the possibility of hearing a self generated sound short from the target. "Ensure the men are aware of and alert to this possibility of a sound short from the target."

"Will do, Captain."

"Good luck, gentlemen. Keep up the good work and thank you," commented the captain as he departed the sonar room.

Bruce toured the crew's dinette and observed the duty cook and his three mess men preparing sandwiches and stacking them high on trays in the chill box. These sandwiches would be much appreciated by the crew later in the day.

He had a friendly chat with this group of men. The mess men had probably the worst job on a submarine. They were the newest seamen and firemen arrivals onboard and were not rated. They keep this job usually for three months before going into a division. Their responsibility was to help prepare the meals with the duty cook and then clean up the space after each meal.

These three mess men were happy shipmates, proud to be serving onboard the *Jackfish*.

During his travels through the submarine, Bruce spent some time talking with the members of the damage control team and the weapons handling team. The team leaders took this opportunity to continue training the team members. Each member of the team had essentially the same questions. Their biggest concern was whether *Jackfish* would be in a torpedo shooting duel and possibly be hit with a weapon.

The captain left each space after satisfying the men that *Jackfish* would be the victor. He thought that if he said "victor" enough times there would not

Mission Complete

be any doubt of the outcome of the fight. Bruce recalled at this time Joseph Conrad's *Command at Sea*. He definitely agreed that the words of this work were certainly correct.

This captain started to feel the loneliness of his job increase along with the pressure of the responsibility for the lives of the *Jackfish* crew. Bruce made it a practice to talk with as many of the men as possible when he toured the submarine. It was obvious that he was extremely proud of his crew and submarine and this pride wore off onto the crew. He was pleased that their confidence seemed to be elevated after he had a conversation with them.

The personnel contact part of being a commanding officer could not be achieved anywhere else nor in any other position in the military or in the civilian environment. Bruce was convinced that the association with such dedicated men was his prime reason for remaining in the Navy and especially in the Submarine Force.

As Bruce sat in his cabin with a large mug of coffee, he started to think of the words to put into his letter to Petty Officer Jackson's wife.

He started writing the letter to Mrs. Jackson slowly and then increased the words, description, and praise for this dedicated young petty officer who was willing to give his life for his country.

When he completed the letter, Bruce thought of many more accolades to describe the petty officer. However, there was enough written so that his young wife would fully understood what tremendous value her husband had been to *Jackfish*, the United States Navy, and his country.

Bococo quietly knocked on the captain's door and reported, "Captain, lunch is being served."

"Thank you, Bococo, I will be there in a couple of minutes."

Dave was in the attack center as the command tactical officer so his absence from the wardroom seating was excusable. Some other officers were not present since they were manning their battle stations assignments. They would be relieved and eat at the second seating in the wardroom.

Bruce entered the wardroom and took his seat at the head of the table. The other officers followed the captain's lead. The captain took this opportunity to provide his officers more tactical information and the approach and attack strategy developed with Nat, Dave, and Ray earlier in the morning.

As to be expected, the eyes of all the officers present opened widely and their mouths dropped as Bruce continued his description of the overall strategy.

After lunch, the captain excused himself and departed from the wardroom.

Bruce took this opportunity to prepare the messages describing the two recent casualties in *Jackfish*. Both messages were to be sent to Captain Bill Walter, the squadron commander and good friend of Bruce, after the "MISSION COMPLETE" message was transmitted.

The first message provided the information germane to the death of Petty Officer Jackson. In this message Bruce asked that Walter inform Bruce's wife, Ann, of the tragic death of Petty Officer Jackson so that she would be able to support Mrs. Jackson when the news of her husband's death was given to her.

The captain included in the message that a recommendation for a meritorious service medal for Petty Officer Jackson was being provided separately. Hopefully, the award would be approved by higher authority expeditiously so that the award could be presented to Mrs. Jackson at her husband's funeral.

Bruce also included in the message the request that the ambulance to pick up the body of Jackson did not appear on the pier until all the *Jackfish* dependents had departed.

The second message described the fire in the main turbine lube oil system in *Jackfish* and the status of the two burn casualties. It detailed the exceptional medical attention provided the casualties on board by the hospital corpsman. Also, Ann should be informed of the casualties and their current medical condition to be able to provide support to their wives if needed.

Bruce included in both messages the statement that *Jackfish* had initiated informal investigations. This saved the squadron commander the burden of initiating his investigations until after he reviewed the results of the *Jackfish* investigations.

Nat was coming off the command tactical watch shortly. Bruce took this opportunity to talk with him before he ate his lunch.

"Nat. After you eat lunch, please generate the movement report for the inbound passage of *Jackfish* to Groton. Plan the departure time from Point Bravo to be zero one hundred Christmas Day." Bruce continued, "Use a speed of advance of twenty knots. At twenty knots, the crew can relax somewhat and come off our anticipated high from the torpedo shooting excitement."

Nat responded, "Captain, at this speed of advance, we would be able to get *Jackfish* back home about zero two hundred on the twenty-seventh of December. However, recommend that we schedule our arrival at zero nine hundred to minimize high speeds, cross the Long Island Sound in good visibility, and allow time for any contingencies."

"Concur with your recommendation, Nat. We certainly don't want to have the ladies and children getting up in the middle of the night to meet the ship. Have the message ready to transmit after we complete this mission."

Nat responded cheerfully, "Yes sir, Captain."

It was about time for Bruce to put his contingency persuasion equipment close to his chest. He slowly spun the dials for his stateroom combination safe, opened the door to the safe, and removed his thirty-eight caliber Smith and Wesson revolver and holster. He strapped the holster around his waist under his blue coverall jumpsuit. The jumpsuit was the standard officer and enlisted uniform for underway operations on a United States nuclear submarine. The loaded revolver was pushed firmly into the holster and then the safety strap was fitted across the revolver hammer.

While sitting in his stateroom, Bruce wrote out a message to Commodore Walter. "Please have someone dress as Santa Claus and be on the pier to meet *Jackfish*. Have plenty of candy and balloons for the *Jackfish* dependents."

The message would be transmitted with the other messages after the "MISSION COMPLETE" message was transmitted.

Bruce felt out of character asking his squadron commander to have a Santa Claus on the pier. However, this was possibly a way for Bruce to lighten up and get ready for the big game tonight.

The captain again had a shuttering thought go through his mind. All planning for this mission was on his shoulders. There could possibly be an error in his assumptions about the *Tigerfish* movements and location.

This would drastically change the complexion of the whole world. Bruce shuttered at the thought and convinced himself that his assumptions were correct. *Jackfish* would be successful before this Christmas Day arrived!

Dave continued to review the performance of the watch section and used much of the time on watch working on training evolutions. He devoted this training period time to addressing different issues with the watch standers. He asked questions about different techniques for solving target solution problems. This leader involvement kept the minds of the watch standers attentive.

Bruce spent some time in the sonar room with Chief Keller.

It was obvious at first glance at the watch standers manning the sonar detection equipment in the sonar room that the pressure and stress was increasing significantly on these sonar technicians. They all were trying to pull a sonar detection signal from the nuclear submarine target with every sweep of the sonar console.

"Good evening, Dave," Bruce said as he walked across the attack center. "It looks like you are getting the plotters and fire control console operators up to speed."

Dave responded to the affirmative. "The battle stations team is performing quite well."

The executive officer continued, "Captain. I have the first draft of the meritorious service medal recommendation for Petty Officer Jackson completed for your review. It is on my desk in the operations officer stateroom."

"Thank you, Dave. I will review it shortly and have the message ready to transmit. Have the conning officer take the submarine to periscope depth to copy the eighteen hundred broadcast. Be very careful to protect the floating wire when baffles are being cleared." The captain continued, "The open window when *Jackfish* will not be detected at periscope depth by the Soviet satellite is between seventeen forty-five and eighteen forty-five."

Bruce completed his tour of the ship and returned to his stateroom.

The messenger of the watch knocked lightly on the captain's stateroom door, opened the door, and reported, "The conning officer reports the ship is at periscope depth to copy the eighteen hundred broadcast. No visual or ECM contacts."

"Thank you."

Bruce used this opportunity to review Dave's draft meritorious service medal recommendation for Petty Officer Jackson. As expected, Dave had provided a thorough and well written document. The captain put his initials on the draft indicating his approval and called the radio room on his stateroom telephone. "This is the captain speaking. Please pick up a draft message from me and type it in the smooth ready for transmittal."

"Yes sir, Captain. Will pick up the message immediately."

When Bruce gave the radio man the draft message, he emphasized that the message was not to be transmitted now, just prepared for transmittal.

When the captain picked up his stateroom telephone, the conning officer reported, "Have copied the eighteen hundred broadcast. No messages for *Jackfish*. Returning to operating depth of two hundred feet."

"Very well, conn. Keep alert."

/11/ MISSION COMPLETE

Bruce fell into a deep trance with thoughts about Tom Morello, the *Tigerfish* crew, and the thirty brave submariners who had been slaughtered in a compound in Cuba.

He realized that the success of his approach and attack phase of the mission depended on Tom and some of his crew aboard *Tigerfish* sending sounds from the submarine by sound shorting some equipment. Again, the captain started to shake a bit and perspire.

Many probabilities associated with this battle scenario must be in Bruce's favor for this mission to be successful for the Unites States. The first significant factor was that the location of *Tigerfish* was based on his best judgment without any outside advice. The second factor was that the self generated noise from the target would be made by the *Tigerfish* crew knowing that they were issuing their own death warrants. Also, the United States sailors were under constant guard by Soviet submariners.

Bruce was startled when Bacoco knocked on the stateroom door and announced, "Evening meal is being served."

"Thank you, Bococo. I will be right there."

The wardroom table seats were half full. Those officers not present were at their battle stations assignments. Each officer had dark rings around his eyes and a show of wrinkles in his forehead. These officers were tired and stressed out working in this current environment. Everyone knew that if it was to happen it was to be tonight, before Christmas. The unknown was the key factor that burdened everyone.

Would *Jackfish* be the last one standing in the ring?

Bruce told the officers, "You do not have to remain at the wardroom table for me to finish." He then directed his officers, "Leave the table when you want after you have eaten."

Evening meal tonight was quiet with minimum conversation taking place. Each officer wanted to finish eating and go back to his battle stations assignment as soon as possible.

Nat ate at this seating while Dave had the top watch in the attack center.

Before Nat excused himself from the table, he reported to Bruce, "Captain, I have the movement report for our inbound leg to Groton completed. I will give it to Dave to review after dinner. The report is basically a reverse of the report we submitted for the outbound leg of the trip."

"Thank you, Nat. I appreciate your promptness in completing the task. After Dave and I approve the report, I will give it to the radio men to prepare it for transmittal after we complete this mission."

Bruce departed the wardroom and proceeded to the attack center. He talked with Dave for awhile to get the overall complexion of the crew.

"Everyone is on edge throughout the ship," Dave responded. "As we approach the end of the day, the stress will increase."

"Keep up the good work, Dave, and try to keep the team on an even footing. I am going to tour the ship and take this opportunity to calm the flock," Bruce said with a smile on his face.

Dave pointed to the search template on the plotter table and directed the captain's attention to the present *Jackfish* location. "This is our location at the present time. All areas have been searched once. Plan on taking a course to head towards Point Bravo and then to search above and below the gradient at five knots." He waited a few minutes to let Bruce catch up with the template. "Making a speed through the water of five knots, *Jackfish* will be at Point Bravo at exactly twenty-two hundred."

Bruce interrupted, "This will give us time at our slow speed to detect the submarine and then maneuver to get into the baffles of the target. We want to stay on the opposite side of the gradient than the target submarine to prevent being detected. I assume that the target will be above the gradient at twenty-two hundred." Bruce continued, "The target will be making noises associated with making weapons ready to launch."

Dave again got very cold, and his face tightened as he shot spears at the captain with his stare. He couldn't understand why Bruce wouldn't give him all the pieces of the puzzle!

Nat entered the scene to relieve Dave of the top battle stations watch. After receiving all pertinent information from Dave, Nat said, "I relieve you of the watch."

It was now twenty thirty on the twenty-fourth of December. Three hours

Mission Complete

and thirty minutes more before Christmas arrived. How this team of proud and dedicated submariners carried out their duties before Christmas would determine the complexion of the world in the future. There either would be many happy Christmases and other religious holidays or the world would be dictated by two tyrant regimes.

"Nat, I am going to tour the ship. Hopefully, I can relieve some of the tension rapidly developing throughout the submarine. Rig the attack center for red, please."

"Yes sir, Captain."

Bruce headed aft to the engineering spaces. The captain smiled as he entered each space and talked with the men manning their assigned battle stations. Everyone was nervous and some men were completely stressed out. The sight of Bruce in their space cut the tension cord and allowed the troops some relief.

Bruce talked with the duty cook and the three mess cooks in the crew's dinette and asked them to start serving sandwiches to their shipmates on station. They rapidly and happily started putting the sandwiches on trays to deliver throughout the ship. Each of these four men were glad and proud to be serving this captain.

Bruce then entered the torpedo room. The torpedo reload team was listening to a training session on the procedure for reloading each weapon.

"Hello, Captain. The troops are ready when you give us the signal," stated the torpedo reload leader. "We have five torpedoes fully ready to shoot with the exception of opening the torpedo tube outer doors."

"Thank you, gentlemen for your continued support." The captain looked them all in the eyes and stated, "Before Christmas we will shoot torpedoes."

The sailors all looked at their watches in unison and thought, *That means less than three hours from now the torpedo tubes will shutter when they discharge torpedoes at our submarine target.*

Bruce returned to the attack center at twenty-one forty-five. He had a good feeling about the spirits of his men. At twenty-two hundred, *Jackfish* was searching above the gradient with its primary sonar equipment. Sonar reported to the conning officer over the sound powered telephone, "Have an intermediate sonar contact detected on bearing one-four-five degrees true."

"Dave. Start tracking this sonar contact on the attack plotter."

"Sonar-conn. I am going below the layer. Let me know if you can hold sonar contact below the gradient."

Sonar reported, "The sonar signal is lost." Sonar continued to report, "The noise was evaluated as a noise source probably caused by a sound short."

The captain directed Dave, "Take the ship above the gradient until we pick up the signal again. By looking at your search template, Dave, it looks like the target is on about the same course as we are and is heading towards Point Bravo. Use these assumptions and put the target range at ten thousand yards from Point Bravo." Bruce continued, "When we get another signal from the target, take *Jackfish* below the gradient and open the outer doors to the five ready torpedo tubes."

Almost ten minutes later, sonar reported that they had regained sonar contact.

Bruce commented to sonar and the operators in the attack center, "The target submarine is most likely sending a sound short signal to us every ten minutes."

After thirty minutes, the battle stations plotter had a relative good track on the target.

"Dave, make course changes to obtain a bearings-only range to the target. Dip under the gradient and increase speed to ten knots to close target range. Also, try to ascertain the target course by sweeping across the submarine's baffle area and locating the dead spots."

Sonar reported to the conning officer, "Have a continuous sound short from the target. Using the frequency spectrum pickup from the target, evaluate the contact to be a submarine of the *Jackfish* class."

There was now deep silence in the attack center with everyone looking at Bruce for a comment.

The captain talked to sonar in an excited tone. "Sonar. This is the target we are attempting to locate. Can you hold the contact without using the floating wire? If you can hold a good signal on the target, reel in the floating wire. Dave, dip under the gradient now and open the outer doors on the five torpedo tubes with ready torpedoes."

"Yes sir, Captain."

Dave had lost his confident behavior. He seemed to be doubting and questioning his actions. He seemed to be saying, "Do you really mean that?"

Dave reported to Bruce, "Captain. Have a good shooting solution; however, would rather fine tune the solution more before shooting."

"Very well, Dave. I want to shoot at five thousand yards. We will launch two conventional torpedoes to run below the layer with the contact detonation mode set. At two thousand yards from the target, program for the torpedoes now to run at a depth of sixty feet."

Mission Complete

Bruce delayed so that all the fire control operators and the weapons officer understood the directive. "If the torpedoes have not detonated after running to the generated range shown on the fire control panel, shift the detonation mode to the acoustic mode." Bruce continued, "One Mark57X torpedo set in the non-nuclear mode will be on standby as a contingency weapon. Continue to trail the contact with *Jackfish* remaining in the target submarine's baffle area."

After a slight delay, Bruce stated, "Should be able to close the range to the target submarine while operating below the gradient. This mode of operation will minimize the possibility of being detected."

Bruce kept thinking that although Dave was not extremely pleased with the scenario taking place in the attack center, he didn't appear to want to jeopardize the mission. Just in case, Bruce would not delay the use of the revolver if conditions warranted.

It was now twenty-three thirty. Sonar reported, "The sonar contact had gone to periscope depth."

Dave reported to Bruce, "Target range is five thousand yards and closing, speed is five knots with course one-five-zero. Have a good shooting solution."

"Very well, Dave. Commence firing two conventional torpedoes."

Dave delayed carrying out the order. Maybe there would be a disagreement between the executive officer and the captain.

All hands in the attack center looked and waited for the resolution of this conflict.

Sonar reported to the conning officer in a frantic voice, "The contact is making torpedo tubes ready, including flooding the torpedo tubes and opening the outer doors."

It was obvious to Bruce that since *Jackfish* was in the baffles of *Tigerfish*, the target submarine could not have sonar contact on *Jackfish*. This only meant the target submarine was getting ready to launch Axehandle nuclear missiles at targets in the United States.

Dave responded to the sonar report by ordering two conventional torpedoes launched.

It would take the sixty knot torpedo two and a half minutes to reach the target. Everyone in the attack center observed their watches and counted down.

Bruce ordered the outer doors closed on all torpedo tubes to minimize any damage to the torpedo tubes and own ship by the impact of the torpedo detonations. The sonar operators were cautioned when the detonation was to occur so that they could train off the explosion to prevent ear damage. On schedule, sonar reported the detonation of the two torpedoes and the breaking up noises of the target submarine.

"Dave, secure from battle stations, restore normal communications throughout the ship and surface the ship." Bruce continued, "Dave, I will go to the bridge. Provide me the course and vector the ship to the impact point of the torpedoes with the target submarine."

Sonar continued to report the breaking up noises from the target submarine. At the vectored location of the torpedo impact with *Tigerfish*, Bruce was able to see oil slicks on the water. No debris was located. Bruce layed below from the bridge.

"Dave, after we have transmitted our messages, submerge the ship and steer course for home. Make ship's speed of twenty knots at a depth of five hundred feet."

"Radio Room-captain. Send FLASH the MISSION COMPLETE message. After receipt of the message, transmit the other messages that I have released."

Bruce took the 1MC general announcing system microphone, pushed the actuator on the microphone and spoke. "Let me have your attention please. First off, I want to wish all hands a Merry Christmas and happy holidays." Bruce paused and then continued. "Because of your professionalism and dedication to duty, the people of the United States and of the free world also will have a Merry Christmas and happy holidays this year and for many more years to come. Thank you."

The captain moved over to Dave in the attack center, looked him in the eye, and shook his hand. "Thank you for your support. Put my night order book on my desk, please."

Bruce entered the sonar room and talked with the eyes and ears of the submarine. "You gentlemen did a superb job throughout the entire trip. Especially at the crucial time during the localize and attack phase."

Bruce vectored Chief Keller into the corner of the sonar room.

"Chief Keller. Please give me the sonar tape recordings of the mission from when we first detected the target submarine until the sinking." Bruce continued, "I can't have any copies made of the tape. Thank you."

"I understand completely what you are telling me." The chief reached out and shook the captain's hand. "It is my distinct pleasure and honor to serve with a captain like you. Thank you."

Mission Complete

Bruce dragged himself into his stateroom. He now was completely exhausted. The loaded thirty-eight caliber Smith and Wesson revolver and holster were removed and returned into the combination safe on Bruce's desk. Bruce wrote his night orders. "Steer course three-three-five degrees true at speed of twenty knots and at a depth of five hundred feet. Take a sounding every hour and randomly clear baffles once an hour." He continued, "Adjust the course as recommended by the navigator. Copy the zero four hundred and the zero eight hundred communications broadcast. Wake me up at zero eight hundred. Well done to all hands!" Bruce called for the messenger of the watch to pick up the night orders and deliver them to the navigator.

After a very short night, the messenger of the watch knocked on the captain's stateroom door, slowly opened itc and reported, "Captain, your zero eight hundred wake up call."

"Thank you."

The captain's sound-powered telephone buzzed twice. "Captain speaking."

"Good morning, Captain. Have just copied the communications broadcast. Have three messages for *Jackfish*. One is for "CO eyes only" and the other is quite interesting. The third is a very favorable weather report for the Groton area. Will have them delivered to your stateroom. Leaving periscope depth en route to our operating depth of five hundred feet."

"Very well, conn. Thank you."

Bruce hit his call button for the stewarts mate as he dressed.

Bococo knocked on the door lightly, opened the door, and placed a large mug of black coffee on the captain's desk. "Good morning, Captain. I have breakfast waiting for you."

"You anticipated that I would be hungry and you are absolutely correct."

The radio man delivered the three messages to the wardroom for the captain. Bruce initialed the weather message and returned it to the radio man. He read the second message and layed it on the table. Bruce took a sip of coffee and then read the message again slowly and smiled at the conclusion.

The message read "To Captain Bruce Stewart and the gallant men of the *USS Jackfish* (SSN 945). Well done! You all have the gratitude of the people of the United States and of all the people of the free world. Happy holidays to all. Thank you. Signed by the president of the United States."

Bruce picked up the 1MC general announcing system annunciator, pushed the actuator button, and spoke. "Please give me attention, this is the captain speaking." The captain read over the general announcing system the message from the president. "You also all have my sincere gratitude. Thank you."

Bruce returned to the wardroom and started to read the for "CO eyes only" message. The message had the title "closure" and was from Commodore Bill Walter.

Bill had dispatched two American attack nuclear submarines in pursuit of the Soviet cruiser that was in Cuba with *Tigerfish*. This cruiser had taken onboard an Axehandle nuclear missile and one of each torpedo carried by *Tigerfish*. Also, copies and information that would put the *Jackfish* class nuclear submarine in jeopardy were removed from the *Tigerfish* and put onboard the Soviet cruiser for transport to the Soviet Union.

As soon as the squadron commander had received the "MISSION COMPLETE" message from *Jackfish*, two United States nuclear attack submarines were directed to attack and sink the Soviet cruiser. The nuclear attack submarines had followed directives exactly.

The message ended: "My congratulations for a job well done. Happy holidays to you and to your expert crew. Thank you. P.S. Santa Claus will be on the pier as requested."